ORATORY SCHOOL
LIBRARY

CLASS 929

BOOK No. 13517

LORDS OF THE LAND

Also by Alison Plowden:

The Young Elizabeth
As They Saw It
Mistress of Hardwick
Danger to Elizabeth
The Case of Eliza Armstrong
The House of Tudor
Marriage with My Kingdom
Tudor Women
Elizabeth Regina
The Young Victoria
Elizabethan England
Two Queens in One Isle

LORDS OF THE LAND

by

Alison Plowden

MICHAEL JOSEPH
LONDON

First published in Great Britain by Michael Joseph Ltd
44 Bedford Square, London WC1
1984

© Alison Plowden 1984

All Rights Reserved. No part of this publication
may be reproduced, stored in a retrieval system,
or transmitted in any form or by any means, electronic,
mechanical, photocopying, recording or otherwise,
without the prior permission of the Copyright owner

British Library Cataloguing in Publication Data

Plowden, Alison
Lords of the land.
1. England—Nobility—History
I. Title
305.5′223′0942 HT653.G7

ISBN 0 7181 2332 8

Typeset by Input Typesetting Limited.
Printed and bound in Great Britain by
Billing and Sons Ltd., Worcester.

CONTENTS

LIST OF ILLUSTRATIONS

ACKNOWLEDGEMENTS

The author and publishers would like to thank the following for permission to reproduce extracts from the publications mentioned:

Blackwell, *Lord Derby and Victorian Conservatism* by William Devereux Jones; Macmillan, *Stags and Serpents: The Story of the House of Cavendish and the Dukes of Devonshire* by John Pearson, and *The House: A Portrait of Chatsworth* by the Duchess of Devonshire.

FOREWORD

> Pride in their port, defiance in their eye,
> I see the lords of human kind pass by.
>
> Goldsmith

By every normally accepted law of logic and common sense there should be no more lords in the land – war, social revolution and taxation, but especially taxation, should have seen to that by now. And yet, against all the odds, the peerage is still very much a part of the English scene. The dukes and the earls, the viscounts and even the barons have turned themselves into charitable trusts and limited companies, turned their houses into tourist attractions, conference centres, safari parks and museums for vintage motor cars, become working farmers and market gardeners, businessmen and impresarios. In short, they provide a remarkably successful example of a threatened species which has adapted to suit an increasingly hostile environment and survived, if in a somewhat attenuated form; although, thanks to the influence of the conservationists and the heritage lobby, public opinion has recently shown a distinct tendency to swing back in their favour. In the 1980s it has suddenly become respectable again to have roots, praiseworthy to strive to preserve an ancestral mansion or hold a family art collection together. When, in the late 1940s and early '50s, the Dukes of Devonshire and Bedford were striving to do just that at Chatsworth and at Woburn Abbey, remarkably little public sympathy or official encouragement came their way. Today it might be different – a fact which both their graces must surely find more than somewhat ironic.

'Gentility', so William Cecil, the first Lord Burghley, once told his son, 'is but ancient riches' – which lofty point of view did not prevent his lordship from going to considerable trouble and expense to investigate of his own pedigree. He came, in fact, of a line of prosperous yeomen farmers from the Monmouth-Herefordshire borders, but his first fully authenticated forebear was his grandfather, David, a younger son who left home to seek his fortune in the train of another adventurer, Henry Tudor, the unknown Welshman who had just come ashore at Milford Haven to make a bid for the English throne. David Cecil rose to become a well-to-do country gentleman and holder of a number of minor court appointments. He settled near Stamford in Lincolnshire, married the daughter of a local civic dignitary and founded the family, which within three generations, had become one of the first in the land. The story of the Cecils' rise, although spectacular, is far from being the only one of its kind. Behind many a noble house – the Howards, the Cavendishes, the Sackvilles and the Russells are all prime examples – there is to be found a sharp lawyer, an enterprising financier or just a restless, energetic young man on the make and not always too particular about the means.

Riches came first, naturally, but then the average successful Englishman turned his attention to achieving gentility. The Elizabethans were especially enthusiastic social climbers. 'Everyone vaunts himself,' complained the contemporary moralist Philip Stubbes, 'crying with open mouth "I am gentleman, I am worshipful, I am honourable, I am noble" and I cannot tell what. "My father was this, my father was that." "I am come of this house, I am come of that. . ." '

It was easy enough to be accepted as a gentleman in England, always providing one could afford it. Thomas Smith, Secretary of State to Edward VI and Elizabeth I, wrote in his treatise on the constitution: 'whosoever . . . can live idly and without manual labour and will bear the port, charge and countenance of a gentleman, he shall be called master . . . and shall be taken for a gentleman'. Those who could afford it and wanted to do the thing properly could pay a herald to provide them with a coat of arms, not infrequently 'newly made and invented, the title whereof shall pretend to have been found by the said herald in perusing and viewing of old registers'.

But although there was nothing to prevent the *nouveaux riches* from buying their way into the landed gentry class, titles themselves came only from the crown and Queen Elizabeth I was notoriously reluctant to create new peerages. Her successor proved less fastidious and by 1615 it had become possible to buy one's way into the aristocracy – the usual price being around £10,000 – though when Lionel Cranfield, the wealthy London mercer, became Earl of Middlesex, one critic remarked sourly that 'none but a poor spirited nobility would have endured his perching on that high tree of honour'.

King Charles I was not a man to hold honour cheap, but nevertheless found himself obliged to be generous with titles as the only way by which he could recompense those wealthy subjects willing to come to his aid in his time of greatest need. The earldom of Sunderland, for example, bestowed on young Baron Spencer in 1643, is said to have been in recognition of financial help from the rich sheep-farming Spencer family. Charles II, too, had obligations towards subjects who had ruined themselves through loyalty to his own and his father's cause, and the dukedom of Newcastle was a relatively inexpensive method of rewarding his former tutor, the stately William Cavendish of Welbeck and Bolsover. Charles II had also rather improvidently raised a fine crop of royal bastards, all needing to be settled in life – hence the dukedoms of St Albans, Grafton, Richmond and Buccleuch.

The next major round of promotions among the peerage came after the Glorious Revolution of 1688 which brought dukedoms to the Chatsworth Cavendishes and the Russells of Woburn. The Percys had to wait until 1766 for their ducal step, the first Duke of Northumberland being the Yorkshire baronet Hugh Smithson who had married the Percy heiress, and who came in for some rather unkind teasing about 'Duke Smithson'. But at no time in its history has the English nobility been a closed caste, and that has always been one of its great strengths. There was another influx of new blood around the end of the seventeen hundreds, and in the nineteenth and twentieth centuries the new industrialists – the tycoons of iron and steel, brewing, textiles, shipping and, of course, the press – were smoothly absorbed into the system.

Always, though, the lords who really mattered have been rooted in the land. From earliest times the ownership of land was their security, the solid foundation of their political influence, the very reason for their being. 'Land is the basis of an aristocracy, which clings to the soil that supports it,' wrote the French historian Alexis de Tocqueville; 'for it is not by privilege alone, nor by birth, but by landed property handed down from generation to generation that an aristocracy is constituted.' Certainly the English aristocracy has always clung to the soil and to its vital territorial power bases. The fourth Duke of Norfolk, he who told Queen Elizabeth I that he thought of himself as a prince at home in his bowling alley at Norwich, could have quickly raised a fair-sized army without looking further than his Norfolk tenantry, moved about the country on his lawful occasions with an escort of five hundred mounted retainers and, from his headquarters at Kenninghall, ruled over the last of the great medieval liberties – some six hundred square miles exempt from the ordinary processes of royal justice. It used to be a common saying that the men of the north knew no other prince than a Percy, and as recently as the present century the seventeenth Earl of Derby could be affectionately nicknamed 'King of Lancashire'.

The aristocratic empires have dwindled now, of course – in some cases, almost to vanishing point. But given the astronomic rise in land values over recent years, ownership of a three- or four-figure acreage today, compared with the five or six figures common in the 1880s, still represents a very sizeable capital asset, while even twenty or thirty acres in central London would be enough to satisfy most people's dreams of avarice – on paper at least.

As well as land, the aristocracy has always depended heavily on the concept of the family – on an extended and complex web of cousinage and inter-tribal alliances in which the ladies played quite as important a part as the lords. A fortunate marriage made all the difference to the upward social mobility of the noble houses of Howard and Stanley, and in later centuries, when it came to choosing brides for its sons, the English peerage was far too shrewd to close its doors to outsiders where money was concerned. The Russells owe the Bloomsbury estate to Rachel Wriothesley, daughter of the Earl of Southampton, but they were not too proud to match the second Duke of Bedford to Elizabeth Howland, daughter of a wealthy City draper and grand-daughter of the banker Josiah Child, who brought the manors of Streatham, Tooting and Rotherhithe into her new family. It's true that the effete son of this marriage contrived to gamble away nearly all his mother's dowry, but that was just part of the luck of the draw. Nineteenth-century peers showed a distinct tendency to marry actresses, and the appearance of American heiresses – dollar princesses like Consuelo Vanderbilt – with title-hunting parents, helped to revive the moulting plumage of some noble families. In general, though, like called to like, and Cecil tended to marry Russell or Cavendish, Percy to marry Seymour, Howard to marry Talbot, Spencer to marry Churchill or Cavendish, Sackville to marry Russell or Stanley.

It's impossible to quantify the contribution which the aristos have made to English life, from the medieval warlords and the tough, hard-working arrivistes of Tudor times to the connoisseurs and collectors, farmers and politicians of the eighteenth century and the farmers and company directors of today. You can approve or disapprove of the whole business of heredity – of the handing on of titles and estates from generation to generation, of elitism or privilege or call it what you will – but there is no denying that the lords have always given and, for that matter, still give, a unique cachet to the land from which they spring. Even in the days when the continental European nobility was still a living entity, the English milord was something a little special. In 1895 the magnificent Lord Ribblesdale believed that to be a lord was 'still a popular thing', and strangely enough he would probably still be right today.

The Percy Out of Northumberland

Esperance en dieu

Henry 9th Earl of Northumberland by Thomas Phillips after Van Dyck *reproduced by permission of His Grace the Duke of Northumberland*

THE PERCY OUT OF NORTHUMBERLAND

Esperance en dieu

THIS ancient and right noble family do derive their descent from Manfred de Percy, which Manfred came out of Denmark into Normandy before the adventure of the famous Rollo thither.

Tradition quite properly plays an important part in family history, especially in the history of so ancient a family as the Percys, but this particular tradition, perpetuated by Dugdale's *Baronage of England*, is no older than the sixteenth century, a period when pedigree-makers were more noted for their flights of romantic imagination than any boring preoccupation with historical fact. There is, needless to say, not a scrap of evidence for the existence of Manfred de Percy among the Viking freebooters who colonised the north-western corner of France early in the tenth century, nor, for that matter, anything to say whether the Percys were of Scandinavian, Frankish or Gaulish origin. They were, however, established in Normandy by the year 1066.

The William de Perci, nicknamed *als gernon*, 'the mustachioed one', who founded the English family, was either a younger son or scion of a cadet branch seeking his fortune. He does not appear to have been present at the Battle of Hastings and most probably crossed the Channel in 1067 in the train of the Conqueror's wife Matilda. Another tradition, recounted by William Peeris, chaplain to the fifth Earl of Northumberland, is that the first Baron Percy was highly regarded by the Conqueror who provided him with a noble bride, Emma of the Port, in consideration of services rendered. This version of the story makes Emma a Saxon heiress, 'the lady of Semer beside Scarborough afore the Conquest'. However, a modern genealogist states categorically that she was the daughter of Hugh de Port, a Norman from the Bessin who had been granted a large fief in Hampshire from which he gave only a single manor on her marriage.

One certain fact is that mustachioed William was among those Norman incomers who benefited from the wholesale confiscation of property in the Saxon north which followed the rebellion of 1069; he appears in *Domesday Book* as the owner of eighty lordships in Yorkshire, where he built and fortified the castles of Spofforth and Topcliffe. A stubborn, cantankerous individual, he presently became involved in a long and bitter legal dispute with the monks of Whitby Abbey, who were doubtless much relieved when the old warrior took the Cross and departed for the Holy Land. He died near Jerusalem in 1096 and was buried at Antioch, although his heart was brought back to Whitby.

A little over half a century later the direct male line came to an end when the first Baron Percy's grandson, another William, left two daughters, Maud and Agnes, to succeed him. Maud's marriage to William of Newburgh was childless, but luckily Agnes proved fruitful, and although her husband Joscelin, the younger son by a second marriage of Godfrey 'Barbatus', Duke of Lower Lorraine and Count of Louvain did not, as is usually stated, take the Percy surname himself, their children carried on the Percy line. Not, however, without some confusion in the next generation between Richard Percy, second son of Agnes and Joscelin, and his nephew William, the rightful heir. Richard, who was evidently a true chip off the old Percy block, remained in possession 'by right of the strong hand' until his death in 1245, and is also notable for the part he played in helping to wrest the Magna Charta from King John. He was one of those who confronted the monarch beside the Thames at Runnymede in the summer of 1215, and a member of the commission of twenty-five barons appointed to act as guardians of the Great Charter.

By the middle of the thirteenth century, therefore, the Percys were strongly established among English baronial families. Henry, the seventh Baron Percy, married into the royal house and fought with King Henry III against Simon de Montfort at the Battle of Lewes in 1264, and was taken prisoner for his pains. But it was his son, another Henry, a skilful warrior and more famous and powerful than any of his predecessors, who forged the family's association with the Scottish Border on which so much of their latter-day renown depends.

It began with Edward I's interference in the dispute concerning the Scottish succession after the death of Alexander III in 1286, and his rather dubious claim to be recognised as feudal overlord by the Scots. The eighth Baron Percy played a prominent part in the conflicts which inevitably followed this unwise attempt to impose an alien system of justice on a primitive tribal society, and in 1309 he bought Alnwick Castle from the Bishop of Durham to give himself a convenient base for cross-Border operations. Thus the Percys came to

> the country called Northumberland . . . a savage and a wild country, full of deserts and mountains, and a right poor country of everything saving of beasts; through the which there runneth a river full of flint and great stones called the water of Tyne.

Succeeding generations of the family fought in France, at Crécy and with the English army in Gascony, but for most of the fourteenth century there was enough fighting to be had against the Scots on their own doorstep to satisfy even the Percy warlords. The eighth baron was present when the English were routed at Bannockburn in 1314, dying of his wounds the following year, while his son saw the Scots defeated at Halidon Hill and again at Neville's Cross in 1346.

By this time the famous blood feud between Percy and Douglas, which arose out of the incessant raiding from both sides of the Border, was already being celebrated in song and story:

> The Percy out of Northumberland,
> And a vow to God made he,
> That he would hunt in the mountains
> Of Cheviot within days three,
> In despite of doughty Douglas,
> And all that ever with him be.

The fattest harts in all Cheviot
He said he would kill, and carry them away:
By my faith, said the doughty Douglas again,
I will let that hunting, if that I may.

There are several versions of the 'Ballad of Chevy Chase' with its rousing descriptions of the exploits of the Lord Percy and his fifteen hundred archers bold pitted against doughty Douglas and his Scottish spearmen in armour bright, until at last the two champions meet in single combat, 'like to captains of might and main'. Neither, of course, will yield and the issue is decided by an English arrow which strikes Earl Douglas 'in at the breast bane'.

The Percy leaned upon his brand,
And saw the Douglas die;
He took the dead man by the hand,
And said: Woe is me for thee!

To have saved thy life I would have parted with
My lands for years three,
For a better man of heart, nor of hand
Was not in all the north country. . . .

There was, however, nothing in the least romantic or chivalrous about the reality of the feud and the *Metrical Chronicle of the Percye Family* is probably a good deal nearer the mark in its description of the vicious petty warfare of the Borders.

They spared neither man or wife,
Young or old of mankind that bore life.
Like wild wolves in furiosity,
Both burnt and slew with great cruelty.

The Percys reached the peak of their political power and influence during the last quarter of the fourteenth century. Henry, the tenth baron, known as 'the little knight' from his unusual shortness of stature, had married into the royal family and had also, by astute and careful management, considerably increased his land holdings in Northumberland.

His son, another Henry, became the close friend and companion of his kinsman John of Gaunt, the great Duke of Lancaster. In the summer of 1377 Percy supported Lancaster in his political quarrel with the bishops and with him championed the cause of the radical Yorkshire priest, John Wycliffe, father of English Protestantism. When Wycliffe was summoned to appear before the Bishop of London in St Paul's Cathedral to answer a charge of heresy, both Percy and Lancaster were present standing guard over their protégé; but the Londoners, already annoyed by Lancaster's high-handed behaviour, were infuriated by this blatant attempt to exercise his authority within the City liberties. In a night of violence they broke into his Palace of the Savoy and sacked Lord Percy's house in Aldersgate. Percy of Northumberland, who never feared the Scots, quailed before the London mob and fled ignominiously across the Thames to seek sanctuary at the Princess of Wales's manor of Kennington.

At the coronation of the child King Richard II which took place about a month later, Percy and Lancaster were both very much on their best behaviour. Riding before King Richard in the recognition procession, they were careful to use themselves 'courteously, modestly and pleasantly'. Wherefore, says Holinshed's *Chronicle*,

> they two, who were greatly suspected of the common people by reason of their great puissance in the realm and huge route of retainers, so ordered the matter that neither this day, nor the morrow after, being the day of the King's coronation, they offended any manner of person, but rather by gentle and pleasant demeanour they reclaimed the hearts of many by whom they were before held in suspicion and thought evil of.

On the coronation day itself, when he acted as Earl Marshal, the Lord Percy was created Earl of Northumberland and his eleven-year-old heir, yet another Henry, was solemnly dubbed a knight by the nine-year-old King. But rumours of trouble in the North soon sent father and son hurrying back to Alnwick and more congenial occupations. By the autumn the familiar battle cry of '*Esperance* and Percy!' was heard again on the Border as the new earl triumphantly swept an invasion of marauding Scots out of Berwick; and the following year, when a party of Scottish raiders again took possession of the town, young Henry, who had now reached the mature age of twelve, was said to have led the victorious Northumbrians himself.

Over the next dozen years, the earl and his son more than upheld the family tradition:

> Knightly men in wars both occupied;
> Beyond the seas great worship had they won
> In many a realm, full greatly magnified
> For martial acts by them multiplied.
> The while were long here to report,
> But in their time they were of noble port.

Young Henry in particular was gaining an international reputation as a fighting man, his restless energy earning him the nickname of Hotspur, ' . . . he that kills me some six or seven dozen of Scots at a breakfast, washes his hands, and says to his wife, "Fie upon this quiet life! I want work!" '

There was to be plenty of such work during the 1380s. Although James Earl of Douglas and Henry Earl of Northumberland had set their hands and seals to a solemn truce in March 1386, no parchment drawn up in monkish Latin could prevent the Scots from descending into the Northumbrian dales, and reiving and raiding, feuding and killing and cattle thieving continued unabated all along the Northern Marches. Matters came to a head in the summer of 1388.

> It fell about the Lammas-tide
> When husbands win their hay,
> The doughty Douglas bound him ride,
> In England to take a prey. . . .

The raid was, in fact, on a larger scale than the ballad suggests: led by the Earls of Douglas, Fife, Moray and Dunbar, it was intended to take advantage of current English weakness, caused by the dissensions developing under the ineffective government of Richard II. The Scots gathered at Jedburgh about the middle of August and according to the *Chronicles* of Jean Froissart:

In threescore years before there was not assembled together

> in Scotland such a number of good men; . . . The lords were well-pleased and were determined they would never enter again into their own houses till they had been in England, and done such deeds there that it should be spoken of twenty years after.

In order to cause confusion and preserve the element of surprise for as long as possible, it was agreed 'to make two armies', the larger force setting off towards Carlisle, leaving the Earls of Douglas, March and Moray to ride down through Redesdale and over the river Tyne into the rich country of the Northumberland/Durham border at the head of a flying column of 'three or four hundred spears and two thousand of other well-horsed'. The invaders succeeded in getting as far as the gates of Durham itself before turning for home, laden with plunder and well satisfied with their exploit.

By this time, the smoke of burning villages and farmsteads had alerted the Percys to the fact that 'the Scots were abroad', and Harry Hotspur, his brother Ralph and all the fighting men of Northumberland were gathering at Newcastle. Here, according to Froissart's account, the young Earl of Douglas added insult to injury by capturing Hotspur's pennon in a skirmish outside the walls, but the Otterburn ballad simply says:

> To the New Castle when they came,
> The Scots they cried on hight,
> 'Sir Harry Percy, and thou bist within,
> Come to the field and fight:
> For we have brent (burnt) Northumberland
> Thy heritage good and right. . .

The Northumbrians and the Scots finally clashed at Otterburn in the wild wooded country north of Newcastle on the evening of 19 August. Again according to Froissart:

> Cowards there had no place but hardiness reigned with good feats of arms, for knights and squires were so joined together at hand strokes that archers had no place. . . . Thus the banners of Douglas and Percy and their men were met each against other, envious who should win the honour of that journey.

The battle, 'as stubborn and hard fought as any in history', raged on through the moonlit summer night and casualties were heavy on both sides.

> There was never a time on the March parts
> Since the Douglas and Percy met,
> But it was marvel and the red blood ran not
> As the rain doth in the street. . .

The Earl of Douglas himself was killed and Ralph Percy seriously wounded and although, for all its ferocity, Otterburn changed nothing and decided nothing, it does seem to have marked a milestone in the Percy/Douglas feud. The Scots had won a victory on points, honour had temporarily at least been satisfied; the ransomed prisoners (who included the Percy brothers) yielded a handsome profit and for the next few years the Border knew some unusual peace.

In 1399 the Percy family used its political influence to help in securing the deposition of King Richard II and his replacement by the Lancastrian Henry Bolingbroke, who was crowned as Henry IV in October of that year. The new king naturally hastened to reward his supportive northern kinsmen with honours and offices, but the honeymoon period was short. The Percys were soon complaining about Henry's failure to reimburse the heavy cost of defending his land frontiers and grumbling about ingratitude, while the king was having misgivings about the Percy connection with the Mortimer family – descendants through the female line from Lionel Plantagenet, Duke of Clarence, one of the all too numerous sons of Edward III and elder brother of John of Gaunt, Duke of Lancaster, father of King Henry IV.

Harry Hotspur was married to Elizabeth Mortimer, so that 'the King began to think that now Hotspur's son had a nearer right to the crown than his own offspring' – a feeling which no self-respecting monarch could afford to entertain for long. To make matters worse, in 1402 Elizabeth's brother Edmund married a daughter of the Welsh chieftain Owain Glyn Dwyr, who was currently causing the English king a great deal of trouble and expense with his guerrilla warfare tactics. And in the same year the Percys won a resounding victory over the Scots at Homildown

Hill and defiantly refused to surrender their noble prisoners (who included the Earl of Douglas) and their ransoms to King Henry. In 1403 they came out in open revolt, and the threat which they and the Welsh insurgents posed to the security of the new royal house of Lancaster was both serious and immediate.

But Hotspur, that gallant impetuous warrior, veteran of a hundred Border frays, was now fighting in quite a different league. When he and his uncle Thomas, Earl of Worcester, reached Shrewsbury on their way to join forces with Glyn Dwyr, they found the king was before them and all efforts to reach a negotiated settlement failed. Shakespeare probably drew the character of Harry Hotspur as accurately as anybody when he put these words into his mouth:

> . . . I profess not talking. Only this –
> Let each man do his best: and here draw I
> A sword, whose temper I intend to stain
> With the best blood that I can meet withal
> In the adventure of this perilous day.
> Now, *Esperance*! Percy! and set on.
> Sound all the lofty instruments of war,
> And by that music let us all embrace;
> For, heaven to earth, some of us never shall
> A second time do such a courtesy.

Hotspur was killed at Shrewsbury, and 'the earth that bore him dead, bore not alive so stout a gentleman'. The old Earl of Northumberland, his father, was forced to submit to the king, but five years later was once more up in arms against the royal forces at Bramham Moor near Tadcaster. Holinshed writes in his *Chronicle*:

> There was a sore encounter and cruel conflict betwixt the parties but in the end the victory fell to the Sheriff of Yorkshire, Rafe Rokesby. As for the Earl of Northumberland, he was slain outright, so that now the prophecy was fulfilled which gave an inkling of his heavy hap long before, namely that the Percy stock shall perish in disordered ruin. For this earl was the stock and main root of all that were left alive called by the name of Percy. . . . For whose misfortunes the

> people were not a little sorry, making report of the gentleman's valiantness, renown and honour. His head, full of silver hoary hairs, being put upon a stake, was openly carried through London and set up on the bridge of the same city.

Despite all the omens the Percy stock did not perish. Harry Hotspur's son, the second Earl of Northumberland, fell fighting on the Lancastrian side at the first battle of St Albans in 1455 and his son, the third earl, was slain at Towton in 1461 and subsequently attainted, but unlike so many other ancient baronial families the Percys narrowly survived the general holocaust of their kind in the Wars of the Roses.

After an uncomfortable and precarious youth, the fourth earl made his peace with the victorious Yorkists and in 1473 was restored in blood by King Edward IV. Although present with King Richard on the field at Bosworth, he took no part in the fighting and advised the citizens of York to accept Henry Tudor, 'that unknown Welshman', as king. Doubtful though his claim might be, he did at least contain in his person the last drop of Lancastrian blood. But for some years the North remained stubbornly Yorkist in sympathy and in 1489 the fourth Earl of Northumberland was killed in an affray in his own park at Topcliffe while attempting to enforce the collection of taxes demanded by the unpopular new dynasty.

His son, known as 'the Magnificent', lived *en prince* on one or other of the family's Yorkshire properties – the Northumbrian strongholds of Alnwick and Warkworth were garrisons rather than homes – spending most of his time at Wressell or Leconfield in the East Riding, when, that is, he was not in London, either at court or accompanying the young Henry VIII on one of his belligerent jaunts into France. He was, in fact, campaigning with the King in Picardy in 1512–13 and so missed the Battle of Flodden, but his brother William was present as second-in-command of the English left wing and was subsequently knighted by the Earl of Surrey.

The Northumberland Household Book gives some idea of the scale of the earl's housekeeping. At Michaelmas 1512 there were one hundred and sixty-six servants officially on his payroll, their wages varying from twenty pounds a year to the treasurer and the comptroller, to twenty shillings to the rockers in the 'nurcy' or nursery. Apart from the usual hordes of grooms, ushers, clerks, cooks, yeomen, footmen and children, the Percys maintained a chapel served by up to a dozen priests and seventeen children and gentlemen choristers, as well as minstrels, schoolmasters, falconers, huntsmen and their own private herald. The sum of £1100 was set aside annually for household expenses, but this modest budget did not cover even the routine extras, such as offerings in the chapel, presents, charities or payments and tips to strolling players and musicians, let alone the lavish hospitality and display expected of a great nobleman.

In 1503 the Earl of Northumberland was called upon to meet the thirteen-year-old Margaret Tudor at York and escort her across the Border on her way to be married to King James of Scotland, and the chronicler Edward Hall reported that

> what for the riches of his coat, being goldsmiths' work garnished with pearl, and what for the costly apparel of his henchmen and gallant trappings of their horses, besides four hundred tall men, well horsed and apparelled in his colours [the earl was esteemed, by both Scots and Englishmen, as] more like a prince than a subject.

This sort of display was not always very wise, or very safe, for the subject concerned, but Northumberland contrived to keep on the right side of his prince – except for an occasion in 1516 when a dispute over his right to certain wardships landed him in the Fleet prison for a spell. Holinshed's *Chronicle* blames the malign influence of Cardinal Wolsey for this unfortunate episode, and certainly the cardinal lost few opportunities to make the nobility feel his power. 'In the Exchequer he them checks' quipped the laureate John Skelton;

> In the Star Chamber he nods and becks,
> And beareth him there so stout,
> That no man dare route
> – Duke, Earl, Baron or Lord –
> But to his sentence must accord.

Nevertheless, in the early 1520s the earl sent his eldest son and heir, yet another in a long line of Henry Percys, to acquire some social polish and experience in the cardinal's household. This was to result in another unfortunate episode.

> When it chanced the Lord Cardinal at any time to repair to the Court [related George Cavendish, the Lord Cardinal's gentleman usher and earliest biographer] the Lord Percy would resort for his pastime unto the Queen's chamber, and there would fall in dalliance among the Queen's maidens, being at the last more conversant with Mistress Anne Boleyn than with any other; so that there grew such a secret love between them that at length they were insured [engaged] together, intending to marry.

As soon as word of this unauthorised wooing came to the cardinal's ears, he took prompt and ruthless action, scolding the unhappy Percy in front of the servants for his 'peevish folly' in so far forgetting himself and his duty as to become entangled with a foolish girl at court, and forbidding him to see her again on pain of incurring the king's severe displeasure. The Earl of Northumberland, in no very good temper, was summoned to London to add the weight of his authority, and between them he and Wolsey had no difficulty in blighting Lord Percy's romance.

George Cavendish believed that the king had already begun to 'kindle the brand of amours' for the young lady in question and had ordered the cardinal to intervene. This must have seemed a reasonable assumption to one writing with the benefit of hindsight, but in fact there is no evidence to suggest that Henry was taking an amorous interest in Anne Boleyn as early as the summer of 1522 when this incident took place. On the contrary, there was a plan under discussion at that time to marry her to one of her Irish Butler cousins, and most probably Wolsey had simply acted to prevent a thoughtless boy and girl from upsetting the arrangements of their elders.

The story had an ironic sequel, for in November 1530, when Cardinal Wolsey had been driven into disgrace and exile by Anne and her friends and was reluctantly travelling north to his archdiocese of York, it was Henry Percy, now Earl of Northumberland, who intercepted him at Cawood with a warrant for his arrest. But the earl was not a vengeful man and seems to have taken no satisfaction in his former guardian's abasement.

Six years later Henry Percy was among the jury of peers assembled to try Queen Anne Boleyn on charges of adultery, incest and high treason, and the occasion was evidently painful for him. The record states that Northumberland was the only peer not to join in the verdict of guilty, and according to one account he left the proceedings before the sentence of burning or beheading at the king's pleasure was pronounced.

Nothing, in fact, ever went right for the sixth earl. His marriage to Lady Mary Talbot had been loveless and childless, and he was now a sick man. The final blow fell at the beginning of June 1537 when his brother Thomas was executed for his part in the rebellion against religious change known as the Pilgrimage of Grace. When the earl himself died a few weeks later, the Percy estates were confiscated and Thomas Percy's two young sons thrown on the charity of friends. The Duke of Norfolk, who had been chiefly responsible for suppressing the Pilgrimage of Grace in the field, nevertheless did what he could for the orphans, the elder of whom, another Thomas, was no more than eleven years old. 'As to Sir Thomas Percy's children', wrote the duke to Mr Secretary Cromwell, 'I have entreated good Sir Thomas Tempest to take them into his custody . . . and have promised him to have their costs paid for.'

The first steps in the restoration of the brothers' civil rights were taken soon after Henry VIII's death, but it was not until the spring of 1557 that Queen Mary Tudor finally reinstated Thomas Percy as Earl of Northumberland – an event greeted by a spontaneous outburst of rejoicing in the clannish and conservative Percy country. Old Bishop Cuthbert Tunstall celebrated High Mass in Durham Cathedral, church bells pealed, oxen were roasted whole on village greens from Berwick to Beverley and bonfires blazed on beacon hills throughout the north-east.

The seventh earl who in 1558 married Lady Anne Somerset, daughter of the Earl of Worcester, and brought her home to Topcliffe, is described by a nineteenth-century chronicler of the family as 'affectionate and simple-minded, a warm friend, a jovial and hospitable neighbour'. He was, it seemed, like so many of his kind, devoted to field sports and martial exercises, of an indolent and irrresolute nature and little intellect, but yet 'by no means devoid of dignity, or of a due sense of the responsibility attaching to him as head of his house and as a great Border chieftain'.

The Border was still a lawless place and, as Lord Warden of the East and Middle Marches, almost an hereditary office in the Percy family, the earl soon found himself called upon to punish incursions by marauding Scots in the good old way. As he reported to Queen Mary in January 1558, he and his brother had felt it necessary to burn a town in the Merse called Langton. 'We crossed over with a thousand foot and one hundred horse at Norham, burnt the town with divers villages thereabouts and a large quantity of corn, and took a great booty of cattle.' It was a situation in which Harry Hotspur would have been perfectly at home, and the seventh Earl of Northumberland can hardly be blamed for failing to guess that the great Border chieftain was already an endangered species: that he and his neighbours and kinsmen the Dacres of Gilsland, and the Nevilles, Earls of Westmorland, feudal magnates ruling their vast territories like petty kings, were becoming anachronisms in a changing world.

The process of change was accelerated by a series of external events beginning with the accession of Elizabeth Tudor and the establishment of a national Protestant church in England. This was rapidly followed by a revolt in Scotland against both the corrupt and moribund Catholic church and the quasi-colonial regime of the French Queen Regent, Mary of Guise. The Scottish rebels, the self-styled Lords of the Congregation of Jesus, appealed to Queen Elizabeth for help, while France prepared to send reinforcements to the aid of the beleagured Regent.

By the summer of 1559 Scottish affairs were reaching crisis point, making it more than ever vital to ensure that the sensitive and strategic Border region was in trustworthy hands – and the government in London had serious doubts as to the loyalty and competence of the Percy family. Sir Ralph Sadler, veteran diplomat and civil servant despatched north on a fact-finding mission, presently reported to his friend, Secretary of State William Cecil, that in twenty years' experience he had never seen the frontiers in such disorder – a state of affairs which, in Sadler's opinion, 'proceedeth of the lack of stout and wise officers'. Not merely were the Percys and Lord Dacre, Warden of the West Marches, all of them 'rank papists', but Henry Percy had not been near the Border for weeks, while the earl his brother, wrote Sir Ralph, 'is, I assure you, a very unmeet man for the charge which is committed unto him here'.

Cecil acted promptly, relieving both Dacre and Northumberland of their commands, and the aggrieved earl retreated huffily to Petworth, the Sussex property brought into the family in the twelfth century by Joscelin de Louvain at the time of his marriage to the Percy heiress. Earl Thomas remained in the South for several years, entertaining the queen at Petworth in 1563 and being created a Knight of the Garter. But he was back in Yorkshire by the spring of 1568 when Mary Queen of Scots made her dramatic escape from Lochleven Castle, landing at the Cumbrian port of Workington a fugitive with nothing but the clothes she stood up in.

To the Earl of Northumberland, head of the proudest family in the North, it was a matter of honour that the Scottish queen should be confided to his charge, and he urged William Cecil to ensure 'that my credit be not so much impaired in the face of the country as she should be taken from me and delivered to any other person in these parts'. But Cecil, wrestling with the intractable problem of what to do with the Protestant Queen of England's Catholic cousin, heiress and competitor, had no time to waste just then being tactful with the Percys. The earl was brusquely warned to stay away from the Queen of Scots, and he complained angrily that he had been treated like a criminal by his social inferiors at Carlisle where Mary was being held. Mary herself, recognising Northumberland and his lady as kindred spirits and influential friends, took care to maintain cordial relations with the earl and countess; and it is scarcely surprising that Thomas Percy, who had small reason to love the Tudor dynasty, should have seen in the sweet-talking captive a potential instrument for revenge on the jumped-up jacks-in-office in London who had consistently slighted, insulted and swindled him over the past ten years.

Certainly treason was brewing in the North and by the autumn of 1569 the Spanish ambassador could report that the Earls of Northumberland and Westmorland and many others, all Catholics, were ready to release the Queen of Scots by force of arms, take possession of all the North Country and restore the Catholic religion. In fact, the rising was precipitated by Queen Elizabeth's peremptory command to the Earls of Northumberland and

Westmorland to appear at court and give an account of themselves. Both refused to obey. But the example of their associate the Duke of Norfolk, now a prisoner in the Tower, was not encouraging, and Northumberland at least was still reluctant to start anything. So much so that his followers, seeing him 'wavering and fearful', are said to have tricked him into action by waking him in the middle of the night with a story that his enemies were at hand, ready to carry him away a prisoner. In fact, by this time he had very little choice. A weak man driven into a corner, he had either to accept the queen's challenge with all that that implied, or else be shamed and discredited for ever 'in the face of the country'.

The Earl of Sussex, the Queen's Lieutenant stationed at York, lived through some anxious days while waiting for reinforcements to reach him from the South, for he dared not rely on his local levies in a region where Catholicism remained so strong. If the rebel earls had succeeded in releasing the Queen of Scots, they might well have found themselves in a position to dictate terms to London. But Mary had already been hurried away out of reach, and without her charismatic presence amongst them the rebel forces, poorly armed and equipped and irresolutely led, could do no more than make a gesture of defiance against the new order: tearing up and trampling underfoot the English Bibles and prayer books they found in the churches, and celebrating Mass 'in all places where they came'.

Well before the end of the year the impetus behind the movement had been exhausted and its leaders were on the run in the desolate bandit country of Liddesdale, where the Countess of Northumberland was driven to seek shelter in a cottage so wretched as not to be compared with an English dog kennel. Charles Neville, Earl of Westmorland, escaped to Flanders and a lifetime of exile. But Thomas Percy was betrayed to the Scots and, after being held for two and a half years at Lochleven in the custody of the Douglas family, was sold back to the English by the then Regent, James Douglas, Earl of Morton, for the sum of £2000. Thus the ancient, romantic story of the feud of Douglas and Percy ended in a sordid financial transaction amid a storm of disapproval by the balladmongers.

Lord Hunsdon, who took delivery of the prisoner in June 1572, found him still his old genial self, 'readier to talk of hawks and hounds than any thing else', but as obstinate as ever in religion and proclaiming his determination to die a Catholic of the Pope's church. This he was shortly to do. The seventh Earl of Northumberland (who joined the official ranks of the martyrs of the Catholic Church at the end of the last century) was executed at York that August as an attainted person and his head displayed on a pole on Micklegate Bar. The death of 'simple Tom' marked the passing of an epoch. According to the French ambassador, it took place 'not without the regret of many, but without any tumult, for the people there respect the justice and authority of the Queen'. The day of the over-mighty subject was over at last, and no longer could it be said that the men of Northumberland knew no other prince than a Percy – indeed it would be almost two centuries before there was a Percy in Northumberland again.

The seventh earl having left no son, the earldom passed to his brother Henry – a somewhat ambivalent character who had played no part in the rebellion, largely it seems because of personal animosity against Charles Neville. But he remained inevitably an object of acute distrust to the authorities and spent a period of preventive detention in the Tower during the early seventies on suspicion of 'unlawful dealings touching the Queen of Scots'. On his release the eighth earl retired to Petworth where, he told William Cecil, now Lord Burghley, he was 'living like a rustic . . . very well content therewith'. Unhappily, though, he was not content with the rustic life for long and the early eighties found him back in prison, accused of involvement in the Throckmorton Plot, yet another in the long line of conspiracies hatched around the Scottish queen, and which was just then coming to light. He died, still in the Tower, in June 1585, and although a coroner's jury returned a verdict of suicide, rumours that he had been murdered grew so persistent that the government was obliged to conduct an official enquiry into the matter, an enquiry which presently confirmed the inquest verdict. A good deal of doubt still surrounds the affair, but it seems most likely that Henry Percy shot himself to avoid the treason trial which would have left all his property in the hands of the Crown, 'the honour and state of his house and posterity utterly overthrown', and his numerous family in the same condition of poverty and dependence he and his brother had known in childhood.

His eldest son, who now succeeded as ninth earl, had been only five years old at the time of the Northern Rising and showed little sign of interest in the Border, except as a source of revenue to pay for his gambling, mistresses and fine clothes. The earl was later to blame this profligacy on his youthful desire to cut a dash in the world and to a general lack of experience and instruction, but he never showed any sign of following in the rugged footsteps of his forebears. A scholar, savant and connoisseur, his fascination for the arcane mysteries of higher mathematics, astronomy, astrology and alchemy soon earned him the soubriquet of the Wizard Earl and he became a prominent member of that coterie of intellectuals, scientists and free-thinkers which included Walter Raleigh, Francis Bacon, John Dee, Richard Hakluyt and Thomas Hariot.

A melancholy, moody, irascible character, the Wizard Earl married Essex's termagant sister Dorothy and their life together was predictably stormy. In October 1599 Robert Sidney's agent at court, the well-informed Rowland White, told his employer that the Countess of Northumberland had arrived late at night at Essex House and 'a muttering there is that there is unkindness grown between her and the Earl her husband, upon which they are parted'. Three years later, only a month after the birth of the son and heir who was to be 'the solder of their reconcilement', the couple were again known to be living apart, but despite frequent rows and separations there were to be four children of the marriage – another son and two daughters.

The accession of the King of Scots to the English throne might have been expected to bring honours and favour to the head of a family which had suffered so much in the past for its support of the new king's mother, and Northumberland was made a Privy Councillor and Captain of the Gentlemen Pensioners or royal bodyguard. He had previously leased Syon House, the former Bridgettine convent at Isleworth on the western outskirts of London, from the crown and the property was now granted to him in perpetuity by King James. Otherwise the earl does not appear to have sought or hoped for preferment and he took no greater part in public life than that which he considered proper to his rank. He had his library and laboratory at Syon, and there he might quite happily have remained had it not been for the activities of his cousin Thomas Percy who, in the autumn of 1605, rented a small house in

Westminster close by the Parliament House and installed as caretaker a certain Guido Fawkes, then going under the name of Johnson.

Whether the Wizard Earl of Northumberland had been in his cousin's confidence or not really mattered very little in the hysterical aftermath of the discovery of 'Gunpowder Treason and Plot'. The fact that Thomas Percy had dined at Syon on 4 November, added to the fact that he had earlier been admitted to the select ranks of the Gentlemen Pensioners on the earl's recommendation, were more than enough to condemn the earl as an accessory before the fact. The Star Chamber found him guilty of misprision of treason, fined him the punitive sum of £30,000 and committed him to the Tower until it was paid. No more than about a third of it ever was paid, and the Wizard Earl's sojourn in the fortress was to last for nearly sixteen years.

During that time he contrived to make himself tolerably comfortable, surrounding himself with his books, zodiacal charts, globes, crucibles, retorts and alembics, and gradually converting his quarters in the Martin Tower into an annexe of Syon House. He conducted his business affairs and entertained his friends from his prison, even keeping a stable for the convenience of his visitors. For recreation he played tennis and battledore, and had a bowling alley constructed at a cost of £14 8s 9d. He also imported the equipment for playing war games: an inlaid table 'for the practice of the Art Militaire' and a brass mould for casting toy soldiers. The earl believed in high living as well as high thinking, and his cellar included a wide variety of choice wines. Like his friend and fellow captive, Walter Raleigh, he was a heavy smoker and bought large quantities of tobacco from the Virginia merchants.

In the circumstances it is perhaps not very surprising that the Wizard Earl should have taken a somewhat misanthropic view of the world, but his tirade on the subject of the general frailty and unreliability of the female sex contained in his well-known *Advice to His Son* (c.1609) was unprovoked. His wife had stood by him bravely in his adversity, even going so far as to make a defiant attack on his arch-enemy Robert Cecil – 'giving the Ferrett a nipp' as she put it. The earl may have believed that wives and daughters should be kept firmly in their place, but he was to have trouble with his own two daughters – both handsome and spirited girls. Dorothy, the elder, married Robert Sidney, son and heir of

Viscount Lisle, later Earl of Leicester, and a great-great-nephew of Elizabeth's favourite, Robert Dudley. Dorothy's marriage, though it turned out very successfully, took place without Northumberland's approval, for he despised the Sidneys and Dudleys almost as much as he did the Cecils.

Worse was to follow in the spring of 1617, when the Court gossip John Chamberlain wrote to his friend Dudley Carleton about the progress of Lord Hay's courtship of the Earl of Northumberland's younger daughter, Lady Lucy Percy, 'with whom he is far engaged in affection, and finds such acceptance both at her hands and her Mother's that it is thought it will prove a match'. But her father was violently opposed and, as Lord Hay, one of those 'Scottish upstarts' who had come flocking to London in the wake of the new dynasty, had previously been one of the homosexual King's 'young men', the earl's attitude was perhaps understandable. He forcibly detained Lady Lucy with him in his prison, declaring 'that he was a Percy, and could not endure that his daughter should dance any Scottish jigs'. A fortnight later it was reported that the Earl of Northumberland was still keeping his daughter in the Tower 'to secure her from the addresses of Lord Hay', but according to John Chamberlain the earl was also using Lucy as camouflage for his frequent visits to the notorious beauty Frances Howard, Countess of Somerset, accused with her husband of the murder of Sir Thomas Overbury.

Eventually of course, Northumberland had to give way. Lucy was married that October and in spite of his father-in-law's unrelenting hostility, the good-natured Hay, later to become successively Viscount Doncaster and Earl of Carlisle, set about organising a campaign for his release. The Wizard, obstinately reluctant to be beholden to any upstart Scot and perhaps genuinely loath to face the outside world again, was not grateful and had to be persuaded by his sons and daughters grudgingly to agree to abandon his peculiar lifestyle when freedom was eventually granted. But at last, on the afternoon of Sunday, 21 July 1621, he was ceremoniously collected by Lord Doncaster in a coach-and-six, while the Tower warders 'made great moan that they have lost such a benefactor'.

The old earl lived on for another eleven years, not noticeably mellowed by age and misfortune. Unimpressed by threats or bribes, he refused to subscribe to the Royal Loan of 1627 and made no secret of his distrust and disapproval of the Stuart kings, father and son, or of their all-powerful favourite the Duke of Buckingham. In fact, if Buckingham had not been assassinated in 1628, the Wizard Earl would very likely have been returned to the Tower. As it was, he died in his bed at Petworth ironically enough on the anniversary of the Gunpowder Plot and was buried in the chapel there beside his long-suffering wife.

His eldest son, christened Algernon, 'somewhat a strange and disused name', spent much of his childhood in the Tower under the earl's supervision and grew up to be just as stiff-necked. Nevertheless, as the mid-century confrontation between king and Parliament approached, it seemed as if so ancient and obstinately right-wing a family as the Percys must surely take their stand on the side of monarchy. Algernon's brother Henry was heavily implicated in the so-called Army Plot of 1641 to seize the Tower and City of London for the king; his sister Lucy, the beautiful and brilliant Countess of Carlisle, was the queen's closest friend and confidante (while at the same time systematically betraying her secrets), but on the outbreak of the Civil War the tenth earl himself emerged as a leader of the moderate Parliamentary party in the House of Lords.

Like all moderates he remained earnestly in favour of a peaceful settlement and in January 1643 moved that 'a Committee be appointed to consider how there might be an accommodation between the King and his people for the Good, Happiness and Safety of both King and Kingdom'. Unhappily, neither of the principals in the quarrel was in the least interested in an 'accommodation', but Northumberland's masters in the Commons were content to let him lead a Parliamentary commission to Oxford that March for propaganda reasons, and two years later he was one of the sixteen commissioners who negotiated, just as fruitlessly, with the king at Uxbridge.

Although he had been wise enough and fortunate enough to pick the winning side, Earl Algernon was by now suffering serious financial embarrassment from the loss of rents and revenue from his northern estates, woods and collieries, and also from the loss of his former office of Lord Admiral. In March 1645, therefore, he was appointed guardian to those of the royal children who had fallen into Parliament's hands and granted a salary of £3000 a year. In September this salary, or allowance, was increased to £5000 and the earl was given the use of Whitehall, St James's, or any other of the king's houses 'as he shall find occasion, with such Hangings, Bedding, plate, silver vessels or other necessary and fitting accommodation as he shall require'.

After the failure of the Uxbridge talks, a plan to depose King Charles and replace him by one of his sons with Northumberland as regent had come under serious discussion, and in 1647 the royal brothers York and Gloucester and their sister Elizabeth were transferred to Syon House. The king being then confined at nearby Hampton Court, the family were able to meet. It was all very civilised, the Earl of Northumberland welcoming His Majesty in his most stately manner and expressing his 'extraordinary contentment to see the King and his Children together, after such various Chances and so long a Separation'. But the Duke of York's daring escape from St James's the following spring while still under Northumberland's charge put an abrupt end to these amenities, while the king's trial and execution put an equally abrupt end to the earl's public career. Deeply and genuinely shocked, he asked to be relieved of his responsibility for the royal children, suggesting that they should be transferred to the care of his sister Dorothy at Penshurst. This done, he went back to Petworth and stayed there throughout the period of the Interregnum.

In October 1635 a family friend remarked that the Earl of Northumberland was 'but a bungler of getting boys'. His first marriage to Lady Ann Cecil produced only daughters – a misfortune widely attributed to a curse laid by the Wizard Earl, who had strongly opposed the match, declaring that 'the blood of Percy would not mix with that of Cecil if you poured them in a dish'. (Lucy Carlisle's failure to have a child was also popularly supposed to have been because she married against her father's wishes.) Ann Cecil died of smallpox in 1637 and the earl subsequently married again, his second wife being one of the Suffolk Howards who presented him with an heir in July 1644. The infant, christened Joscelin – thus reviving another strange and disused family name – was a sickly child whose health continued to cause his parents anxiety.

After the Restoration, Northumberland and his brother-in-law the Earl of Leicester received a summons to appear at Whitehall. 'We went together,' recorded Leicester, 'not knowing for what, and having stayed awhile in the King's Withdrawing Chamber, we were called into the Council Chamber and there, contrary to his or my expectations, we were sworn Privy Councillors.' At the outbreak of the Great Plague of 1665, the Council transferred its deliberations to Syon House, but in general the tenth earl preferred to hold aloof from politics, devoting the closing years of his life to cultivating his garden at Syon and to his stud at Petworth – the state papers of the time contain numerous warrants authorising him to import 'barbs', that is barbary or Arabian horses, free of duty. He died in 1668 to be buried like his father at Petworth, his last months gladdened by the birth of a grandson. But although the feeble Joscelin Percy had survived long enough to marry Lady Elizabeth Wriothesley and to sire two daughters and a son, the baby, Henry, died at eight months 'from sheer poverty of blood' and the elder girl, Henrietta, lived no more than four years. In May 1670 Earl Joscelin himself succumbed to a fever while travelling in Italy, thus leaving his second daughter, three-year-old Elizabeth, as sole heiress and representative of the senior line. Or was she?

Early in 1671 one James Percy, derisively nicknamed 'the Trunkmaker' from his having once followed this perfectly respectable trade, came forward to challenge Lady Elizabeth's title, presenting a petition to the House of Lords praying for recognition in his person of the style, honours and dignity of Baron Percy and Earl of Northumberland, as a great-grandson of Sir Richard Percy, fifth son of the fifth earl. While it is not impossible that the Trunkmaker may have possessed legitimate Percy blood, he had hopelessly confused his dates and generations which, together with his inability to produce any documentary evidence to substantiate his claim, told heavily against him. He received some support from the old Countess of Pembroke (born Lady Anne Clifford), who remembered hearing of some Percy children being smuggled out of Yorkshire at the time of the troubles in 1569; but the family, headed by the formidable Dowager Countess of Northumberland, grandmother and guardian of the heiress, closed their ranks against the claimant. The case dragged on for nearly twenty years, and it was June 1689 before the Lords finally found against the Trunkmaker, ordering him to appear in Westminster Hall wearing a placard round his neck with the words 'The False and Impudent Pretender to the Earldom of Northumberland'. There is no record that this vindictive punishment was ever carried out, but James Percy was by now a broken man and is generally believed to have died shortly afterwards.

Meanwhile, Elizabeth Percy had been growing up and in 1679 King Charles II approached the dowager with an application on behalf of his son George, hoping that her ladyship would at least promise him first refusal. But although George – the king's third son by Barbara Villiers – was described by John Evelyn as being of all His Majesty's children 'the most accomplished and worth the owning', the dowager was not interested in helping her sovereign lord to provide for his bastards. Instead, she proceeded to match or, more accurately, to sell the red-headed Elizabeth to Lord Ogle, the Duke of Newcastle's sickly and feeble-minded heir. 'My lord Ogle does prove the saddest creature of all kinds that could have been found fit to be named for my Lady Percy,' wrote Lady Percy's cousin, the Countess of Sunderland; 'as ugly as anything young could be.'

Perhaps fortunately for all concerned, Lord Ogle died within six months of the wedding, but the next bridegroom selected for Elizabeth Percy was scarcely any more congenial. Thomas Thynne of Longleat, generally known as 'Tom o' Ten Thousand', may have been one of the richest and best-looking men in England, but he also boasted a reputation second to none as drunkard, womaniser and scoundrel. This marriage, too, was in name only – in fact, the bride appears to have promptly fled the country – and it ended violently in Pall Mall one Sunday evening in February 1682, when Tom Thynne was set upon in his coach by a gang of armed desperadoes. As the magistrate, Sir John Reresby, was going to bed that night, he received an urgent summons to go to Mr Thynne's lodgings and found him 'mortally wounded by five bullets which had entered his belly and side, shot from a blunderbus'.

The assassins, two Swedes – Christopher Vratz and John Stern – and a Pole called Borosky or Boratsky were quickly arrested, brought to trial and subsequently hanged although the man who had hired them, the Swedish adventurer Count Königsmarck who, it was said, had hoped to marry Mr Thynne's widow, was acquitted by a corrupt jury and escaped. The affair naturally created a considerable scandal – some unkind people not hesitating to accuse Elizabeth Percy of having encouraged Königsmarck's attentions, even of having planned her husband's murder. Five months later the widow, still only fifteen years old, took as her third husband Charles Seymour, Duke of Somerset, and this time settled down to married life, although the union was more one of convenience (especially financial convenience) than affection.

The Somersets became close friends of Queen Anne and Duchess Elizabeth held the office of Mistress of the Robes after the Queen's great quarrel with Sarah Duchess of Marlborough. With the advent of the Hanoverians, however, she stayed away from court, ostensibly on the grounds of health but really because her aristocratic Percy soul revolted at the prospect of having to associate with George I's German cronies. She lived either at Northumberland House in Charing Cross or at Petworth, not caring for suburban Syon which she dismissed as 'a hobbledehoy place, neither town nor Country'. She died at Petworth in 1722, and her eldest son Algernon succeeded her as Baron Percy and Earl of Northumberland.

In the next generation the Percy honours were once more transmitted through the female line, through Algernon's daughter, another Lady Elizabeth, more usually known as Lady Betty. In 1739 Lady Betty was being courted by a young Yorkshire baronet and, like a dutiful daughter, wrote to her mama:

> I never felt so awkwardly about writing to you as I do at present; nor indeed had I ever before so odd a subject to write about. However . . . I shall proceed to tell you that Sir Hugh Smithson the other day asked me to let him speak to me, which was to inform me that he designed proposing himself to my papa. You will easily guess how much I was surprised and confounded at so extraordinary a compliment. However, I mustered up my courage and told him that I could not give my consent to his doing it . . . but all I could prevail upon him was to promise to defer mentioning it till I came to London

A few days later, Lady Betty admitted she was by no means indifferent to her good-looking and exceptionally well mannered suitor. 'Nay, I shall not scruple to own that I have a partiality for him,' she informed her parents. 'His estate, I have been told, will be greater than what I believe you apprehend; and he has an extreme good character.'

Sir Hugh, it emerged, was already worth a snug £4000 a year, with further expectations from his cousin, Mr Smithson of Tottenham High Cross. Originally Yorkshire tenant farmers and yeomen, the family fortunes had been founded by the first baronet, Sir Hugh's great-great-grandfather, haberdasher and citizen of London, who had purchased the manor of Stanwick from Anthony Catterick in 1638 and was connected on his mother's side with the old Catholic aristocracy of the North.

When the matter of his granddaughter's betrothal was tactfully broached to that family tyrant and ogre of family pride, the sixth Duke of Somerset, his Grace responded that he did not know Sir Hugh Smithson nor his fortune, but if upon enquiry he should find out that he was gentlemanly and respectable and with sufficient means to settle £2000 on Lady Betty by way of jointure and £500 a year pin money, he should not object to the match.

Of course, Hugh Smithson, however gentlemanly and respectable, would never have stood a chance with the Seymours had Lady Betty then been a great heiress, but in 1739 it was expected that her younger brother George, Lord Beauchamp, would presently succeed to both the Seymour and Percy titles. Unhappily George was to die of smallpox five years after his sister's marriage and although the old Duke of Somerset, in a frenzy of rage and bitterness, did his utmost to prevent the lowly baronet from reviving the Percy name, he was frustrated by Sir Hugh's superior command of diplomacy and tactics. After the death of her father in 1750, therefore, Lady Betty Smithson and her husband succeeded to the earldom of Northumberland, assuming the name and arms of Percy by special Act of Parliament. Sir Hugh had to put up with a good deal of ill-natured teasing but he was, after all, doing no more than Joscelin of Louvain had done seven centuries earlier, and he turned out to be the best thing that had happened to the Percy family since the days of Harry Hotspur.

Created Duke of Northumberland in 1766 after an active political career, Sir Hugh rescued the ancient castle of Alnwick and the northern estates from virtual dereliction after years of neglect and mismanagement. 'He found the country almost a desert', remarked an admiring contemporary, 'and he clothed it with woods and improved it with agriculture.' As well as replanting trees, improvidently cut down for timber and not replaced, rebuilding ruined cottages and implementing drainage projects and other agricultural improvements, the first Duke of Northumberland soon showed himself to be a shrewd businessman. Petworth and the Sussex estate had passed to the Wyndham family by the terms of the Duke of Somerset's will, but development of the mineral resources – especially coal – on the Percy lands in the North brought an increase in the annual rent-roll from around £8500 in the late 1740s to £50,000 by 1778.

The Northumberlands were famous for their lavish hospitality and the magnificence of their establishment – 'as magnificent as it was possible for any English nobleman's to be'. The duke also built up a reputation as a generous patron of 'the polite arts', spending impressive sums of money on pictures, landscape gardening and building and interior decoration by the Adams brothers.

The duchess, good-humoured, robust and plain-spoken, played a leading part in mid-eighteenth-century high society. A lady of literary tastes and, according to James Boswell, 'of excellent understanding and lively talents', her diary contains some unexpected glimpses of contemporary events and personalities. Of Colonel Clive newly returned from India: 'his complexion bears a near resemblance to mahogany and had his dress been Oriental he might easily have been taken for the Nabob himself'. Of the twenty-three-year-old King George III, she tells us he was blue eyed, with auburn hair, a fresh complexion but with a tendency now and then to throw out pimples. She describes the disconcerting blue, scarlet and black faces of three Cherokee Indians come to negotiate a lasting peace with England; and, in 1770, was present at the wedding in Paris between the Dauphin and the fifteen-year-old Austrian princess Marie Antoinette, 'very little and slender' and not looking more than twelve years old.

The duchess had by this time resigned her post as Lady of the Bedchamber to Queen Charlotte and was indulging her passion for foreign travel. Two years later she paid a visit to Voltaire in his retreat at Ferney near Geneva: 'He is tall and rather genteel and has a Fire in his Eyes I never saw in those of a Man of 25.' (He was then in his late seventies.) In 1774, when she herself was in her late fifties, she set off again, following the course of the River

Rhône, exploring the sights of Avignon, and being driven round Marseilles. Down on the quay, although 'from the want of Tide the smell here is intolerable', the intrepid traveller got into her boat and 'row'd about the Harbour where there was a prodigious number of Ships and Boats of all sizes Shapes and Nations', but only four galleys now, she noted, and two thousand slaves, 'the rest being sent to Toulon'.

The second Duke of Northumberland revived the family's ancient military tradition. As Earl Percy he served as a volunteer under the Duke of Brunswick in the Seven Years' War and rode in Lord Granby's famous charge through the French lines at Minden. He also played a reluctant part in the American War of Independence, writing to his father from Boston in 1774: 'As I cannot say this is a business I very much admire, I hope it will not be my fate to be ordered up the country. Be that as it may, I will do my duty as long as I continue in the service.'

Twenty years later, when England was threatened with invasion by Napoleon, there was happily no conflict between duty and inclination and the duke raised, paid and clothed a volunteer force of some 1500 of his own tenants – riflemen, cavalry and artillerymen – under the command of his eldest son. 'This spirited energy, so worthy of a Percy,' exclaims the author of a nineteenth-century guide to Alnwick, 'combined to form a glorious spectacle which dissipated every apprehension at home, and penetrated with despair the hirelings of ambition.' It was a Major Henry Percy who brought the news of Waterloo to London, arriving in St James's Square where the Prince Regent was attending a reception, a travel-stained figure in a post chaise with three French eagles sticking out of the windows. Another Percy of the blood of Harry Hotspur won the V.C. in the Crimea at the Battle of Inkerman; and yet another – the ninth Duke of Northumberland – was killed in action in France in May 1940.

The third duke, who succeeded in 1817, was a moderate Tory described by Charles Greville as 'a very good sort of man, with a very narrow understanding; an eternal talker and a prodigious bore'. He married Charlotte, daughter of the Earl of Powis and a grand-daughter of Clive of India – 'a sensible, amiable and good-humoured woman ruling her husband in all things' – who was for a time State Governess to the young Princess Victoria. The marriage was a childless one and the third duke was succeeded in 1847 by his brother Algernon.

After service in the navy as a young man, the fourth duke had chosen to devote himself to intellectual pursuits. Created Baron Prudhoe in 1816, he travelled extensively in the Middle and Near East and joined a group of pioneer Egyptologists studying the mysterious monuments of that antique land. In 1834 his scientific curiosity led him to join Sir John Herschel's expedition to South Africa to observe the constellations of the southern hemisphere, and in the 1840s, he encouraged and financed the scholar Edward Lane in the preparation of his monumental *Arabic Lexicon*.

In that age of philanthropy all wealthy and powerful men were expected to dispense constructive charity as a matter of plain duty and, with his naval background, Duke Algernon paid particular attention to projects for the welfare of sailors and fishermen, his special interest being the Royal National Lifeboat Institution. At the time of the Great Exhibition of 1851 he offered a prize for the best designed model lifeboat and was instrumental in bringing into practical use the first self-righting boat, as well as promoting the building of lifeboat stations all round the coast of the British Isles. It was also Duke Algernon who was responsible for transforming the interior of Alnwick Castle into an Italianate palace. From the outside the building still presents the appearance of the archetypal romantic medieval castle, but inside it is rich in eighteenth-century paintings, porcelain and furniture, and further embellished by the collections of Egyptian and other exotic antiquities amassed by the fourth duke on his travels.

Nineteenth-century Dukes of Northumberland lived in style, as, of course, they were expected to do.

> The magnificence of Alnwick Castle . . . the elegance of Syon House, which for taste and beauty is scarcely to be paralleled in Europe; the stateliness of Northumberland House, the finished model of a palace for the town residence of a great nobleman; were all kept up with unrivalled splendour, and at the same time with a judicious and well-regulated economy.

Today Northumberland House in London is commemorated only by a street name, but the elegance of Syon remains to be enjoyed both by the public and the family, and after six hundred and fifty years there are still Percys at Alnwick, which has become the family's principal home, although part of the castle is now used as a teacher training college. The present, tenth, duke has followed in the footsteps of the first Duke of Northumberland as a dedicated planter of trees and, as a practical, hardworking farmer and land-owner, has devoted his life to watching over the inheritance handed down through the centuries.

Nine hundred years have gone by since the first William de Perci came to Yorkshire and during those years the exploits of the family founded by that rugged young Norman adventurer have woven a glowing thread of courage and violence, tragedy and romance into the dense tapestry of history and legend which makes up the story of England's past.

The Sackvilles of Knole

Jour de ma vie

Knole from the north-west, and the Stone Court, Knole, drawn by J. Fulleylove and engraved by C. Carter *Mary Evans Picture Library*

THE SACKVILLES OF KNOLE

Jour de ma vie

LIKE the Percys and a handful of other noble English families, the Sackvilles can legitimately claim pre-Conquest Norman origins – though whether they can also legitimately claim to have come into Normandy with Rollo the Dane in 876 is perhaps open to doubt. The English Sackvilles begin with Esbrandus, or Herbrand, de Sackville, or Sauqueville of Sauqueville sur Scie in Normandy, the seneschal to William Giffard, who was summoned to England by his lord shortly after the Conquest, possible as early as 1070. He is recorded in *Domesday Book* as holding the manor of Fawley in Buckinghamshire. Another Sackville, Richard, from Secqueville-en-Bessin, probably a relation and possibly a brother of Herbrand, also appears in the Domesday survey – as the holder of manors in Essex and Hertfordshire – and he may well have arrived even earlier than Herbrand. But it is from Herbrand that the family descends and, as was so often the way, the first important step in its upward progress was marked by a marriage: that of Jordan, Herbrand's grandson, to Ela, daughter and coheiress of Ralph de Dene, who brought her husband important estates in Sussex, including the manor of Buckhurst near Withyham on the Kent-Sussex borders.

As well as being rich, Ela was also fruitful, bearing a family of five sons. The eldest, another Jordan, died round about 1208 and Buckhurst passed to his younger brother Geoffrey. Succeeding generations of Sackvilles pursued uneventful but by no means unprofitable careers, marrying shrewdly and consolidating their territorial assets; performing their duties as citizens, but wisely steering clear of politics. It was another marriage at the beginning of the sixteenth century which finally brought the family into prominence, though when John Sackville of Chiddingley allied himself to Margaret, daughter of William Boleyn of Blickling and Hever Castle in Kent, neither family could have foreseen the notoriety to be achieved by Margaret's niece Anne, born in the same year as Richard, eldest child of the Sackville marriage.

It was this Richard who, long afterwards, told Queen Elizabeth's former tutor Roger Ascham that a harsh schoolmaster had driven him from all love of learning before he was fourteen years old – a confession which is supposed to have helped to inspire Ascham to write his famous treatise on education. But Richard Sackville's unhappy schooldays do not appear to have impeded a career which took him first to Cambridge and thence to Gray's Inn and in November 1529 to the House of Commons as member for the borough of Arundel, giving the young man from Sussex a ringside seat at the great take-over battle for control of the wealth of the church in England as it was fought in Parliament.

He married Winifred Bruges, or Bridges, daughter of a former Lord Mayor of London, and his eldest son Thomas was born in 1536 – the year which also saw the beheading of his cousin Anne Boleyn. Not that the queen's misfortune had any effect on his prospects. Towards the end of the 1530s Sackville became Under Treasurer of the Exchequer and in 1548 he won the important and lucrative appointment of Chancellor of the Court of Augmentations, which was still engaged in processing the transfer of religious real estate into lay hands. Sackville was knighted in 1549 and the following year nominated Lord Lieutenant of Sussex. In 1553 he was one of the witnesses to King Edward VI's controversial will which bequeathed the Crown to Lady Jane Grey, but managed to remain *persona grata* with Queen Mary Tudor. On the accession of Elizabeth he became a member of the new Privy Council and during the next eight years up to his death, his name recurs regularly: the queen's representative at a memorial service in St Paul's for the King of France; one of a panel of commissioners appointed to supervise the repair of Rochester Bridge; inspector of coastal defences at Rye, and custodian of Lady Margaret Lennox when she was suspected of illicit match-making on behalf of her son Lord Darnley. A widely varied list, but no more than was expected of any Tudor government official.

Like his contemporary William Cavendish, Richard Sackville possessed an enviable flair for finance which had already earned him the punning nickname of Fillsack, and throughout his professional career he had been quietly acquiring manor after manor in the south-east. The Sackville empire covered many thousands of acres in Surrey, Kent and Sussex, acres of good meadow, pasture and woodland – an especially valuable commodity this last at a time when the timber of the Wealden forests provided the essential fuel for an expanding iron-founding industry. But it was in 1564 that Sir Richard made his most significant purchase from the point of view of the Sackville family fortunes, paying the sum of 'sixe hundred and forty one pounds, five shillings and tenpence halfe penny of lawfull money of England' for the mansion known as Salisbury House situated within the parish of St Bridget in Fleet Street in the suburbs of the City of London. The Salisbury House estate, also known as Salisbury Inn or Salisbury Court, and belonging to the bishopric of Salisbury, comprised all the land lying between Fleet Street and the River Thames, between St Bride's church and Whitefriars Street, together with its shops, houses, tenements, gardens, orchards and wharves and, by any standards, represented a first rate capital investment.

When Sir Richard died, therefore, Thomas Sackville became a very rich man and, almost as important, he was already being singled out by Queen Elizabeth 'by her particular choice and liking . . . to a continual private attendance upon her own person'. Although Elizabeth was seldom, if ever, heard to mention the name of Anne Boleyn, it was noticeable that her maternal relations could always rely on her favour and protection – they were 'of the tribe of Dan' according to the Earl of Leicester. She had extended this favour towards the Sackvilles by helping Sir Richard in the matter of his purchase of Salisbury House and allowing his wife, a well-known Catholic sympathiser, to escape prosecution when she was caught in the act of attending mass at Lady Carey's house in Fetter Lane in 1562. But Thomas was not only the queen's cousin, he was her close contemporary and an agreeable, cultivated man whose company she enjoyed for its own sake.

In his early years Thomas Sackville had acquired a certain reputation as a poet and man of letters, best known for his 'Induction' and 'Complaint of the Duke of Buckingham' in a long philosophical poem by several hands entitled *A Mirror for Magistrates*, and *Gorbudoc* or *Ferrex and Porrex*, a five act tragedy based on the legendary history of Geoffrey of Monmouth. His contributions to *A Mirror for Magistrates* are still highly regarded, and pronounced by one authority on Elizabethan literature to 'contain the best poetry written in the English language between Chaucer and Spenser', the originals 'or at least the models of some of Spenser's finest work'. *Gorbudoc*, written in collaboration with the radical politician Thomas Norton, has the distinction of being the first English blank verse tragedy and is said to have introduced 'the true mode of tragic expression' to contemporary audiences. But when the piece was first performed by the young gentlemen of the Inner Temple in the early 1560s, it is probably fair to assume that the audiences were a good deal more interested in identifying the numerous political allusions lurking in the text. Although *Gorbudoc* is certainly entitled to its landmark status in the history of English drama, today it is of concern only to dedicated students of English Literature.

Thomas Sackville himself regarded his versifying in the light merely of a youthful hobby to be discarded along with student days – the serious business of his life being to follow in his father's footsteps as a landowner, businessman, courtier and public servant. In the year of his father's death he received two unmistakable indications from the queen that an honourable career of public service was his for the asking when Elizabeth, always parsimonious with honours, created him Baron Buckhurst and granted him the reversion of the manor of Knole at Sevenoaks in Kent.

Now so closely associated with the Sackville name, Knole already had a long history. It is possible that a Roman building once occupied the site, and medieval Knole first appears in the record in 1291. In 1456 it was sold by Lord Saye and Sele to Thomas Bourchier, Archbishop of Canterbury, for £266 13s 4d and Bourchier and his successor Cardinal Morton are responsible between them for most of the fabric of the present house, which they converted from the original rustic manor to an archiepiscopal palace. In 1538 Henry VIII cast covetous eyes on Knole, forcing an unwilling

Thomas Cranmer to 'deliver his house up into the King's hands'. Edward VI gave it to the Earl of Warwick, and Mary Tudor gave it to Reginald Pole. When Elizabeth gave it to Thomas Sackville, it had already been leased (to the Earl of Leicester) and sublet, so that, as the sitting tenants showed no sign of obliging the new owner by removing themselves, he had to wait until 1603 before getting vacant possession.

Lord Buckhurst was however kept fully occupied during the intervening years with two diplomatic missions to France in the late sixties and early seventies – both connected with the Anjou marriage negotiations. He was twice in the Netherlands during the 1580s and in France again at the beginning of the nineties. At home he was regularly employed as a commissioner at state trials and he was among those appointed to sit in judgement on Thomas Howard Duke of Norfolk, Philip Earl of Arundel and Mary Queen of Scots. It was Lord Buckhurst who was sent to Fotheringay with the news that sentence had been passed, while in January 1601 he presided as Lord High Steward over the trial of the Earl of Essex. He was sworn a member of the Privy Council in 1586, made a Knight of the Garter in 1589, elected Chancellor of the University of Oxford in 1591 and in May 1599 nominated to succeed the late Lord Burghley in the office of Lord Treasurer. Rich, dignified and respected (except by Leicester – they loathed each other) Buckhurst was a pervasive presence on the political stage. Never a leader of men or an initiator of policies, his personality as a statesman made little impact on his times. Nevertheless he served queen and country faithfully, one of those steady, reliable bureaucratic workhorses without which the government machine could not have functioned.

When Elizabeth died, Lord Buckhurst was in his late sixties and in poor health, being much afflicted by a weak chest and 'rheums'. But Tudor public servants never retired of their own free will and Buckhurst set out to travel as far as Broxbourne on the Great North Road to meet the new king, who received him graciously and confirmed him in the office of Lord Treasurer. The following spring he was created Earl of Dorset and appointed one of the English commissioners at the Somerset House conference, where peace with Spain was finally negotiated that summer. In October he was directed by the king to impose a greatly increased duty on tobacco in the hope of discouraging those lieges whose 'great and immoderate taking' of the noxious weed was seriously damaging their health, and in 1605 he was called upon to entertain the royal family at Oxford in his capacity as chancellor of the university. In 1606 he was involved in the important constitutional case of a merchant named Bates, who had refused to pay a new duty on imported currants levied by the Crown without parliamentary authority. The barons of the Exchequer Court duly gave judgement for the Crown and its servant the Lord Treasurer – but it was a portent of a future with which Thomas Sackville would not be concerned.

As well as his continuing public duties, the Earl of Dorset had at last obtained possession of Knole, and in 1605 he embarked on an ambitious programme of rebuilding and refurbishing. The accounts show that in the last ten months of his life he spent over four thousand pounds on the house, from which Charles Phillips, a previous family historian, concludes he must have spent between ten and fifteen thousand altogether. It was he who built the Great Staircase leading to the ballroom, once the solar or upper chamber, added the oak wainscoting to the Great Hall and put in the elaborately decorated plaster ceiling and equally elaborate carved screens surmounted by an achievement of the Sackville arms.

Sadly though, old Thomas was not destined to enjoy his new grandeur at leisure. He died quite literally in harness, struck down by what was probably a coronary while sitting at the council table at Whitehall where he had spent so much of his life, in April 1608 and was buried in the family vault at Withyham parish church. His marriage, to Cicely Baker, daughter of John Baker of Sissinghurst, appears to have been an entirely happy one, with four sons and three daughters reaching maturity, but Robert, second Earl of Dorset, survived his father by less than a year, dying in London most likely of the plague, in February 1609 at the age of forty-eight.

Richard, the third earl, who thus came into his inheritance in the month before his twenty-first birthday, was the son of Robert's first marriage, to Margaret Howard whose father, the fourth Duke of Norfolk, had been executed for his part in the Ridolfi Plot to free Mary Queen of Scots. Richard proved a disaster for the family – self-indulgent, spendthrift and shallow. His extravagance became a byword and his 'excessive prodigality in housekeeping and other noble ways at court, at tilting, masqueing and the like' came very close to ruining the Sackvilles and losing Knole.

Apart from his prodigal habits, Richard is chiefly remembered for his wife, the famous and formidable Lady Anne Clifford. Lady Anne – and it is a tribute to the strength of her personality that despite being twice married she remains best known by her maiden name – was the daughter of George Clifford, Earl of Cumberland, the Elizabethan magnifico, buccaneer, sportsman and courtier. In the famous miniature by Nicholas Hilliard, he is depicted as the Queen's Champion and Knight of Pendragon Castle – a glamorous figure dressed for the Accession Day tilts in star-studded armour and embroidered surcoat, his helmet at his feet, the queen's glove, or favour, proudly displayed in his hat.

Although no disaster ever succeeded in quenching George Clifford's 'spark of adventure' or in discouraging his compulsive urge to go off on yet another unprofitable treasure hunt in Spanish waters, he still contrived to retain great estates in Cumberland, Westmorland and Yorkshire, and Lady Anne was his only surviving child. Unhappily, when he died in October 1605, he was found to have left a will bequeathing the northern property to his brother Francis, with reversion to his daughter only in the absence of other male heirs, having apparently either forgotten or ignored the fact that the estates were already entailed on his child, regardless of sex, by a deed executed in the reign of Edward II. This, of course, opened the way for a legal battle which was to rage intermittently over the next forty years, between Francis Clifford, who was not unnaturally determined to defend his position against all comers, and his niece Anne, just as determined to enforce her claim to her rugged ancestral domains of Appleby and Pendragon, Brougham and Brough, Barden and Skipton. The dispute overshadowed Lady Anne's first marriage. As she herself records:

> With my first Lord I had contradictions and crosses about the desire he had to make me sell my right in the lands of my ancient inheritance for money, which I never did nor never would consent unto; insomuch as the matter was the cause of a long contention betwixt us.

Lord Dorset, needless to say, was in no way concerned over the justice of his wife's title to her 'ancient inheritance'. He was only interested in the financial compensation which might be wrung from the Cliffords, and Lady Anne's celebrated diary, which gives a minute account of her daily life during the years 1616, 1617 and 1619, tells the story of his bullying attempts to break her resistance. His family and friends – from the Archbishop of Canterbury downwards – are all co-opted into the struggle to induce the Lady Anne to sign away her rights. Their tactics are sometimes terrifying, sometimes flattering: she is not to be allowed to live at Knole; her two-year-old child, Margaret, is taken away; her husband will not come to see her any more. On 12 May 1616 she writes:

> All this time my Lord was in London where he had all and infinite great resort coming to him. He went much abroad to Cocking, to Bowling Alleys, to Plays and Horse Races, and commended by all the world. I stayed in the country, having many times a sorrowful and heavy heart, and being condemned by most folks because I would not consent to the agreements, so as I may truly say, I am like an owl in the desert.

But still the young Lady Dorset was not to be moved. Not even by King James himself. In January 1617 husband and wife were summoned to the royal presence in the Drawing Chamber at Whitehall. The diary records:

> He put out all that were there and my Lord and I kneeled by his chair sides when he persuaded us both to peace and to put the whole matter wholly into his hands, which my Lord consented to, but I beseeched His Majesty to pardon me for that I would never part from Westmorland while I lived upon any condition whatsoever.

There is a note by the side of this entry: 'The Queen gave me warning not to trust my matters absolutely to the King lest he should deceive me.'

Three days later there was another confrontation, with all the parties to the dispute present, plus an impressive array of legal talent. 'The King asked us all if we would submit to his judgement in this case, my uncle Cumberland my Coz. Clifford, and my Lord answered they would, but I would never agree to it without Westmorland at which the King grew in a great chaff.'

After all this excitement Lady Anne went back to Knole to worry about her little girl's ague, nose bleeds and teething, to sit over her stitchery, read her Bible and walk in the gardens, or lose at cards with the steward, Edward Legge, and Peter Basket, Gentleman of the Horse. It is clear that she was often lonely and often bored. 'The time grew tedious, so as I used to go to bed about 8 o'clock'. When her husband did condescend to come and see her, he was moody and irritable – 'sometimes I had fair words from him and sometimes foul' – and before long they would be quarrelling again over the everlasting business of her land, on which neither was prepared to give an inch. He accused her of being 'devoid of all reason' on the subject, while she believed some evil spirit was at work, making him 'as violent as possible'.

But apart from this, and in spite of the earl's infidelities and his neglect – 'my lord being in the midst of his merry progress far out of Sussex' – the couple were not always at odds. There are references in the diary and in Lady Anne's letters to my lord's goodness and kindness, to his sitting and reading with her, or their playing together at Barley Break on the bowling green at Knole. Occasionally, too, she came up to town to stay at Dorset House in Fleet Street, and in November 1617 she was at court wearing a 'green damask gown embroidered without a farthingale'. Christmas that year was also spent in London, there being 'great housekeeping' at Dorset House. The Sackvilles dined in state on Christmas Day, and on 28 December entertained a great company of neighbours to eat venison.

Lady Anne kept their tenth wedding anniversary, 25 February 1619, 'as a day of jubilee'. Her health was bad during this year and she was saddened by the death of her infant son, Thomas, Lord Buckhurst (she lost three babies altogether). But her husband seems to have been rather kinder to her and in general there seems to have been less 'falling out', although she continued to worry about her money affairs and her jointure, which had still not been secured to her.

Lord Dorset wasn't well either. Perhaps all that racketing about – the country house visiting, card playing, cockfighting and theatre-going – described in his wife's *Day-by-Day* book was beginning to take its toll. Five years later, on the morning of Easter Sunday 1624, he wrote to Lady Anne from Dorset House, saying that he had intended to come down to Knole and to have received the sacrament with her, but had been prevented by illness – vomiting and a fit of fever. However, 'I thank God I am now at good ease, having rested well this morning'. By noon that day he was dead. He was, wrote his widow, 'just 35 years old at his death, and I about 10 months younger, but I was not with him when he died, being then very sick and ill myself at Knole House in Kent, where I and my two daughters then lay.'

Lady Anne Clifford was to survive Richard Sackville by more than half a century, and her second husband, Philip Herbert, Earl of Pembroke, by more than a quarter of a century, dying at last in her eighty-seventh year on 22 March 1676 in her own chamber at Brougham Castle overlooking her beloved Westmorland fells. She had, needless to say, triumphantly outlived all the male Cliffords and long since come into the lands of her ancient inheritance. A sturdy, autocratic and indomitable old lady, she had, as a girl, stood among the crowds in Westminster Abbey to watch the solemnities of Queen Elizabeth's funeral performed and, as a young married woman had defied King James in his own withdrawing chamber. She had seen the Stuarts humbled, and lived through the Commonwealth (sharing Appleby Castle for a time with a Parliamentary garrison commanded by the regicide Thomas Harrison) to see the king come into his own again – and had not, one suspects, been unduly impressed by any of it. Her real interests had always lain in the North Country: her lifelong obsession had been with the preservation of her ancient rights in Westmorland and the Clifford inheritance which eventually passed through her to the Tufton family – descendants of her daughter Margaret, 'the Child' whose clothes, ailments and progress figure so prominently in the Knole diary.

As all three of his sons by Anne Clifford had died in infancy, Richard Sackville was succeeded by his brother Edward, a handsome, hot-tempered individual who, in 1613, became notorious for killing Lord Bruce of Kinloss in a duel over a woman. In spite of this not very creditable episode, Edward Sackville led a busy public life. He was knighted in 1616, when Prince Charles was created

Prince of Wales, travelled extensively in France and Italy and was an active member of the House of Commons. He spoke out in defence of his friend the disgraced Lord Chancellor Francis Bacon and was an active supporter of the Protestant cause in Germany. This was a burning issue of the day, and Edward Sackville formed part of a tiresomely insistent Parliamentary lobby urging the king to intervene on behalf of his embattled son-in-law the Elector Palatine, drawing a pathetic picture of the plight of the Elector's wife, the English Princess Elizabeth. 'The Foxes have holes and the Birds of the air have nests, but the daughter of our King and Kingdom scarce knows where to lay her head, or if she do not where in safety.' This championship of the Elector's cause, and with it encouragement of the widespread anti-Spanish feeling in the country at a time when King James was trying to arrange a Spanish marriage for the Prince of Wales, did not endear Edward Sackville to his sovereign. There was trouble, too, over the management of the Virginia Company and Bermuda Islands Company, in both of which Sir Edward was a major shareholder. A quarrel had arisen between two factions on the board of the Virginia Company, and in April 1623 'the two parties appeared before the King with their accusations and allegations, when Sackville carried himself so insolently that the King was fain to take him down soundly and roundly'. Matters were not improved by the king's suspicion that the settlements which Sackville was helping to finance in the New World were dominated by Puritans.

The fourth Earl of Dorset was, therefore, a tough, hardbitten, experienced politician and man of the world in his mid-thirties by the time he succeeded to the heavily encumbered and much reduced family property. The third earl, who had 'lived in the greatest splendour of any nobleman in England', had been selling land steadily during the last ten years of his life, but still left debts amounting to approximately half a million pounds by today's values. It was to take his brother years to restore the estates to solvency and he complained constantly about his financial difficulties.

The fourth earl maintained his transatlantic interests though, and in 1637 he petitioned the king for the grant of 'certain islands on the south of New England, viz. Long Island, Cole Island, Sandy Point, Hell Gates, Martin's [Martha's?] Vineyard, Elizabeth Islands,

Block Island, with other islands near thereunto' which had been 'lately discovered by some of your Majesty's subjects, and are not yet inhabited by any Christians.' And a year later, he petitioned for 'an island called Sandy, lying near the continent of America, in height of 44 degrees', recently discovered by one Rose, who had suffered shipwreck and, finding no inhabitants, had taken possession. From the endorsements scribbled on these documents, it would appear that both petitions were granted but unfortunately their later history is lost. The real estate value of the eastern seaboard of the United States from Cape Cod to Delaware Bay, even when uninhabited by Christians, thus so casually demanded, beggars the imagination. But for a Sackville all the riches of the New World could not compete with the beauties of Knole, impoverished as they were (the total income from the Knole estate in 1628 had been just over £100). A delightful description survives of the rooms of the old house perfumed for a banquet with orange flower water and by sweetbrier, sweet-scented stocks, gillyflowers and wallflowers in 'glasses and pots in every window and chimney'.

The master of Knole was still following an active career of public service and consequently spent much of his time in London, sitting on commissions appointed to enquire into such matters as the decrease in the wool trade or the enforcement of building regulations. He was concerned with Irish affairs, ecclesiastical affairs, revenue and naval affairs. He was a Knight of the Garter, a Privy Councillor, Lord Chamberlain to the Queen, High Steward of the Honour of Grafton, joint Lord Lieutenant of Sussex and Middlesex and Master of Ashdown Forest, while his wife held the influential post of governess to the royal children.

Lord Dorset was, in short, very much an establishment figure and when the Civil War broke out naturally ranged himself on the royalist side of the barricades. His name is on the list of forty-two peers who subscribed to the 'Engagement of York', promising to defend the king's 'Person, Crown and Dignity . . . against all persons and power whatsoever', drawn up in the spring of 1642. He was still with the King when three troops of Parliamentary horse arrived at Knole one Sunday morning that August, rudely arresting his cousin Sir John Sackville as he was on his way to morning service at Sevenoaks parish church, and seizing the substantial store of arms (enough for five or six hundred men, according to the Parliamentary account) which was being held in the house. Some damage was done. Locks were broken. Gilding on a couch in the gallery, embroidered satin cushions and plumes from the tester of the earl's own bed were cut away, torn down and despoiled, and six trunks broken open – the very trunks which Vita Sackville-West as a child at the beginning of this century remembers finding still stacked in the attics at Knole – and money stolen from one of them, but 'what is lost we know not, in regard the keeper of it is from home'. The troopers also invaded the painter's chamber and spoilt his oil and committed other atrocities to the value of forty pounds, took oats and peas from the granary and finally rode away with their booty of five wagonloads of arms.

But the Dorsets were to suffer more grievously than this for their loyalty to the Crown. Lord Dorset, though now over fifty, was present at Edgehill in October and, as King James II was to recall years later, 'being commanded by the King my father to carry the Prince [of Wales] and myself up a hill out of the battle, refused to do it, and said he would not be thought a coward for ever a King's son in Christendom'. Of his own sons, Richard Lord Buckhurst and Edward, so delightfully portrayed at Knole in their lovelocks and lace collars, Richard was captured by Parliamentary forces at Mile End Green that November while returning from a recruiting foray in Kent. He was held for a year and does not seem to have taken any further part in the war. Edward fought as a volunteer in the royalist ranks at the Battle of Newbury in 1643 and was wounded there. Two years later he, too, was taken prisoner by the enemy, at Kidlington near Oxford, and shortly afterwards was stabbed to death by one of his guards. He was probably no more than twenty-two years old at the time.

The bereaved Lady Dorset remained steadfast at her post in London, caring for the king's two younger children, the Princess Elizabeth and Henry Duke of Gloucester. She was now homeless, inasmuch as Knole had been sequestrated and in 1643–4 was being used as the headquarters of the Committee of Sequestration for Kent which, according to tradition, held its meetings in the room known as the Poets' Parlour.

The Countess of Dorset died in May 1645 and was voted a public funeral by both Houses of Parliament in tribute to her devoted service to her young charges. The earl, although increasingly depressed and disillusioned, and increasingly anxious to see an end to the war, remained with the king at Oxford until after Charles had delivered himself up to the Scots in the spring of 1646. He was then among those who negotiated the surrender of the town to Sir Thomas Fairfax. Later that year he agreed to 'compound' for his estates by paying a fine of one-tenth of their value, a sum computed at £4360, although this was later reduced on appeal to £2415; Lord Dorset himself maintained that his loyalty to the Stuarts had cost him £40,000 altogether. He did not, in fact, long survive the king he had served so faithfully. He died in London in 1652 having, so it is said, made and kept a solemn vow never to leave his house after the king was executed until he was carried out in his coffin.

His son Richard, the fifth earl, married Frances, the daughter and eventual sole heiress of Lionel Cranfield, a Dick Whittington character who had begun life apprenticed to a London mercer, married his master's daughter and set up in business on the strength of her dowry of £800. Cranfield's financial acumen brought him to the notice of King James I and he subsequently progressed rapidly up the social and political ladder, becoming first Earl of Middlesex and Lord Treasurer of England.

The Cranfield marriage brought the Sackvilles considerable estates in Gloucester and Warwickshire, as well as the ancient manor of Copt Hall in Essex, whose furnishings are now at Knole and include some of the finest pieces in the house. Frances Sackville, however, did not come into her inheritance until after the death of her brother in 1674 and Richard, too, had to wait for the death of his apparently indestructible aunt Anne Clifford to secure the reversion of her jointure lands, so that the greater part of his life was harassed by the debts and financial problems carried over from the Civil War.

Frances bore thirteen children, of whom only six reached maturity. But her eldest son, Charles, Lord Buckhurst, survived to become one of the leading bloods at the early Restoration court: drinking, brawling and whoring round London in the company of such kindred spirits as his brother Edward, Charles Sedley, Thomas Ogle, George Etherege and John Wilmot Earl of Rochester. In general these activities were harmless, if tiresome, though there was certainly one occasion when a prank went badly wrong and ended in the death of an innocent by-stander.

In 1664 Buckhurst enlisted as a volunteer in the Dutch wars and was present in the Duke of York's entourage at the naval battle fought off Lowestoft the following June. This was the occasion of his best known poetic effusion: a jolly, jingling ballad later set to music and reprinted, anthologised and parodied relentlessly over succeeding centuries:

> To all you ladies now at land
> We men at sea indite;
> But first would have you understand
> How hard it is to write;
> The Muses now, and Neptune too,
> We must implore to write to you.
> With a fa, la, la, la, la,

and so on over another ten stanzas full of topical jokes and allusions.

Lord Buckhurst returned to London and his former raffish way of life and proceeded to fall for the charms of a young actress who had started her career selling oranges to the audiences of the London theatres. In July 1667 Samuel Pepys recorded that 'Buckhurst hath got Nell away from the King's house [that is, Drury Lane Theatre], lies with her, and gives her £100 a year, so she hath sent her parts to the house and will act no more'. Nell Gwynn – pretty witty Nelly the Protestant whore and the original tart with a heart of gold – remained under Lord Buckhurst's protection for a year, or possibly less. She apparently did go back to acting at Drury Lane during this time and by 1669 had become the king's mistress. There was some speculation that Buckhurst had demanded payment for giving her up and it is true he was made a Gentleman of the Bedchamber around this time and given a pension of £1000 a year for life. But this sort of small scale money-grubbing hardly seems to agree with the lavish frivolity of the rest of Lord Buckhurst's highly-coloured persona.

During the 1670s, Lord Buckhurst succeeded to the earldoms of Dorset and Middlesex, to the Sackville and Cranfield estates, was given the Garter and the position of Lord Chamberlain. He also married – first the widowed Lady Falmouth and secondly Mary Compton, daughter of the Earl of Northampton – and embarked on his career of patron of the arts. John Dryden, Matthew Prior, Edmund Waller, William Congreve, William Wycherley, Samuel Butler, Thomas Otway, and Alexander Pope were all his friends. It is said that Wycherley owed the success of his play *The Plain Dealer* to Lord Dorset and that it was his influence which brought Butler's poem *Hudibras* to the notice of the court. Dryden was a regular visitor to Knole: Dorset gave him a pension after he lost the poet laureateship. He also paid for the early education of Matthew Prior whose portrait hangs in the Poets' Parlour at Knole, together with those of many other members of the earl's literary circle.

The death of Charles II in 1685 brought to an end that cultivated yet delightfully free and easy court society which Dorset and his cronies had always found so congenial. The pompous, humourless and Catholic James was very little to their taste, and although the new king reconferred the Lord Lieutenantship of Sussex upon him and paid the arrears of his salary as a Gentleman of the Bed-chamber, the earl came less and less to Whitehall. Never much of a political animal, he was nonetheless moved to take an active part in the rebellion of 1688 when William of Orange was invited to take the throne and personally supervised the Princess Anne's unobtrusive departure from town, escorting her first to Copt Hall, where she stayed a few days, the Countess of Dorset lending her anything she needed in the way of clothes, and thence to Nottingham.

Dorset continued as Lord Chamberlain under William and Mary and in February 1689 was sworn a member of the Privy Council, but the excesses of his youth were now visibly beginning to catch up with him. Kneller's portrait of the fifty-one-year-old earl, which is probably a flattering likeness, shows all the marks of self-indulgence in the double chins and heavy, empurpled features coarsened by drink and dissipation. Dorset certainly had a longstanding reputation as a heavy drinker, and the cellar accounts at Knole record the purchase of alarming quantities of strong liquor: eighty-five gallons of sherry, seventy-two gallons of canary wine and over five hundred gallons of port between August 1690 and January '91. His wine bill for the period from July 1690 to November '91 came to almost six hundred pounds, and this at a time when sherry cost around six shillings and eightpence and port five shillings a gallon!

The earl had disappeared from public life by the end of the 1690s. In his last years he married Anne Roche, a woman 'of very obscure connections', and lived with her in Bath where she is said to have kept him virtually a prisoner – a grossly fat, senile old man. Although Matthew Prior, sent down by the family to report on the situation, loyally maintained that Lord Dorset '*drivels* so much better sense even now than any other man can *talk*, that you must not call me into court as a witness to prove him an idiot'. It was a sad and sordid, but perhaps not entirely surprising end for Dorset, the generous patron, 'the grace of courts, the Muses' pride', whose own light-hearted occasional verses, 'gay, vigorous and airy', have earned him a minor place among the Restoration poets. He died in 1705 – a relic of the reign of the Merry Monarch, when the world had been young and hopeful and that 'bold merry slut' Nell Gwynn had kept house with him in their Epsom love nest. He was buried among his ancestors at Withyham, Alexander Pope composing the epitaph on his monument in the Sackville Chapel:

> '. . . Blest courtier! who could King and country please,
> Yet sacred kept his friendships and his ease. . . .'

Lionel, the son of his second marriage to Mary Compton, the seventh Earl and first Duke of Dorset, made his first appearance on the public stage at the age of four as 'Lord Buck' playing with a toy cart in the gallery at Kensington Palace, and knocking imperiously on the door of the King's Closet to tell His Majesty that he must come to tea directly, as the queen was waiting for him. Whereupon, so the story goes, the normally stern and forbidding William at once threw down his pen, scooped Lord Buckhurst up in his arms and merrily pulled the child in his little cart down to the room where the queen and the company were sitting.

Lionel Cranfield Sackville was eighteen when he succeeded to his father's honours. 'He had the good fortune', said Lord Shelburne, 'to come into the world with the Whigs, and partook of their good fortune to his death'. In August 1714 he was commissioned to go with Lord Halifax to Hanover to inform the Elector of his good fortune and subsequently accompanied the new King George I back to England. Thereafter his career continued its smooth upward progress, as befitted one who seemed 'in all respects a perfect English courtier and nothing else'. He was appointed Groom of the Stole and First Gentleman of the Bedchamber, elected a Knight of the Garter, sworn a member of the Privy Council and, in 1720, created Duke of Dorset. He was Lord Lieutenant of Ireland in 1731 and again in 1750; Lord President of the Council, Lord Steward of the Household, Constable of Dover Castle, Master of the Horse, Lord Lieutenant of Kent, Lord Warden of the Cinque Ports – all these honours fell effortlessly to one who never expressed an awkward opinion about public affairs and who, again according to Lord Shelburne, 'preserved to the last the good breeding, decency of manners, and dignity of exterior deportment of Queen Anne's time'.

Duke Lionel lived *en prince* at Knole, and on Sunday mornings 'the front of the house was so crowded with horsemen and carriages as to give it rather the appearance of a princely levee than the residence of a private nobleman'. An affectionate husband and father, a genial host and, despite the gravity of his public demeanour, in private 'the greatest lover of low humour and buffoonery', the duke was, in short, a perfect eighteenth-century type of English country squire.

He married a soldier's daughter, Elizabeth Colyear, his 'dear dear Colly', to whom he was devoted and who gave him three sons and three daughters. The family at Knole was completed by the duchess's bosom friend, Lady Betty Germain, born Lady Betty Berkeley, who had once been a lady-in-waiting to Queen Anne and whose late husband is thought to have been an illegitimate son of William III. Lady Betty lived contentedly in her rooms at Knole, occupied with her needlework, her correspondence and the potpourri which she made every summer from her own recipe. She died in 1769 in her ninetieth year, bequeathing her considerable fortune to the Dorsets' youngest, and favourite, son George.

The Sackvilles had never been a martial family and Lord George's decision to embrace a military career, which may have been due to the influence of his maternal grandfather Marshal Colyear, was untypical and, as it turned out, unfortunate. Commissioned into the 6th Dragoon Guards at the age of twenty-one, he saw some active service in Flanders during the early 1740s, accompanying

George II, the last English warrior king, on an expedition against the French. In 1744 he was present at the Battle of Fontenoy, was seriously wounded and is said to have led his regiment so far into the enemy camp that when he fell – shot in the breast, he told his father – he was carried into the King of France's own tent to receive first aid. He subsequently served under the Duke of Cumberland, in Scotland during the Forty-Five and was warmly praised by the Butcher, both for his courage and 'a disposition to his trade that I don't always find in those of a higher rank than him in the Army' – a testimonial which would have had more value had it come from a commander with a better disposition to his trade himself. In 1751 Lord George went with his father to Ireland, where he quickly gained a reputation for bullying and haughty behaviour, or initiative and toughness, according to point of view. Either way he looked to be on his way up. Promoted to major-general by 1755, he had become, at thirty-nine, a force to be reckoned with in both the military and political spheres – able, aggressive, ambitious and possessed of a quite unusual talent for annoying people.

Nemesis caught up with him four years later at the Battle of Minden, where he was commanding the British and German cavalry. The Anglo-Hanoverian infantry having repulsed the French cavalry and a brigade of infantry, a timely intervention by the British cavalry should, according to all the military experts, have turned a French defeat into annihilation. Instead, Lord George either ignored or misunderstood the orders of his superior officer, Prince Ferdinand of Brunswick, and for a crucial forty minutes or so the British horse remained inactive, allowing the French to regroup and withdraw behind their fortifications at Minden.

Whether this was due to a failure of nerve, a genuine misunderstanding or plain bloody-mindedness on Lord George's part probably no longer matters very much, but it proved disastrous for Lord George himself. While a more likeable personality might perhaps have been given the benefit of the doubt, George Sackville, who, as Horace Walpole put it, 'never had the art of conciliating affection', was now brought face to face with the unwisdom of having made so many unnecessary and unforgiving enemies. He became the target of a campaign of public vilification out of all proportion to his alleged offence, he was stripped of his command and his army rank, and informed that the king had no further use for his services. When it came to exacting revenge the royal Hanoverians were in a class of their own.

Lord George, for his part, furiously denied all the charges of cowardice and treachery being made against him and demanded a court martial to clear his name. When this opened, in March 1670, he assumed 'a dictatorial style', attempted to browbeat the witnesses and treated the judge advocate with contempt. His own replies were quick and spirited and 'nothing was timid, nothing humble, in his behaviour'. 'An instant of such resolution at Minden had established his character for ever,' commented Horace Walpole.

But despite 'the unembarrass'd countenance, the looks of soveraign contempt and superiority, that his Lordship bestow'd on his Accusers during the tryal . . . his Cause would not support him'. The court found him guilty of having disobeyed orders given him by his commander in chief, according to the rules of war, and judged him 'unfit to serve his Majesty in any military capacity whatsoever' in the future. Some felt he was lucky not to have been shot, but his disgrace, both military and social, was nevertheless complete, and the blow to Sackville family pride a very dreadful one. 'The poor old Duke can hardly bear the sight of anybody,' wrote the poet Thomas Gray, and indeed Dorset spent the remaining five years of his life in sorrowful retirement at Knole. Lord George, however, was of too restless and dynamic a temperament to accept defeat and began almost immediately to plan the long, hard and often painfully humiliating route-march which would get him out of the wilderness and back into public life and politics.

When he finally emerged, fifteen years later, as Secretary of State for the Colonies, it was as Lord George Germain – a condition of Lady Betty Germain's will having been that he should change his name – the affluent owner of Lady Betty's property at Drayton in Northamptonshire. He had not, however, changed in any fundamental respect. He was still a hard man – 'distant' was an adjective frequently used – cold, acerbic, with a reputation for 'decision and dispatch in business' and generally still more feared than trusted.

In the circumstances, therefore, it was particularly inopportune that Lord George's period at the colonial office should have coincided almost exactly with the American War of Independence, which Charles Fox, a Whig statesman who had opposed taxation of the American colonies, accused him not merely of provoking but fatally mismanaging. Obviously, Lord George alone cannot be held responsible for London's total failure to understand the real nature of the conflict with the rebellious colonists; at the same time, he was emphatically not the man for the job and was later to become a convenient scapegoat. Even when Lord Cornwallis's surrender at Yorktown had made the outcome of the war inevitable, he told the House of Commons that

> let the consequences be what they may, I will never put my hand to any instrument conceding independence to the colonies. My opinion is, that the British Empire must be ruined, and that we can never continue to exist as a great, or as a powerful nation after we have lost or renounced the sovereignty over America.

After this, of course, it was obvious that he would have to go. His price for going quietly was a peerage and George III was persuaded by the harassed prime minister, Lord North, to make Lord George a viscount – though his elevation led to an unpleasant scene in the Upper House, when certain of their lordships protested violently against having the notorious 'man of Minden' thus foisted upon them.

But the new Viscount Sackville was now content to retire from public life, and spent the three years of life which were left to him partly at Drayton and partly at Stoneland Lodge near Tunbridge Wells. He was, as might be expected, 'extremely precise in the movements of his large domestic establishment' and on Sunday mornings 'as if he was dressed for a drawing-room', marched his whole family in grand cavalcade to church. 'He had a way of standing up in sermon-time', remembered his friend Richard Cumberland, 'for the purpose of reviewing the congregation and aweing the idlers into decorum.' He would also, it seemed, be ready to encourage the preacher with 'cheering nods and signals of assent', not to mention occasional cries of 'Well done, Harry!', and paid careful attention to the performance of the 'corps of rustic psalm-singers' which he nurtured in each of his parish churches.

'Once,' wrote Cumberland, 'when his ear had been tortured by a tone most glaringly discordant, he called out loudly "Out of tune, Tom Baker." '

In spite of his glaring egotism and other dislikeable qualities, there still remains a good deal more to be said for the first Viscount Sackville of Drayton than for either of his brothers. Charles, Earl of Middlesex, who succeeded as second Duke of Dorset in 1765 when he was already, perhaps fortunately, well into middle age, had always been unsatisfactory. Eccentric to the point of mental instability, he squandered enormous sums of family money on financing London opera. 'We are likely to have no Opera next year,' wrote Horace Walpole in 1743. 'Handel has had a palsy, and can't compose, and the Duke of Dorset has set himself strenuously to oppose it, as Lord Middlesex is the impresario and must ruin the House of Sackville by a course of these follies.'

Lord Middlesex's other 'follies', drink and ladies of easy virtue, were equally expensive and though he temporarily improved his finances by marrying an heiress, Grace Boyle, daughter of the second Viscount Shannon, he soon ran through his wife's money as well. The further lapses of taste committed by this 'proud, disgusted, melancholy, solitary man' included having himself painted in the costume of a Roman Emperor, bare knees, plumed helmet and all, writing a quantity of bad verse and, more serious, cutting down the timber – 'even the trees of his father's planting' – in the park at Knole. The situation got so bad in the end, that the family were obliged to take steps to have him declared mentally incompetent to make a will.

As the second duke left no legitimate issue, the title passed in 1769 to his twenty-four-year-old nephew – son of the middle brother John, who also suffered from melancholia and had been sent to live in exile in Switzerland in sadly shabby conditions. The third duke, who reigned at Knole for the remainder of the eighteenth century, was a romantically beautiful and exquisite young man. He belonged, wrote his descendant Vita Sackville-West, to

> an age of quizzing glasses, of flowered waistcoats, of buckled shoes, and of slim bejewelled swords. When he had his mistress sculpted it was lying full length on a couch, naked save for a single rose looping up her hair. When he had her

> drawn, it was pointing her little foot in the first step of a dance. . . .

This particular mistress was the Italian dancer Gianetta Baccelli, whom the duke encountered in Paris towards the end of his career. But there had been others. When he set out on a grand tour of France and Italy in 1770, he took with him the celebrated and accomplished courtesan Nancy Parsons; and Nancy was succeeded by Elizabeth Armistead. Nor was his grace content to amuse himself only with professional ladies of pleasure – witness his famous affair with the young Countess of Derby. 'I have always looked upon him as the most dangerous of men,' wrote Georgiana Duchess of Devonshire to her mother, 'for with that beauty of his he is so unaffected, and has a simplicity and a persuasion in his manner that makes one account very easily for the number of women he has had in love with him.'

The fascinating duke continued to devote the greater part of his time to 'gallantry and pleasure among the fashionable circles, as well in France and Italy, as in England', but he was fond of Knole and spent money on improvements and repairs, putting in new windows and floors, re-leading the roof over the Great Hall and restoring the gateway towers. He also invested nearly £2500 in a magnificent set of new table silver from Jefferys & Jones of Cockspur Street, and replanted the trees so improvidently vandalised by his uncle. He brought back pictures from Italy, and patronised native artistic talent at a time when it was flourishing as seldom before or since. Reynolds, Gainsborough, Romney, Opie, Hoppner and Ozias Humphrey were all well represented at Knole. Hoppner received a hundred guineas for a delightful portrait of the ducal children painted in 1796. Twelve years earlier Gainsborough had been paid the same amount for two three-quarter length portraits of the duke, a full-length of the Baccelli, two 'landskips' and a sketch of a beggar boy and girl thrown in. But in 1769 the price for a Reynolds was three hundred guineas. Another of the duke's interests was cricket, which he played himself in his younger days. He is supposed to have given the Vine Ground to Sevenoaks in 1773, and he was a member of the committee which drew up the original rules of that sacred institution the MCC.

Unlike so many of his predecessors, the third duke showed no sign of being politically minded, but in 1783 he was appointed to the position of Ambassador Extraordinary and Plenipotentiary to the Court of France. He was a great social success in Paris, although he did not greatly care for the French, whom he considered 'capricious and inconstant', and was obliged to spend £11,000 a year on entertainment 'for to do honour to those who have never shown me the smallest mark of attention or civility'.

The duke reported on the progress of the scandalous affair of the disappearance of Marie Antoinette's diamond necklace (there is a tradition that he subsequently bought some of the smaller stones himself from Jefferys the London jeweller), and on the 'extraordinary proposal' made to the French government by a M. Montgolfier 'to construct a balloon of a certain diameter to carry sixteen persons'. It seems he intended to use it to trade between Paris and Marseilles, and was asking for an advance of 60,000 livres. Despite the fact that 'great credit is given to M. Montgolfier's superior skill in these matters', his grace plainly found it hard to take the project at all seriously, especially as 'the weight he proposes to carry *exceeds that of a waggon-load*!' Occasionally more serious matters creep into the despatches from Paris. M. de Calonne, the Finance Minister, was finding himself very much embarrassed by the enormous demands upon him for the expenses of the court, and in August 1787 the mob burnt the Edict and Declaration (of the Stamp Act and Land Tax) in front of the Palais de Justice.

> These excesses of the populace have made it necessary for the Government to double the Guards in Paris . . . an order has been issued for the suppression of all Societies under the denomination of Clubs etc.'

Two years later:

> The greatest revolution that we know anything of has been effected with, comparatively speaking . . . the loss of very few lives. . . . At least 200 workmen are employed in pulling down the Bastille, but as it is a construction of uncommon strength, it will require some time to erase it completely.

According to his contemporary Nathaniel Wraxall, the duke, while displaying 'neither shining parts nor superior abilities', possessed good sense, a mature knowledge of the world and, since he had travelled over a considerable part of Europe, should have been 'well calculated' for the post of ambassador. But his 'soft, quiet, ingratiating' manners were formed for the courts of the *ancien régime*. His grace was all at sea with the new dispensation in France and seems to have put his foot in it with his masters in London by humbly soliciting an 'audience' with the President des Etats and being refused. 'So undignified, so humiliating,' wrote the Marquis of Buckingham crossly. So the Duke of Dorset received his letters of recall and returned home to Knole. Although there was some talk of sending him to Ireland, nothing came of it and his diplomatic career ended without glory. He does not appear to have regretted it, however. He was now approaching his forty-fifth birthday and felt it was time to settle down and start a family. He parted with the plump, merry Baccelli in December 1789 and a month later married Miss Arabella Diana Cope, cool and stately daughter of an Oxfordshire baronet who brought with her a dowry of £140,000.

The children of the Hoppner portrait now began to arrive – Mary in July 1792, George John Frederick in 1793 and Elizabeth in 1795. By this time, though, their father was beginning to show ominous signs of personality change, and the beautiful, hedonistic youth, whose 'raven locks and milk-white vest' had once caused a great fluttering of hearts among feminine spectators at Kentish cricket matches and in London drawing-rooms, degenerated steadily into a morbidly suspicious, irritable and quarrelsome old man. 'His decease', says Wraxall, 'was preceded by a long period of intellectual decay and mental alienation,' and he seems indeed to have exhibited all the symptoms of the depressive illness which had afflicted his father and uncle. He died in 1799, still only fifty-four, leaving his five-year-old son to succeed him.

The fourth duke and his sisters were brought up by their mother and her second husband Charles, Earl Whitworth, in what appears to have been an atmosphere of loveless and chilly severity. The French artist, Madame Vigée Le Brun, who stayed at Knole in the early 1800s, remembered that when the young duke, then about eleven or twelve years old, came into the dining-room after dinner for dessert, his mother hardly spoke to him and presently 'sent him away without giving him the least sign of affection'.

Whereas earlier generations of Sackvilles favoured Westminster School, Duke George was educated at Harrow, where he became Lord Byron's fag.

> Whom, still, affection taught me to defend,
> And made me less a tyrant than a friend,
> Though the harsh custom of our youthful band
> Bade *thee* obey, and gave *me* to command;
> Thee, on whose head a few short years will shower
> The gift of riches, and the pride of power. . . .

These lines from an '*Ode to the Duke of Dorset*', composed in the summer of 1805, were not perhaps the most inspired to come from Byron's pen, but they acquired a certain poignancy ten years later when the Duke of Dorset was killed by a fall from his horse while coursing hares near Dublin with his friend and another former school-fellow Lord Powerscourt. The appealing child of Hoppner's portrait in frilled shirt and long trousers had grown into a good-looking young man – at least according to the drawing reproduced in Charles Phillips's *History of the Sackville Family*. He was, inevitably, described as being 'of amiable temper, warm and steady in his affections, endowed with considerable judgement, and possessing, with the accomplishments of a perfect gentleman, all the qualities that constitute an honest man'. He was twenty-one years and three months old.

The title now passed to Charles Sackville-Germain, eldest son of Lord George Germain, Viscount Sackville of Drayton, but by the terms of the third duke's will, Knole and all the family estates remained in the possession of the dowager duchess – or Lady Whitworth as she had become – for her lifetime, and thereafter would be divided between the coheiresses, the Ladies Mary and Elizabeth Sackville. The fifth duke lived on until 1843, when he died unmarried, and the dukedom of Dorset died with him.

Duchess Arabella Diana, meanwhile, had died in 1825 and Knole had been awarded to Mary, the elder daughter, who married twice, outlived both husbands and died childless in Bournemouth in 1864. Elizabeth Sackville acquired the mansion and park of Buckhurst on her mother's death, at which time she was already married to George West, fifth Earl de la Warr (who later adopted the surname of Sackville-West) and the mother of several children – she was to have six sons and three daughters, one of whom became Duchess of Bedford and another Countess of Derby. On Countess de la Warr's death in 1870 the whole question of the succession developed complications highly productive of lawsuits, but put at its simplest, the earldom of de la Warr and the barony and estate of Buckhurst devolved upon Reginald, the eldest surviving son, while Mortimer, next brother in order of seniority, inherited Knole and in 1876 was created first Baron Sackville.

When Mortimer died childless in 1888, he was succeeded by his brother Lionel. The second Baron Sackville had been a career diplomat – a stiff, shy, unsociable man whose life had nevertheless contained one great romance. In 1852, while on leave in Paris, he had met and fallen in love with the exotic Spanish gipsy dancer known as Pepita, and billed as 'the Star of Andalusia'. Although she did not immediately abandon her stage career, Pepita lived under Lionel Sackville-West's protection as his mistress until her death nineteen years later. There was never any question of marriage – in any case Pepita already had a husband – but they were a devoted couple and when Pepita died giving birth to a stillborn son (her seventh child), the normally taciturn Lionel was distraught with grief.

In 1880 Pepita's eldest daughter, Victoria Josefa Dolores Catalina, now eighteen years old, was taken from her French convent school and brought over to London to be inspected by her English relations, in particular her kind aunt the Countess of Derby. Her father had just been appointed British Minister to Washington and after much anxious consultation, involving Queen Victoria, the British Foreign Secretary, and the American president's wife, and the ladies of Washington, it was agreed that Victoria Josefa should be sent to join him and act as his hostess. She was, by all accounts, an extraordinarily captivating and beautiful girl and was also, of course, surrounded by the glamorous aura of her romantic origins. The experiment proved a triumphant success: Washington society flocked, fascinated, to the British Legation and the bewitching Miss West was besieged by suitors, all of whom she rejected without apparent hesitation.

In September 1888 Lionel was foolish enough to allow himself to be tricked by the 'Affair of the Murchison Letter' into seeming to take sides in the presidential election campaign and was consequently dismissed from his post. But, perhaps providentially, his brother Mortimer died the same month, giving him an unexceptionable excuse for resigning from the service and bringing himself and his daughter back to Europe. After a pause for the inevitable family lawsuit, they moved into Knole and Victoria Josefa was soon being courted by her cousin, another Lionel Sackville-West and heir to Knole and the barony, who had fallen head over heels in love with her on sight. They were married in June 1890 and their first and only child, Victoria or Vita, was born in March two years later.

The second Baron Sackville, by now 'very old, and queer, and silent', died in 1908 and immediately another lawsuit threatened, this time brought by Victoria Josefa's brother Henri. He claimed that Pepita the gipsy dancer had never been legally married to her husband Juan Oliva, and that the second Baron Sackville had married her in secret so that Henri, as their only surviving son, was the legal heir to Knole.

Lawyers for both sides scurried round Spain delving into the records – and revealing, incidentally, that the entry in the register of the church where Pepita and Juan Antonio Oliva were married in January 1851 had been rather obviously tampered with. Nevertheless, 'The Case' – predictably described by the popular press as 'the Romance of the Sackville Peerage' – was duly heard in the High Court of Justice in a blaze of publicity in February 1910. Judgement was given for the Sackville-Wests, and Lionel, third Baron Sackville, Victoria Josefa and the seventeen-year-old Vita returned to Knole in triumph. The horses were taken out of the traces of their carriage and they were pulled through the streets of Sevenoaks by the local fire brigade.

Two years later, Lady Sackville, who attracted drama as a magnet attracts iron filings, was involved in yet another sensational 'case' when the relatives of her old friend Sir John Murray Scott contested his will in which he had left her a legacy of £150,000 plus the extremely valuable contents of his Paris apartment. Undue influence was alleged and Victoria Josefa, refusing an opportunity to settle out of court, fought and won the battle in another blaze of publicity, effortlessly disposing of Mr F. E. Smith, the eminent counsel appearing for the plaintiffs. She was, as the judge observed in his summing-up, 'a lady of high mettle – very high mettle indeed', but she was also becoming very difficult to live with. While she unquestionably possessed dazzling and sometimes irresistible charm – 'one forgave her everything', wrote her daughter, 'when one heard her laugh and saw how frankly she was enjoying herself' – she could at the same time be irresponsible, ruthless and sometimes cruel. 'Like a child she neither analysed nor controlled her moods; they simply blew across her'. It is hardly surprising, therefore, that the marriage between this child of nature and Lord Sackville, the quiet, courteous, conscientous, English country gentleman should have cracked under the strain. They separated in 1919 and Lady Sackville went to live in Brighton, where she remained until her death in 1936.

Of all the twentieth century Sackvilles, by far the most interesting and significant was the daughter of this unlikely union. In 1913 she married Harold Nicolson, diplomat, diarist and minor political figure of the 1930s and '40s, and became the mother of two sons. But it is as Miss V. Sackville-West, poet, author, novelist, literary journalist and gardener, that she has won herself a place in the story of her times.

Vita Sackville-West loved her childhood home with an all-consuming passion and when her father died in 1928 and Knole passed into the possession of her uncle, Charles John Sackville-West, fourth Baron Sackville, it was like an expulsion from Eden to which she never became fully reconciled but which, ironically and indirectly, led to what was perhaps her greatest achievement – an achievement which began in 1930 when she and her husband bought for £12,000 the semi-derelict property of Sissinghurst Castle, near Cranbrook in Kent. The surviving buildings at Sissinghurst were in an advanced state of dilapidation and the grounds a dispiriting rubbish dump of old iron bedsteads, chicken wire, sardine tins and other detritus. But what mattered to Vita was that it had once been a great Tudor mansion, the home of the Baker family whose daughter Cicely had married Sir Thomas Sackville in 1554. Sissinghurst thus became some compensation for the loss of Knole. Her husband, who pointed out that they would probably have spent almost £30,000 by the time they had put the house and garden into anything like habitable order, went on to write rather wistfully that for £30,000 it would be possible to buy 'a beautiful place replete with park, garage, h. and c., central heating, historical associations, and two lodges 1. and r.' However, he realised that for Vita Sissinghurst would fill a genuine need, that it would be for her 'an ancestral mansion' and that this would more than make up for the lack of company's water, h. and c. and other desirable mod. cons.

So, in May 1930 the Nicolsons bought Sissinghurst replete with its historical associations, its Elizabethan tower, its cottages, adjoining farmhouse and five hundred acres of land, and thereafter the creation and upkeep of the beautiful garden – one of the most beautiful in England – out of a tangle of bindweed, ground elder, nettles and old iron became a joint passion which lasted until Vita's death from cancer in 1962. She poured her love of the Kentish countryside, of gardens in general and Sissinghurst in particular into her poetry, and expressed her fascination with her roots in books such as *Knole and the Sackvilles*, *Pepita*, her edition of Anne Clifford's diary and, probably her best known novel, *The Edwardians*, which describes in detail life as it was lived in a great house like Knole at the turn of the century.

In 1967 her son Nigel Nicolson, who had inherited Sissinghurst, gave it to the National Trust. Knole, with its thousand-acre park and more than three acres of courtyards, galleries, state apartments, state bedrooms, staircases, passages, stables and outbuildings, had already, in 1946, passed into the Trust's keeping, although the sixth Baron Sackville and his family still keep a home there. The great house, described by Vita Sackville-West as having the personality 'of some very old woman who has always been beautiful, who has had many lovers and seen many generations come and go', now sees the visitors come and go, climb the Great Staircase, walk the Brown Gallery and the Leicester Gallery, stare at the famous Knole settee and the Charles I billiard table, the copies of the Raphael cartoons in the Cartoon Gallery, the portraits and elaborate French furniture in the ballroom, the ornately carved marble mantelpieces, the Gainsboroughs and the Reynolds and the Hoppners, the Caroline and Georgian silver, the panelling and the embroidery – all the treasures amassed over four centuries and ten generations.

The house, serene in its mellow old age, remembers Lady Anne Clifford sewing at her cushions of Irish stitch work and weeping and falling out with her querulous, extravagant husband, who sold or mortgaged so much of the London property on which the family fortunes had been based. It remembers the Restoration Earl, that 'rakish, witty and florid figure' entertaining Dryden and Wycherley and Matthew Prior in the Poets' Parlour. It remembers Signora Baccelli – 'Madam Shelley' the English servants called her when the third duke brought her back from Paris – whose nude plaster form now reclines at the foot of the Great Staircase. It remembers the boy who died in Ireland and the silent, reclusive old man, the second Lord Sackville, playing draughts with his granddaughter, herself a withdrawn and secretive child, and sometimes telling her stories of when he was a little boy, travelling by coach from Knole to London with his parents. It remembers the young Vita rummaging in the attics and occasionally meeting a stag that had strayed through the open door into the banqueting hall, 'puzzled but still dignified'.

You would not meet a stag in the banqueting hall today, and the earls and the dukes, their wives and mistresses and children have all been tidied away too, their sorrows and laughter long since dissolved into dust. But the house remains, its grey-brown Kentish ragstone roofed in reddish tiles, its jumble of chimneys and turrets, Tudor gables and battlemented towers giving it more the appearance of a small medieval town than of a single house. There is nothing symmetrical or Italianate about Knole, no deliberate attempt to impress or overawe. Rather it looks somehow native to the soil, to the green of the Kentish countryside. Maybe a day will come when there are no more Sackvilles, perhaps even no more visitors. But surely Knole will always be there with its memories – tranquil, cradled in trees, an English house beneath a pale English sky in 'a beautiful decent simplicity which charms one'.

The Stanleys of Knowsley

Sans changer

Charlotte de la Tremoille, married the 7th 'Great' Earl of Derby
by courtesy of the Victoria and Albert Museum

THE STANLEYS OF KNOWSLEY

Sans changer

UNTIL exposed to the unromantic scrutiny of modern scholarship, the Stanleys, like almost every other noble family worth the name, laid confident claim to that essential adjunct of true gentility, a knightly Norman ancestor. In fact, the earliest forebear who can be traced with confidence is one Liulf or Lydulph of Aldithley, Aldelegh or Audley, living in the time of Stephen and Henry II, that is, mid-twelfth century, whose name declares him to have been of native English stock. The name Stanley, or Stanelegh or Stoneley, a township of Leek in Staffordshire and also of Saxon origin was subsequently acquired by marriage.

From this stem descended the Stanleys of Hooton, but the fortunes of what was to become the best known and most influential branch of the family tree were founded by John Stanley, a younger son and professional soldier. John fought under the Black Prince at the battle of Poitiers and went on to achieve international distinction as a champion in the dangerous art of single combat in the lists – prowess which earned him his knighthood and the sort of fame enjoyed today by a sporting superstar. It may very well also have helped him to win a rich bride, for he married Isabel, daughter and heiress of Sir Thomas Lathom, who brought the estates of Lathom and Knowsley into the Stanley family, as well as the famous badge or crest of the Eagle and Child.

Legend has it that a former Thomas Lathom and his wife were walking in their park when they came to an especially wild and deserted spot where an eagle usually built its nest. Hearing the cries of a young child, they ordered their attendants to investigate, whereupon a suspiciously well-dressed male infant was discovered lying in the eagle's eyrie. Lady Lathom, who had borne no son herself, took the baby as a gift from heaven to be adopted as her own. This she did and the child grew up to be heir to the estate and father of Isabel, Sir John Stanley's bride. Legend, of course, also has it that the foundling was a Lathom bastard, and that Sir Thomas had chosen this way of persuading his credulous wife to accept it.

John Stanley's status was naturally enhanced by his marriage, but he had also proved himself to be a useful and reliable man in his own right. Richard II employed him as Lord Deputy in Ireland and after the *coup* of 1399 he won the esteem of the new King Henry IV who, as well as creating him Knight of the Garter and Constable of Windsor Castle, made him generous gifts of land in Cheshire. This proved a wise investment, for when Owain Glyn Dwyr and the Percys revolted in 1403, the Stanleys, strategically placed in the north-west, stayed loyal to the Crown. Their reward was the grant of the lordship of the Isle of Man, that curious, romantic amalgam of Celtic and Norse culture seized from the Scots by Edward III but still retaining a measure of independence and national identity. John Stanley seems never to have visited his domain in the Irish Sea, which he now held 'with the style and title of King of Man' from the crown of England '*per homagium legium*, and paying to the King, his heirs and successors a cast of falcons at their coronation . . . and carrying the Lancaster sword on the left side of the King at every coronation.' It was his son, another John Stanley, who first made the sea crossing in 1417 and held a Tynwald, or council, at which the barons, deemsters (justices), officers, tenants and commons of the land were summoned to attend according to custom. It was agreed that he should come in 'royal array' and sit upon the Hill of Tynwald under a canopy of estate 'with his visage unto the east, his sword before him, holden with the point upward'. Those barons who had not already done so swore fealty to him and the commoners showed him their charters. John Stanley II was in Man again in 1422 and appears to have acted as a sensible and progressive overlord: he had the ancient Manx laws set down in writing for the first time and conceded the islanders their traditional form of representative government by the deemsters and 'the Twenty-Four' worthiest men.

The Stanleys had no time to spare for their 'kingdom' of Man during the remainder of the crowded fifteenth century. John Stanley II died in 1437 and his son Thomas was fully occupied with the administration of the family estates, now extending into large areas of North Wales, and as a servant of the Crown. As Sir Thomas Stanley he represented the county of Lancaster in Parliament as Knight of the Shire, and followed in his grandfather's footsteps as Lord Lieutenant in Ireland, as well as holding office as comptroller and chamberlain of the royal household. In 1456, three years before his death, he was raised to the peerage as Baron Stanley and, in the words of a nineteenth-century chronicler, left behind him 'the character of being brave in the field, wise in the Senate and an ornament to his family'. He married Joan, daughter and co-heiress of Sir Robert Goushill of Heveringham, who was related through her mother to the bluest blood in the land – FitzAlan, Bohun and Plantagenet. Fruitful as well as well-connected, Joan presented her lord with four sons, one of whom founded the line of Stanley of Alderley, and three daughters.

Thomas Stanley II's succession to the barony coincided closely with the outbreak of the Wars of the Roses, and Lord Stanley prudently allied himself with the winning Yorkist side, becoming a trusted councillor of King Edward IV and Steward of the Household. Like his forebears he was also a useful man in a fight. He was with the king in France in the 1474 campaign, raising a force of forty men-at-arms and three hundred archers; and in 1482 he and Richard of Gloucester wrested the border town of Berwick from the Scots after a particularly bitter and sanguinary battle.

Lord Stanley's first wife was Eleanor Neville, sister of Warwick the Kingmaker, who bore him six sons, but it was his second marriage which brought the family their moment of glory on the stage of English history. Some time at the beginning of the 1480s, the widowed Lord Stanley married the twice-widowed Lady Stafford, born Margaret Beaufort, great-great-granddaughter of Edward III and the heiress of the House of Lancaster. Lady Margaret was also the mother of a son by her first husband, the long dead Edmund Tudor, Earl of Richmond. Henry Tudor, now a political refugee in Brittany, was the object of some intermittent disquiet on the part of the House of York, but during the lifetime of King Edward and his two sons, any real danger from the exiled Tudor/Lancastrian claimant seemed too remote to be of serious concern.

Then suddenly, in April 1483 Edward IV was dead. His two young sons passed into the care of their uncle Richard, Duke of Gloucester, and were lodged in the Tower of London pending the coronation of the thirteen-year-old Edward V. But before this could take place, Gloucester made the interesting discovery that their father's marriage to Elizabeth Woodville had been invalid and that the children were therefore illegitimate. By the end of June Richard of Gloucester had been proclaimed king and it was noticed that the young princes were no longer to be seen 'shooting and playing in the Tower gardens'.

In that period of acute political tension no one in high places, however apparently favoured, could count on survival. At the famous council meeting in the Tower on 13 June, when Gloucester turned on his friend Lord Hastings, Lord Stanley was hit on the head by a soldier's halberd in the general confusion and dragged off to gaol with the Archbishop of York and Bishop John Morton of Ely. Although his period of confinement was brief – he was released in time for Richard's coronation, made a Knight of the Garter, appointed High Constable of England and assured by the king that

> I am thyne and thou art myne,
> And soe two fellowes wyll we bee,
> I sweare by Marye maiden mylde
> I knowe none such under the skye

– the shrewd and cautious Stanley was not greatly impressed and asked permission to return to his estates to attend to his personal affairs.

To what extent at this stage his affairs were connected with those of young Henry Tudor it is impossible to say, but there can be little doubt that Stanley was at least aware of his wife's activities. Lady Margaret, intelligent, formidable, strong-willed and utterly single-minded when it came to promoting the 'well doing and glory' of the son she had scarcely seen since he was a child of five, spent that summer working to gather support for a Tudor bid for the throne; and already couriers bearing news, instructions and substantial sums of money were slipping unobtrusively across to Brittany.

But the conspirators were playing a dangerous game. Before the end of September King Richard had discovered what was going on and by mid-October the plot had collapsed. The Duke of Buckingham, Margaret Beaufort's principal ally, was executed, and the fact that Lady Margaret herself escaped a similar fate is usually attributed to Richard's reluctance to antagonise the influential Stanleys. Instead she forfeited her property, which was transferred to her husband for his lifetime, and Thomas Stanley was ordered to keep his wife under better control in future and make sure she could not pass messages to her son or his friends, 'nor practise against the King'.

The cornerstone of the Tudor plan had always been a marriage between Henry, last surviving male of the Lancastrian line, and the Yorkist heiress, King Edward's daughter Elizabeth. But early in 1485 a rumour began to circulate that King Richard, now a widower, was planning to marry his niece himself. Whether true or not this caused great alarm in the pro-Tudor faction and according to the contemporary ballad, 'The Most Pleasant Song of Lady Bessy', Elizabeth sent for Lord Stanley, 'father Stanley', telling him she would rather die – 'with sharp swords I will me slay' – than become her uncle's leman, and begging his help for the exiled Henry.

> You may recover him of his care,
>   If your heart and mind to him will gree:
> Let him come home and claim his right,
>   And let us cry him King Henry!

Stanley hesitates. He is afraid of Richard, and besides it would be deadly sin to betray his king,

> . . . then should I lose my great renown!
> I should be called traitor thro' the same
>   Full soon in every market town!
> That were great shame to me and my name . . .

But Bessy persists, flinging her headdress on the ground and tearing her hair, while tears 'fell from her eyes apace'. Stanley's heart is touched by her distress, but still he hangs back. 'It is hard to trust women' and Bessy might betray him. He also protests, rather feebly, about the difficulties of communicating with Henry. He himself cannot write and dare not confide in a secretary. But dauntless Lady Bessy meets all his objections. She can read and write, if necessary in French and Spanish as well as English, and she will act as scrivener. Amazed by the talents of this 'proper wench', Stanley finally capitulates and late that night, closeted behind the locked doors of Bessy's chamber and fortified with mulled wine, and sweetmeats, they concoct a series of letters to Stanley's friends and to 'the Prince of England' in Brittany.

'The Song of Lady Bessy', most probably written by Humphrey Brereton, a squire in the Stanleys' service, contains some unmistakably authentic touches (as well as a good deal of poetic licence), and Henry Tudor had undoubtedly received promises of help from Lord Stanley and his brother William, who between them controlled North Wales, Cheshire and Lancashire, before he landed at Milford Haven on 7 August 1485. But as the royal army mustered and marched, and Henry continued his advance northward through Wales, gathering support as he went, the Stanleys were not yet prepared to commit themselves openly. The fact that George Lord Strange, Lord Stanley's son and heir, was being held hostage in Richard's camp no doubt affected his father's position. But this was poor comfort to Henry, for whom his step-father's support was going to be crucial.

On 14 August the Tudors were at the gates of Shrewsbury and three days later 'the unknown Welshman' had a brief and apparently inconclusive meeting with William Stanley. On Sunday 21 August there was another conference at the village of Atherstone near Tamworth with both Stanleys present. But on the following morning, as the two sides confronted one another across the flat marshy ground a few miles south of Market Bosworth, the Stanleys with their contingent of about three thousand men were still holding aloof, stationed somewhere 'in the mid way betwixt the two battles' (that is, the two armies). Exactly where isn't clear. One thing, though, had become very clear – they meant to be on the winning side.

Henry, outnumbered almost two to one, was naturally counting on the Stanleys to join him before rather than after the issue had been decided, and sent an urgent message to Thomas asking him 'to come with his forces to set the soldiers in array'. The reply, that Henry should 'set his own folks in order' and Thomas would arrive in due course, must have come like a blow in the face. Henry indeed 'began to be somewhat appalled', but there was no time to argue. The main body of the Tudor army, estimated at no more than a bare five thousand, was deployed in a wedge formation, with 'a slender vanguard' of archers in the centre commanded by the veteran Earl of Oxford, and as they began to advance across the open ground towards the ridge known as Ambien Hill where Richard was waiting, the king gave the signal to attack.

Oxford, anxious to prevent his small force from being overwhelmed in the first onslaught, had given orders that no one was to move further than ten paces from the standards, and after an exchange of arrow shot and some hand-to-hand skirmishing there was a lull. The royal troops drew off and Oxford and his companions, scenting a certain lack of enthusiasm, were encouraged to renew the attack. In the fierce fighting which followed the Duke of Norfolk and several other prominent Yorkists were killed and Norfolk's son, Thomas Howard Earl of Surrey, was taken prisoner.

So far only the two front lines had engaged, and Lord Stanley, though said to have dismissed Richard's threat to kill his son with the remark that he had more sons who would not hesitate to avenge their brother's murder, still hesitated to commit himself. By this time the king had been able to pick out his adversary from the general confusion of the battlefield, and the sight of that impudent adventurer who, against all the odds, had reached the very heart of his kingdom, seemed to madden him. Whatever the reason, he suddenly made up his mind to settle the issue man to man. Surrounded by his household troops, he set spurs to his horse and launched himself straight for the spot where the red dragon of Cadwaladr was being borne over Henry's head by his standard-bearer William Brandon.

It was the act of a berserker, and in the first fury of his attack Richard personally overthrew the red dragon and slew William Brandon, 'making way with weapon on every side'. For a while the issue hung in the balance, but Henry's guard closed round him, and Henry himself stood his ground bravely, 'bearing the brunt' longer than his own soldiers, who were now, according to the chronicler Polydore Vergil, beginning to lose all hope of victory, would have thought possible. This, if ever, was the moment for a dramatic intervention and, at this very moment, the Stanleys came thundering down to the rescue. Richard was killed in the thick of the fighting and after that the Earl of Oxford, assisted by the massive Stanley reinforcements, experienced no difficulty in putting the rest of the royal army to flight. The Tudors and Stanleys were left in undisputed possession of the field and Richard's crown, or circlet, was retrieved from the debris of the battle – hanging in a thorn bush, so the old story goes – and handed to Thomas Stanley who, with his brother William standing by, placed it solemnly on his stepson's head.

The Stanleys had now very definitely 'arrived'. At Henry Tudor's coronation, two months after Bosworth, Thomas Stanley was created Earl of Derby, while William was appointed Lord Chamberlain and both were awarded confiscated Yorkist estates. Not that the Yorkists were finished yet. Two years later John de la Pole, Earl of Lincoln, with a businesslike force of German mercenaries and Irish tribesmen hoping for plunder, crossed from Dublin to the Pile of Fouldry on the north Lancashire coast, bringing one Lambert Simnel, son of an Oxford organ-maker, who was being passed off as the Earl of Warwick, nephew of the late King Edward. This attempted coup was frustrated at Stoke, properly the last battle of the Wars of the Roses, at which George Stanley Lord Strange (his title derived from the barony inherited by his wife) played a distinguished part; as a result the Earl of Derby was further rewarded by the grant of the estates of Thomas Broughton of Furness, who had been unwise enough to join forces with the invaders.

Considerably less happy for the family were the consequences of the second Yorkist attempt to dislodge the new Tudor dynasty. In the early 1490s another handsome youth, Perkin Warbeck or Osbeck, was being paraded in France and Flanders as Richard Duke of York, the younger of the two 'little Princes in the Tower', miraculously spared by the murderers of his brother. Just enough doubt remains about Perkin Warbeck's origins to give him a faint aura of romantic mystery, and it is just possible that he may have been a bastard of the House of York. But to Henry Tudor all that mattered about this latest 'apparition' was how many and which important men were planning to support him. The king's intelligence service was an extremely efficient one, but it was December 1494 before it tracked down one of the ringleaders – no less a person than Sir William Stanley himself.

Francis Bacon says that 'the King seemed to be much amazed at the naming of this lord, as if he had heard the news of some strange and fearful prodigy'. Henry had apparently had his suspicions about his step-uncle for some months past, but it must nonetheless have been a shock to have those suspicions confirmed and to learn that a man who had so recently helped to put the crown on his head, 'a man that enjoyed by his favour and advancement so great a fortune both in honour and riches', and a member of his immediate family circle should have been so ready to betray his trust.

Stanley's motives for dabbling in treason were apparently compounded of greed and resentment that he had not been given a peerage. According to Bacon, 'his ambition was so exorbitant and unbounded' that he coveted the royal Earldom of Chester. He also appears to have believed that the king would not dare to proceed against him, hardly bothering to deny the accusations made by the Yorkist defector Sir Robert Clifford on whose evidence he was condemned. But although Henry was naturally reluctant to offend Thomas Stanley, he could not afford to show a leniency which would, in the circumstances, at once have been interpreted as weakness. William Stanley was, moreover, becoming rather too rich and powerful for the king's comfort. Bacon says he was 'the richest subject for value in the kingdom', having an income of £3000 a year from his rents, while forty thousand marks' worth of cash, plate, jewels and other household stuff was found at his stronghold of Holt Castle near Wrexham.

William Stanley, therefore, paid the usual price of treason in February 1495 but in spite of this unfortunate episode, relations between the Tudors and the Stanleys remained entirely cordial and in 1496 Henry VII visited his stepfather at Lathom, where the earl was now building himself a suitably palatial residence. The story that the family jester took the opportunity to urge his master to push the king off the battlements to avenge his brother's death should probably not be taken too seriously.

George Stanley, the hostage of Bosworth and hero of Stoke, predeceased his father by seven years and the first earl was succeeded in 1504 by his grandson, another Thomas, who campaigned with the young Henry VIII in France in 1512. His uncle Edward, meanwhile, was distinguishing himself at the infinitely more momentous Battle of Flodden:

> Where shivered was fair Scotland's spear
> And broken was her shield

and her power to inflict damage on her southern neighbour for a generation to come. Edward Stanley was in command of the English left wing, where his Cheshire archers wrought terrible havoc among the fleeing Highlanders before engaging the flank of the King of Scotland's own division, which was already being attacked by Edmund Howard, commanding the right wing. Edward Stanley was created Baron Monteagle by a grateful sovereign, and his stirring deeds at Flodden Field were later recalled by Walter Scott:

> 'Charge, Chester, charge! On, *Stanley*, on!'
> Were the last words of Marmion.

The second Earl of Derby's unremarkable career ended in 1521, but during the lifetimes of the third and fourth earls, which spanned the remainder of the Tudor century, the family continued to reign like petty kings, not only in Man but over huge areas of the north-west, much as the Percys did over the north-east of England. Unlike the Percys, though, the Stanleys chose to remain consistently loyal to the crown.

Edward, the third earl, was not yet twenty when he succeeded his father. One of his guardians was Cardinal Wolsey and he served as cup-bearer at Anne Boleyn's coronation, escorting her from Greenwich to the Tower in his own barge. His was an unexceptional existence as a great noble under Henry VIII, accompanying the monarch to his ostentatious encounter with the French King at the Field of the Cloth of Gold, helping to suppress the

'Pilgrimage of Grace', the religious disaffection which followed the dissolution of the smaller monasteries, and profiting comfortably from the spoils of the Reformation. Notwithstanding his outspoken opposition to the new vernacular *Book of Common Prayer*, the earl became a Privy Councillor under Edward VI, though he seldom took his seat, and contrived to avoid involvement in the deadly intrigues of the reign. The political climate under Mary being more to his conservative taste, he appeared more frequently at the council table and took an active part in the anti-heresy campaigns of the mid-1550s. He retained his place on the Council after the accession of Elizabeth – he was too influential in the north, always a turbulent area, for the new regime to want to risk offending him – but again he seldom appeared at court and held no great office of state. The queen and William Cecil were never entirely happy about the soundness of Edward Stanley's politics but, despite his well-known Catholic sympathies (and it was no coincidence of course that the north-west, especially Lancashire, remained stubbornly and predominantly Catholic), the Earl of Derby stood aloof from the treasonable Percy-Neville-Dacre-Howard alliance in 1569 and scrupulously observed his promise to use all diligence to keep the county of Lancaster in obedience to the sovereign.

Earl Edward, who died in 1572 at the age of sixty-four, is chiefly remembered for his princely lifestyle and the legendary hospitality dispensed at Lathom House during his reign. He normally kept over two hundred servants on his payroll, fed seventy old and decrepit poor twice a day and all comers three times a week, besides giving meat, drink and money to over two thousand people every Good Friday for thirty-five years. Generous though he was, and it was said at his death that 'the glory of hospitality seemed to fall asleep', the earl was also 'an excellent economist' who kept a shrewd Lancastrian eye on the accounts and conducted his affairs in an admirably business-like fashion. 'Every month he looked into his income, and every week into his disbursements, so that no one should wrong him, nor any be wronged by him' – a system which produced the eminently satisfactory result that the earl 'never exceeded his comings in, and died rich'.

The third Earl of Derby had married three times. His first wife, Dorothy Howard, the Duke of Norfolk's daughter, bore him a family of three sons and five daughters. Their eldest son was the second Stanley to be honoured with a royal bride. In 1555, at Westminster, Henry, Lord Strange, married Lady Margaret Clifford, the fifteen-year-old daughter of the Earl of Cumberland and his wife Eleanor Brandon, whose mother had been Mary, Duchess of Suffolk, younger sister of King Henry VIII. The match had the blessing of Queen Mary Tudor and the wedding was graced by the presence of her consort King Philip, whose Spaniards added a touch of extra glamour to the proceedings with a torchlight display of the intricate Moorish war game of hurling and twirling canes.

The new Lady Strange was not only a great territorial heiress, she also stood very close to the throne – her great-uncle Henry having arbitrarily disinherited the Stuart descendants of his elder sister Margaret in favour of the junior, Suffolk line, a deadly legacy which had already killed Margaret's cousin Jane Grey and was to poison the lives of the other Suffolk girls Katherine and Mary. Margaret Strange's own life was not a happy one, blighted by ill health and quarrels with her husband and his parents. She was a silly woman in many ways. The contemporary historian William Camden said of her that 'through an idle mixture of curiosity and ambition, supported by sanguine hopes and a credulous fancy, she much used the conversations of necromancers and figure flingers.' An interest in any form of fortune-telling was a dangerous hobby for one in Margaret's position and, for a time, earned her the serious displeasure of Queen Elizabeth. But in spite of chronic toothache and rheumatism, her husband's infidelity, their acrimonious financial disputes and various other miseries, Countess Margaret produced a family of four sons and a daughter and lived on into the mid-1590s, the last survivor by nearly twenty years of the unlucky posterity of that long-ago Tudor-Brandon love match.

The fourth Earl of Derby lived, like his father, *en prince* at Lathom and Knowsley. His household was, in fact, a miniature court and in May 1587, 'at which time his lordship did begin to set up house at Lathom after his return from the Court', there were 117 persons listed by name on the check-roll of his servants – from the steward, with a salary of twenty pounds a year, down through the seven gentlemen waiters, two ushers of the chamber, six grooms and two sub-grooms of the chamber, two clerks of the kitchen, two master cooks, two slaughtermen, porters, butlers, pantlers, yeomen of the ewery, the cellar and the wardrobe of beds, footmen, carpenters and gardeners, the laundresses Margaret Scarisbrick and Ellen Gaskell, Gilbert Prestcote the coachman and 'Henry the fool'.

Like his father, the fourth earl held no great office of state but he was summoned to sit on the commission which tried Mary Queen of Scots in 1585, and in December 1587 was appointed to lead a delegation which was to attempt to negotiate a peace with the Duke of Parma, King Philip's commander in the Netherlands. This despite the fact that the earl's kinsman, William Stanley of Hooton, an ardent Roman Catholic, had recently defected to the enemy, betraying the Dutch town of Deventer to Spain.

The fifth earl, who survived his father by only a couple of years, is better known as Ferdinando Lord Strange, courtier, man of letters, poet in a small way himself and friend and patron of poets and actors. He had his own company, as did a number of other prominent Elizabethans, and Lord Strange's players were among the foremost in the profession. He married Alice, daughter of Sir John Spencer of Althorp, and after his early and rather mysterious death – he was only thirty-four and there was some suspicion of poison – his friend Edmund Spenser celebrated him as Amyntas and his wife as Amaryllis in *Colin Clout's come home again*.

> Help, O ye shepherds! help ye all in this,
> Help Amaryllis this her loss to mourn;
> Her loss is yours, your loss Amyntas is,
> Amyntas, flower of shepherd's pride forlorn.
> He, whilst he lived, was the noblest swain
> That ever piped on an oaten quill:
> Both did he other, which could pipe, maintain,
> And eke could pipe himself with passing skill.

Earl Ferdinando having left no son, the title passed to his brother William whose principal claim to fame seems to have been an adventurous journey he made to Palestine, Turkey and on as far as Russia. It is said he was in Moscow when news of his father's and elder brother's deaths reached him. He married Elizabeth de Vere, old Lord Burghley's granddaughter and the wedding, which took place at Greenwich Palace in January 1595, was the social event of the season. The Tudors and the Stanleys had been bound together by strong ties of kinship, shared interests and old memories, but now the Tudors were about to make way for another dynasty and loyalty to the House of Stuart was to prove an expensive business for the House of Stanley.

James, seventh Earl of Derby, known as the Great Earl, was not a particularly likeable character. Tall, graceful and good-looking in a dark, florid style, he was also vain, arrogant, self-centred and when crossed could play very rough indeed. He seems, in fact, to have inherited quite a few of the less attractive traits of his maternal grandfather, William Cecil's unsatisfactory son-in-law Edward de Vere Earl of Oxford. Born in 1607, he married at nineteen the well-dowered and impressively well-connected Charlotte de la Tremoille, whose widowed mother – a daughter of the Dutch national hero William the Silent by his third wife Charlotte de Bourbon – had come to England in the train of Charles I's Queen, Henrietta Maria. The marriage, which took place at The Hague in June 1626, succeeded remarkably well, Mademoiselle de la Tremoille proving to be a lady of courage, intelligence and commonsense.

The outbreak of the Civil War coincided almost exactly with James Stanley's succession to his father's title. He was later to be accused of having caused the first casualties of the war by his unsuccessful attempt to seize the arms depot at Manchester – a strongly Puritan community of weavers and clothiers. But this is disputable, for as early as the summer of 1642 fighting was beginning to break out all over England in pustules of fear, rancour and petulance.

The Earl of Derby, who tended to regard the war in Lancashire as a personal insult to the authority of the Stanleys, would no doubt have taken a good deal of satisfaction in revenging himself on the impudent psalm-singing Mancunians, but he left it too late. In September he received orders to join the king at Shrewsbury, and on 1 October he raised the siege, leaving Manchester unsubdued and aggressive – and a useful strategic base for future Parliamentary operations in the north-west. Loyalties in Lancashire were divided, but the unpopularity of the Earl of Derby and the thuggish behaviour of his forces – he had raised and armed somewhere between three and five thousand auxiliaries who roamed in undisciplined bands over the countryside – did serious damage to the royalist cause.

In March 1643 a Spanish ship carrying a cargo of arms and ammunition to the Netherlands was stormbound in the Wyre estuary and plundered of 'divers goodly pieces of ordnance' by the Parliamentarians.

> These cannons [Derby informed Prince Rupert] being carried to the Castle of Lancaster – which is strong for the enemy . . . I ventured with some few forces to go there; and by the way, the people had the grace to rise with me. . . . When I came before the town I summoned it in His Majesty's name, and the Mayor (as I heard) counselled by the commanders of the Parliament made me so slight an answer . . . that I, enraged to see their sauciness against so good a Prince, made bold to burn the greatest part of the town, and in it many of their soldiers, who defended it very sharply for two hours, but we beat them into the Castle.

But the earl failed to take the castle and later that spring he lost the loyal towns of Wigan and Warrington. By mid-summer rumours of trouble in the Isle of Man (where his attempts to bring the ancient Manx system of land tenure into line with mainland practice had already caused acute local irritation) obliged him to abandon Lancashire for a visit to his island kingdom. During his absence, the Parliamentary forces seized the port of Liverpool, captured Preston and gained control of the Lune valley in the north, so that by the end of the year Lathom House itself was virtually the only royalist stronghold left in the whole county.

Ancient Lathom, with its yard-thick walls and wide moat, its seven towers and medieval drawbridge, would have been a tough proposition even if it had not contained the formidable Countess of Derby commanding a garrison of three hundred determined and well-drilled defenders – 'a desperate and too-well provided enemy', wrote Colonel Alexander Rigby mournfully from the trenches. Sir Thomas Fairfax, Parliament's northern general, formally demanded the surrender of Lathom in February 1644, offering a pardon for the earl and safe conduct for the countess and her children to Knowsley or New Park. But her ladyship defied him. She might be a woman and a stranger, she retorted, but she had not forgotten her duty to the Church of England, her prince or her lord her husband, and meant to defend her home to her last breath.

The epic siege of Lathom House lasted three months, effectively tying down a large proportion of the Parliamentary army in the north-west – for the garrison was by no means content to remain on the defensive only. Led by Captain Ogle, they made several daring sorties, killing a number of the besiegers, taking prisoners, seizing arms and ammunition and, on one triumphant occasion, capturing and dragging away with them a heavy mortar which had been tormenting them with its 'grenadoes'. The countess herself remained undaunted by stray bullets landing on the dinner table or coming through her bedroom window, and only consented to move her quarters after several such incidents. She continued to insist that 'she would keep the house while there was building to cover her head' and indignantly rejected all calls for surrender – she would burn Lathom to the ground and immolate herself and her children in the flames rather than fall into the hands of that 'insolent rebel' Alexander Rigby.

Fortunately her ladyship was never called upon to make good these self-dramatising threats. The earl, who had spent the winter with the king at Oxford, was now back in some force in the Wirral peninsula and contriving to find means of communicating with his wife and the Lathom household. 'I did write letters to them in cipher as much in as little compass as I could,' he remembered afterwards. These were then rolled in a pellet of lead or wax, so that 'if the bearer suspected danger of discovery he might swallow it, and Phisick would soon find it again.' How many postmen were thus inconvenienced is not recorded.

According to the reports of Colonel Rigby, the earl was succeeding in making 'inroads on the Parliamentarians' and keeping them in 'continuall alarms', but the siege of Lathom was not finally raised until the end of May, when Prince Rupert came storming into Lancashire to retake the port of Liverpool – vital for the king's communications with Ireland. He was rapturously received at Lathom, where the countess embraced her young kinsman and received from him the colours captured in his successful assaults on Preston and Bolton.

Rupert could not stay long in the north-west. Having temporarily restored the royalist position there, his next task was to relieve the hard-pressed Duke of Newcastle at York; but before he left he advised Lord Derby to send his wife and children away to the comparative safety of the Isle of Man. After the disaster at Marston Moor later that summer, the earl followed his family into exile, leaving Lathom still held for the king under the command of Colonel Rawsthorne. The garrison was finally starved out and forced to surrender in December 1645, whereupon the house was ransacked and virtually demolished by the Parliamentarians – the parish records of nearby Ormskirk contain receipts for the sale of planks, beams and lead from the old building.

The Derbys remained on the Isle of Man, which they continued to hold as a royalist outpost, and in 1649 the earl spurned a call for its surrender from Cromwell's son-in-law General Ireton.

> I scorn your proffers [he wrote furiously on 12 July from Castle Rushen] disdain your favour and abhor your treason; and am so far from delivering up this Island to your advantage, that I will keep it to the utmost of my power to your destruction. . . . If you trouble me with any more messages on this occasion, I will burn the paper and hang the bearer.

Some six months had now passed since the trial and execution of the king for whose sake the Stanley family had suffered and lost so much – all their mainland property sequestered, Lathom destroyed, Knowsley occupied by strangers, their goods scattered, pillaged and 'divided amongst the robbers' as his lordship put it sourly. But Stanley loyalty – and thirst for revenge – burnt as fiercely as ever, and lying low on the Isle of Man the earl patiently waited his chance. In the summer of 1651 it came. The dead king's son, recently crowned Charles II by the Presbyterian Scots, was preparing to invade England with Presbyterian Scottish help and summoned his faithful and well-beloved Earl of Derby to meet him in Lancashire.

The earl sailed on 12 August and thereafter events moved swiftly and disastrously. On the twenty-sixth Lord Derby's forces were badly mauled at Wigan by the local militia under Colonel Robert Lilburne. The earl himself was wounded and only narrowly escaped capture. He found temporary refuge at Boscobel, a remote house hidden in the Shropshire oak woods and occupied by a family of humble Catholic foresters, and reached the king just in time for the last act of the tragedy.

Although two thousand royalists were killed in the reeking streets of Worcester on that hot September afternoon and three thousand or so taken prisoner, Charles himself miraculously escaped unwounded. Towards dusk, as the scale of their defeat became starkly obvious, a tiny group of desperate men led by Lord Wilmot, the Duke of Buckingham and the Earls of Derby and Lauderdale closed round the young king and got him out of the town. They were riding north with no very clear idea of where they were going, conscious only of the need to put as much distance as possible between themselves and Cromwell's army. There was some talk of trying to get back to Scotland, and Charles wanted to make for London, but the most urgent necessity was to get him under cover, into some safe hiding place until the first hue and cry had died down. Then Lord Derby remembered the honest Penderels of Boscobel. Guided by Charles Giffard, another Catholic, and his servant Francis Yates, the party reached Whiteladies, a manor on the Boscobel estate, at about four o'clock in the morning. William and Richard Penderel were sent for and taken to an inner parlour where Charles was resting and being revived with sherry and biscuits. 'This is the King,' said Derby simply. 'Thou must have a care of him and preserve him, as thou didst me.'

There was nothing more to be done, and the little party of Cavaliers split up to seek their own safety. Derby, Lauderdale, Lord Talbot, Charles Giffard and about forty horse continued northwards, hoping to catch up with the retreating Scots. But later that day, harassed by the enemy, hungry, exhausted and dispirited, they surrendered to one Captain Oliver Edge a little beyond the town of Newport.

Lord Derby was taken to Chester Castle as a prisoner of war, but soon discovered that he was to be treated as a war criminal and on 30 September was tried by court martial on charges of having invaded the realm with intent to levy war on the Parliament and Commonwealth of England, and to set up Charles Stuart, a declared traitor and enemy of the people, as king. The outcome of these proceedings was never in doubt. Other considerations apart, James Stanley had made too many personal enemies since the outbreak of war, and memories of the burning of Lancaster and the sack of Puritan Bolton in the spring of 1644 were still green – it was no coincidence that his execution took place in Bolton market-place.

In his last letters to his wife, the earl warned her that a force under Colonel Duckenfield, the Governor of Chester, would soon be coming to demand the surrender of the Isle of Man. 'And however you might do for the present,' he wrote, 'in time it would be a grievous and troublesome business to resist, especially them that at this hour command three nations.' Duckenfield himself was a gentleman who might be trusted to deal fairly and therefore, despite his great affection for the island, the earl's advice to his lady was that she should submit to the will of God and make the best conditions she could for herself,

> and children, and servants, and people, and such as came over with me, to the end you may go to some place of rest where you may not be concerned in war. . . . I conjure you, my dearest heart [he went on] by all those graces which God hath given you, that you exercise your patience in this great and strange trial. If harm come to you, then I am dead indeed. . . .

Whatever the countess was planning to do, and there is some reason to believe that she had been hoping to use the Isle of Man as a bargaining counter in the stakes for her husband's life, she was frustrated by the prompt action of Manx patriot William Christian, also known as Illiam Dhone or Blond William. Christian, a member of one of the most influential island families and already at loggerheads with the Stanleys over the land tenure question, had no intention of allowing the heroine of Lathom to put his people at risk by staging a repeat performance at Castle Rushen. He therefore mustered the community leaders, and as soon as the commonwealth force arrived at Ramsey a deputation of Manxmen formally surrendered to Colonel Duckenfield without reference to the countess.

The 'Rebellion of Illiam Dhone' was to have unpleasant consequences after the Restoration, when the Stanleys were reinstated as Lords of Man and Earl James's son Charles, eighth Earl of Derby, sought revenge. He had William Christian tried and convicted of treason – the sentence of death by shooting being carried out in January 1662. The earl maintained that he had acted according to Manx law, but the Privy Council in London disagreed, ruling that the indulgence offered by the Act of Indemnity passed by Parliament in 1660 applied equally to the king's Manx subjects, and as a mark of displeasure the royal assent was refused to a measure restoring the rest of the sequestered Stanley estates. Although the eighth earl did eventually succeeed in recovering most of his patrimony, memory of this episode rankled. Nearly fifty years later the tenth Earl of Derby had an inscription set up at Knowsley in memory of his martyred grandfather and publicly proclaiming royal ingratitude in refusing to restore property lost through loyalty to the Stuart cause.

The eighth earl had intended to rebuild Lathom House but the plan was never carried out and, instead, Knowsley, about eight miles from Liverpool and originally a Stanley hunting lodge, became the principal family home. The tenth earl improved and enlarged it. An eighteenth-century visitor remarked that the oldest part of the house, of dark brown stone dating back to Tudor times and beyond, looked like an ancient castle, but that 'in the year 1731 there was added to it a brick wing and a large range of stables. The front looks neat', he observed kindly 'and some of the apartments are handsome; but the whole building, taken together, is a piece of patchwork.'

As well as adding a modern wing, the tenth earl, a younger son and professional soldier who had spent many years of his life abroad campaigning with the Prince of Orange, acquired a collection of Flemish and Italian pictures and opened the gallery at Knowsley to students of drawing and architecture. When he died childless in 1736, the barony of Strange and the Isle of Man passed out of Stanley hands into those of the Dukes of Atholl through the female line, but thirty years later the third duke sold out to King George III for £70,000 and the Lordship of Man reverted to the English Crown.

The Earldom of Derby passed to Sir Edward Stanley Bt. of Bickerstaff Hall near Ormskirk and Patten House in Preston, MP for Preston and one-time mayor of the town. Sir Edward, who was well into his forties when he succeeded, was a sixth cousin of the Knowsley Stanleys, but could trace direct descent from the younger brother of the second earl. His eldest son married an heiress, Lucy, daughter of Hugh Smith of Weald Hall in Essex, adding her surname to his, and followed an active career in politics. He predeceased his father who lived on to the great age of eighty-seven.

In 1774 the eleventh earl's grandson and heir, another Edward, announced his engagement and Horace Walpole wrote on 8 June:

> This month Lord Stanley marries Lady Betty Hamilton. He gives her a most splendid entertainment tomorrow at his villa in Surrey and calls it a *fête-champêtre*. It will cost five thousand pounds. . . . He has bought all the orange trees around London and the haycocks, I suppose, are to be made of straw coloured satin.

The wedding took place on 23 June at the home of the bride's mother – once the Duchess of Hamilton, now Duchess of Argyll and born Elizabeth Gunning, one of those fabulous Irish beauties who had taken London by storm in the 1750s. The young couple spent their honeymoon at The Oaks, the villa at Banstead in Surrey where their bethrothal party had been held, and presently set up house in Grosvenor Square where their parties continued to be famous. 'Last night and the night before I supped at Lady Betty Stanley's,' wrote the contemporary gossip and diarist George Selwyn. 'Their suppers are magnificent but their hours are abominably late.'

The Stanleys were prominent Whigs – in January 1775 Lord Stanley made his maiden speech in the Commons where he sat as member for the county of Lancaster – and their wealth and rank entitled them to a leading place in the glittering society ruled by Georgiana Devonshire and the Devonshire House set. Lady Stanley was almost as compulsive a gambler as the Duchess of Devonshire and in some ways their lives followed a curiously similar pattern – both were recklessly indiscreet and both were dominated by anxious and ambitious mamas. Lady Stanley was more fortunate than Georgiana in that she was able to present her husband with a son and heir punctually ten months from their wedding day, but her marriage was not a happy one and soon gossip was linking the names of Betty Stanley, or the Countess of Derby as she became in 1776, with that of the Duke of Dorset. There was talk of a divorce for the Stanleys and Lady Sarah Lennox confided to a friend: 'It is no scandal to tell you it is imagined that the Duke of Dorset will marry Lady Derby, who is now in the country keeping quiet and out of the way.' But there was no divorce and no reconciliation either. Lord and Lady Derby separated in 1778 and never spoke to one another again.

The earl consoled himself with the friendship of a charming and talented young actress, Elizabeth Farren, and with his numerous sporting interests. A member of the Jockey Club, he was often at Newmarket, but in 1779 he inaugurated a race for three-year-old fillies to be run at Epsom over a mile and a half and called The Oaks after his own house near the course on Banstead Downs. Lord Derby won the first Oaks with his filly Bridget, and the following year came the first running at Epsom of the Derby Stakes, arguably the most famous horse race in the world. Originally run over two miles, it was open to colts and fillies. The entry fee was fifty guineas, and on that first occasion the winner was Sir Charles Bunbury's Diomed. The earl won the race himself in 1787 with Sir Peter Teazle – a feat which was not repeated until 1924 when the seventeenth earl won with Sansovino, and again in 1933 with the legendary Hyperion.

The twelfth Earl of Derby also established the racecourse at Aintree, but in his own lifetime he was best known as a champion cockfighter and breeder of game cocks, developing a strain known as Derby Reds, or the Knowsley Breed. This cruel and ancient sport was popular with all classes of Englishmen and, though prohibited, was sanctioned in the eighteenth century by aristocratic interest and patronage. Lord Derby constructed his own cockpit at Preston and sponsored numerous 'mains', as each series of contests was known.

That great explosion of energy and inventive genius known as the Industrial Revolution brought new wealth to the Stanleys, just as it had to many other landed families fortunate enough to own real estate in the once comparatively barren north. Liverpool's growth as a port, trading with the West Indies and North America carrying rum, sugar, tobacco and raw cotton in one direction, and slaves and finished cotton goods in the other, had been steady since the early part of the century. But it was the spinning jenny and Richard Arkwright's improved spinning frame which, by the 1770s, had begun to transform quiet little agricultural communities like Bolton, Preston, Wigan and Warrington into thriving industrial centres, with cotton mills and the housing needed for their workers springing up on Stanley land. By the end of the first quarter of the nineteenth century the process was being accelerated by the building of the Manchester to Liverpool railway, and in November 1829 Thomas Creevey wrote from nearby Croxteth, where he was staying with Lord Sefton:

> Today we have had a *lark* of a very high order. Lady Wilton sent over yesterday from Knowsley to say that the Loco Motive machine was to be upon the railway at such a place at 12 o'clock for the Knowsley party to ride in if they liked, and inviting this house to be of the party. So of course we were at our post in 3 carriages and some horsemen at the hour appointed. I had the satisfaction, for I can't call it *pleasure*, of taking a trip of five miles in it, which we did in just a quarter of an hour – that is, 20 miles an hour.

Lord Derby's estranged wife had died in the spring of 1797, whereupon the patient Miss Farren bade farewell to the stage and a few weeks later became Countess of Derby in a quiet ceremony in Grosvenor Square. The marriage was an entirely happy one and although the new Lady Derby was by this time in her late thirties, she produced several children in quick succession. Of these only the youngest daughter survived into adult life, marrying the Earl of Wilton and returning to Knowsley to keep house for her father after her mother died.

The extended family at Knowsley included not only the children and grandchildren of the earl's first and second marriages, but also the four illegitimate offspring of his great friend General 'Gentleman Johnny' Burgoyne, who were adopted by Lord Derby after Burgoyne's death in 1792. Creevey, who was a regular visitor, commented more than once on the cheerful atmosphere in the house. 'My Lord and Lady were all kindness to me,' he wrote in 1822. '. . . I must say I never saw a man or woman live more happily with nine grown-up children. It is my Lord Derby who is the great moving principle.' But Lady Derby deserves credit too, having clearly made a noticeable success of her change of role and surpassing, in Creevey's opinion, 'all your hereditary nobility I have seen'. She also seems to have possessed a sense of humour. Creevey records an occasion at Knowsley soon after the new dining-room came into use.

> It is 53 feet by 37, and such a height that it destroys the effect of all the other apartments. . . . You enter it from a passage by two great Gothic church-like doors the whole height of the room. . . . Ly Derby (like herself) when I objected to the immensity of the doors, said: 'You've heard General Grosvenor's remark upon them, have you not? He asked in his grave pompous manner, "Pray are those great doors to be opened for every pat of butter that comes into the room?" '

In April 1822 Creevey had spoken of 'little Derby . . . very *very* old in looks, but as merry as ever'. 'Little Derby' was then in his seventieth year, but was to live on into his eighties, surviving his beloved wife by five years and dying at last in October 1834 after a reign of nearly sixty years. He was buried in the family vault at Ormskirk and his funeral was attended by almost the whole of Lancashire. They came to pay their respects to a 'venerable and highly, nay universally, respected and beloved Nobleman' and 'one of the brightest ornaments of the British Turf'. Though perhaps not universally beloved (an especially bitter political feud had raged between his lordship and the Corporation of Preston over their rejection of his grandson as their elected representative), the twelfth Earl of Derby had long since become a familiar, even a reassuring landmark typifying an England which was already beginning to fade into legend. As the *Sporting Magazine* solemnly assured its readers, 'We ne'er shall look upon his like again.'

Certainly the thirteenth earl did not much resemble his father in his sporting tastes. An enthusiastic amateur naturalist and zoologist, President of the Linnean and Zoological Societies, he collected over twenty thousand stuffed specimens for the museum he bequeathed to the City of Liverpool. He also assembled at Knowsley an unrivalled menagerie of rare animals and birds, which was indirectly responsible for one of the comic masterpieces of English literature. Invited to sketch the collection, the poet and artist

Edward Lear was employed at Knowsley from 1832 to 1836, composing his Nonsense Rhymes for the entertainment of the earl's children.

Although he had fulfilled his obligations by sitting in the Commons as member for Preston, the thirteenth earl, a quiet mannered, blue-eyed, rosy cheeked man, never displayed any enthusiasm for politics. His son and heir was a very different proposition. Born at Knowsley in 1799, Edward Geoffrey Smith-Stanley was the old earl's favourite grandchild and had been groomed from infancy for a public career. He also had the advantage of elocution lessons from his actress step-grandmother and even those who disliked him, such as Charles Greville, conceded his remarkable powers of oratory. 'His voice and manner are so good that no one can hear him without listening to him,' wrote Lord Campbell, and Lord Aberdeen declared that, at his best, Stanley excelled masters of the art such as Fox, Pitt, Grenville and Whitbread.

Edward Stanley entered the unreformed House of Commons in 1822 as member for the rotten borough of Stockbridge, exchanging it four years later for the family seat at Preston. In 1830, however, to the fury of his grandfather, he was rejected by the electors in favour of the radical Henry 'Orator' Hunt and obliged to turn to a 'safe' seat in the South.

Stanley had, of course, been bred in the family Whig tradition and held office as Secretary of State for Ireland and Colonial Secretary under Lord Grey. But while he voted for the Great Reform Bill of 1832, he was far from being a convinced liberal with a large or small '1', and in 1834 resigned from the government over the Irish Tithes question. Not yet ready to throw in his lot with Robert Peel and the Tories, he tried to form a third, middle-of-the-road party. This was neither a large nor a successful venture and became known at the time as the Derby Dilly, a nickname coined by the Irish MP Daniel O'Connell from a political squib by George Canning which had appeared in the *Anti-Jacobin*:

> Still down thy steep, romantic Ashbourne, glides
> The Derby dilly with its six insides. . .

By September 1841, the Dilly abandoned, the new Viscount Stanley had crossed the great divide and joined the Conservative Party, returning to the Colonial Office as a member of Peel's second cabinet.

When he first began to make his mark in public life, it was said of him that 'at thirty he was by far the cleverest young man of the day; and at sixty he would be the same, still by far the cleverest young man of the day'. He was certainly a good all-rounder. A classical scholar, he had won the Chancellor's Prize for Latin verse at Oxford and towards the end of his life he published a new translation of Homer's *Iliad*, which went through nine British and five American editions. As well as his intellectual pursuits, he maintained the family's interest in the turf, becoming a Steward of the Jockey Club in 1848, and in April 1851 Charles Greville recorded in his diary that if any grave Parliamentary gentleman or distinguished foreigner who knew Lord Stanley only in his dignified public persona had found themselves

> in the betting room at Newmarket on Tuesday evening and seen Stanley there, I think they would have been in a pretty state of astonishment. There he was in the midst of a crowd of blacklegs betting men and loose characters of every description in uproarious spirits, chaffing, rowing and shouting with laughter and joking. . . . It really was a sight and a wonder to see any man playing such different parts so naturally and obey all his impulses in such a way utterly regardless of appearances and not caring what anybody might think of the minister and statesman as long as he could have his fun.

It was a couple of months after this episode that Stanley became Earl of Derby and in February of the following year he became Prime Minister for the first time, with Benjamin Disraeli as his Chancellor of the Exchequer. He was to hold prime-ministerial office twice more, in 1858 and 1866, being succeeded in 1868 by Disraeli. Primarily associated with his opposition to Free Trade and the disestablishment of the Irish Church, Lord Derby's career, in the words of his most recent biographer,

> seemed to be a process of gradually compromising the special privileges of his class, and changing the old society into some-

thing new and less attractive. But he had no grudges or hard feelings towards anyone, or any class. As a sincere Christian, such malice had no place in his life; as a sportsman, it was not his way to condole with himself or others regarding his losses.

The fourteenth earl died in his seventieth year after a twilight period of retirement at Knowsley. His son wrote to Disraeli in September 1869; 'I cannot report very well of my father, he has become more of an invalid in his habits, goes out but little, and is seldom quite free from gout in some form. . . . He thinks badly of the political future, but speaks of it without excitement or annoyance.'

The fifteenth earl also followed a political career – doing the rounds of the Colonial, India and Foreign Offices – but never achieving anything approaching his father's distinction. In fact he made a palindrome of his father's politics by crossing back from the Conservative to the Liberal Party, although he eventually broke with Gladstone over the Home Rule question. His liberal proclivities, though, encouraged the Greeks to offer him their throne after the deposition of Otto of Bavaria in 1862. 'This beats any novel', wrote Benjamin Disraeli. 'Had I his youth I would not hesitate. . . . It is a dazzling adventure for the house of Stanley, but they are not an imaginative race, and I fancy they will prefer Knowsley to the Parthenon and Lancashire to the Attic Plains.' He was quite right. They did, and sadly there was no adventurous Stanley King of Greece. The job went instead to Prince George of Denmark.

The fifteenth earl died childless in 1893 and was succeeded by his younger brother Frederick, whose wife Constance (born Constance Villiers, daughter of the Earl of Clarendon) presented him with a quiverful of ten children. The eldest of these, Edward George Villiers, born at his grandfather's town house, 33 St James's Square, on 4 April 1865, was to become the seventeenth – and first twentieth-century Earl of Derby. He inherited his father's dignities in June 1908 and with them an estate of some seventy thousand acres. A modest patrimony compared with some of the Scottish ducal estates, but the Derby acres were exceedingly valuable in real terms – especially those in urban Liverpool and industrial East Lancashire – and brought in a rent-roll which gave the earl a net taxable income of approximately £100,000 a year, at a time when the standard rate of income tax was a shilling in the pound.

Lord Derby sold his birthplace in St James's Square and acquired an ostentatious mansion in Stratford Place on the north side of Oxford Street. He also extended the Newmarket estate purchased by his father but Stanley family life remained firmly centred on Knowsley. Emily Lytton (later Emily Lutyens) whose mother was Constance Derby's cousin, stayed at Knowsley as a girl in the early 1890s, and wrote:

> This house is enormous and very rambling. There are something over 80 bedrooms, all very small. None of the house is pretty, though some very old, but it has been so patched and pulled about by different owners . . . that it is really hideous. [The stables, however, with over forty splendid occupants, were 'magnificent' and kept] spotlessly clean which they ought to be considering that they have twenty men to look after them. The gardens are large and ugly, and these require twenty-four gardeners. Thank goodness I am not obliged to live here. The luxury of a small home and a few servants can only be properly appreciated by coming to a house like this.

But she did admit the convenience of having electric light in both the house and stables.

The way of life at Knowsley, with its platoons of domestic staff (thirty-eight indoor servants in 1910), its big dinners and shoots and the grand annual house party for the Grand National, when the king and queen were frequently among the guests and forty people filed through the 'Gothic church-like' doors into that enormous dining-room, followed the usual pattern of large scale political country house living, but Knowsley, unlike Chatsworth or Woburn for example, was never a treasure house of works of art. The Stanleys, with the possible exception of the tenth earl, had never pretended to be connoisseurs. Indeed, it is said that when a knowledgeable lunch guest complimented the seventeenth earl on a fine set of Charles II dining-room chairs, Lord Derby was much inclined to take offence. 'Damn cheek, that fellow noticing my chairs!' he grumbled afterwards.

The seventeenth earl's political career spanned more than thirty years and both his sons followed in his footsteps, so that from the Glorious Revolution to the outbreak of the Second World War, there was scarcely a period when there was not a Stanley in Parliament, in government, or both. A large, genial, sociable man, Lord Derby's talents lay chiefly in oiling the wheels, and his appointment as British ambassador to France at the end of the First World War probably initiated the happiest and most successful period of his public life.

Although much of that public life was necessarily spent in the South, his connections with Lancashire remained extremely close and meant a great deal to him. In 1911 he was elected Lord Mayor of Liverpool, thus maintaining a family tradition going back to 1568, and flung himself wholeheartedly into a hectic round of social, charitable and welfare work – from the distribution of Christmas hotpots to organising a fund for the Titanic survivors. He always spoke with the trace of a Lancashire accent, and in January 1914 the Irish Nationalist MP for the Scotland Division of Liverpool wrote in the *Pall Mall Magazine* of 'the present head of the Stanleys', that he had the bluff manner and brusque jerky speech of the Lancashireman. 'If you did not know that he was a great noble,' Mr O'Connor went on, 'you might take him for the heir to some vast cotton-spinning business . . . he has also a good deal of Lancashire doggedness underneath all his air of bonhomie and easy-goingness. . . . And he has enormous influence over men – at least in Lancashire.'

Not everyone, of course, was convinced that the Stanley influence in Lancashire was entirely beneficial. In 1913, Lloyd George, then Chancellor of the Exchequer, took a side swipe at the earl as an owner of slum property where 'it was almost impossible for people to preserve their own health and . . . the health and the lives of the little children'. The wicked landlord was always a useful political Aunt Sally – especially at election time – and during the campaign of 1923 the Labour candidate for the Edgehill Division of Liverpool attacked the ground rents being drawn from the county by the Stanley family, describing them as a 'toll which is strangling the economic life of our people'. This provoked Lord Derby into retorting that such was the ever increasing burden of taxation that he saw the time coming when he might be forced to give up the home of his ancestors. 'The Stanleys to leave

Knowsley!' exclaimed the Manchester *Evening News*. 'It is unthinkable to those who have felt a county pride in possessing the greatest host in the north of England,' and the paper went on to express the hope that his lordship had not been in earnest. But a Labour spokesman, reported by the *Liverpool Post*, predictably hoped that when Lord Derby was looking for a new home, he would put his name down on the Liverpool Corporation housing list where, if he waited his proper turn, he would be about fifteen-thousandth from the top. Needless to say, the Earl of Derby's name never did appear on the waiting list for a Liverpool council house, but by the end of the twenties he had sold all his property in Liverpool as well as the East Lancashire estates.

None of this had any effect on the strong mutual attachment which existed between the earl and the people of Lancashire. In the words of Mr Randolph Churchill, his official biographer:

> There was no Lancashire activity too large or too small to lay claim to his interest, encouragement and support. . . . It was not merely that he was more assiduous than others in a like situation; he genuinely enjoyed local functions, particularly when they were small. No bazaar or fête was too remote for him to attend, no foundation stone too small for him to lay; no swimming pool too unimportant for him to open.

Thus it was that he earned his soubriquet of 'King of Lancashire' and on his seventieth birthday in 1935, nearly five thousand people gathered in Preston Public Hall to witness the moving ceremony at which he was presented with a piece of gold plate as a token of their 'admiration and regard'. With it came a gift of jewellery for the countess and twenty-two stout volumes bound in red morocco containing the signatures of the eighty-three thousand Lancastrians who had each subscribed a shilling to the presentation, and conveying a message of affectionate greeting to his lordship.

Politics and Lancashire aside, the earl's lifelong passion was for bloodstock and racing, an enthusiasm which endeared him both to his native county and the nation at large. This dated back to 1893, when he first persuaded George Lambton to undertake the training of his father's horses and restore the prestige of the family stable, which had languished since the death of the fourteenth earl. In the forty years from 1908 until his death, the seventeenth earl's bulky top-hatted figure became a familiar sight at Epsom and Ascot, Newmarket and Doncaster. He was to win twenty classic races, including the Derby three times, the Oaks twice, the St Leger six times, the 1000 Guineas seven times and the 2000 Guineas twice. The Derby stud produced a string of fine horses, all of them bred for stamina as well as speed, to enable them to win over the classic Derby distance of one and a half miles.

Always a devoted family man, in 1889 the earl had married Lady Alice Montagu, daughter of the Duke of Manchester and his German wife Louisa (later the famous Double Duchess of Devonshire). It was a happy and successful partnership, but the couple were to know the sorrow of losing two of their three children. Their only daughter, Victoria, to whom her father was especially attached, was killed in an accident in the hunting field in 1927 and in 1938, in the month after Munich, their elder son died after a long illness.

Lord Derby was in his seventy-fifth year at the outbreak of the Second World War and viewed the future with undisguised foreboding.

> I wish I knew what we are fighting for [he wrote to Lord Beaverbrook in September 1939] – if to beat Hitler to a pulp I understand and strongly sympathise, but if it is to reconstitute Poland, I am not so enthusiastic . . . if it is to reconstitute Poland, when we have beaten Hitler we shall have to fight and beat Russia, a tough proposition. Altogether things are *hell*.

In 1940 the old man suffered a car accident which left him partially crippled and progressively more infirm. Two years later he won his third and last Derby (run at Newmarket like all the wartime classics) with Watling Street ridden by Harry Wragg. But the earl was not there to lead in the winner. Typically, he had promised to open a big gymkhana in north Lancashire, an engagement he 'did not like to chuck'. The King of Lancashire died at Knowsley in 1948 at the age of eighty-three. He was the last of his kind, the last of the old-style Earls of Derby, 'so grand and rich and beloved that he had no ambition for himself except to do his duty in the spacious world into which he had been born'.

His grandson, Edward John, who succeeded as eighteenth earl, had to adjust himself to less spacious surroundings and in 1953 literally reduced the size of those surroundings by demolishing all the Victorian additions to Knowsley, so that the huge, rambling old house regained its more manageable eighteenth-century proportions. An 'L' shape now, the longer arm is formed by the eighteenth-century building and the shorter by the Royal Chambers, reputed to include the hall rebuilt by the first Earl of Derby for the reception of his stepson, the first Henry Tudor. Even so, it is still very large, and the present earl lives in a more convenient house in the park.

Until the First World War Knowsley and its park, although close to Liverpool, had remained pleasantly rural, but today the city has extended to enclose both Knowsley and neighbouring Croxteth Hall. Knowsley's two-and-half thousand acres of parkland, once the enclave of a privileged few, has now, with the help of the Chipperfield circus family, become in part a safari park where lions, elephants and tigers roam their mini-Africa almost within sight of the glass factories of St Helen's. The thirteenth earl would have been quite at home amongst these incongruous tenants.

The present earl, who with his younger brother served in the Grenadier Guards during the Second World War and was awarded the Military Cross for gallantry on the Anzio beachhead, has maintained the family's tradition of service to crown and country. President, like his grandfather, of the Liverpool Chamber of Commerce and subsequently of the Merseyside and District Chamber of Commerce, Alderman of the Lancashire County Council until 1974, Pro-chancellor of Lancaster University, Lord Lieutenant and Custos Rotulorum of Lancaster, Constable of Lancaster Castle, he has also nobly maintained the tradition of service to Lancashire; while his brother Richard, as MP for the North Fylde Division of Lancashire from 1950–66, has followed the family's political tradition.

It is now very nearly five hundred years since Thomas and William Stanley retrieved the crown from a thorn bush on the bloody field of Bosworth. The dynasty they helped on to the throne that day has long since vanished from the scene, as has that other royal house for whose sake they all but ruined themselves. But the

Stanleys, tough and tenacious as the Lancashire folk they have adopted as their own, are still with us; and for as long as the English, from the monarch downwards, continue to flock to Epsom on Derby Day, their name is likely to remain familiar in our ears.

The Noble House of Howard

Sola virtus invicta

Thomas 3rd Duke of Norfolk by Hans Holbein the Younger
reproduced by permission of His Grace the Duke of Norfolk

The Noble House of Howard

Sola virtus invicta

THE origins of the noble house of Howard can be traced to the Norfolk village of East Winch – a fact commemorated by a plaque in the parish church which states, with due solemnity, that: 'As from a spring bubbling in a dell a river rises to flow to the sea, so from a ruin in this place flowed the broadening line of the Howards, Dukes of Norfolk, into English history.'

It was to East Winch, in or about the year 1277, that a rising young lawyer – one William Howard or Haward, of King's Lynn – came to make his home and start buying up small parcels of land. In the days of their later glory, a somewhat optimistic attempt was made by the Howards, Dukes of Norfolk, to claim descent from Hereward the Wake, but in fact nothing definite can be proved about the first William Howard's parentage. The likelihood is that he came either from a burgess family of Lynn or of local yeoman stock, and that his patronymic was an occupational one derived from the hayward – the parish officer responsible for the upkeep of the fences and enclosures which prevented cattle from straying off the common grazing land onto the village fields.

Whatever his background may have been, William Howard was clearly a man of exceptional natural ability for, without any advantages of aristocratic connections or inherited wealth, his career prospered in a most satisfactory fashion. Not long after he settled at East Winch he became legal adviser to the Corporation of Lynn, then a flourishing port on the River Ouse. In 1293 he was appointed a Justice of Assize for the northern counties and, two years later, he was summoned to Parliament. Before the end of the century he had been knighted by Edward I and had risen to the dignity of Chief Justice of the Common Pleas.

Sir William was now a man of considerable importance in his native Norfolk and the burgesses of Lynn were at pains to keep on good terms with him, the town rolls containing a number of entries relating to gifts for their distinguished counsel and his wife Alice. For example, in 1306 the Corporation spent six shillings on the carcase of an ox for Lady Howard, thirteen shillings and eightpence on wine for Sir William, two calves and a shield of brawn, and eleven shillings on two salmon sent over to the manor house at East Winch on 'the vigil of Easter'.

None of Judge William's descendants followed him into the legal profession. Instead they concentrated their energies on establishing themselves as a 'county' family, serving the crown in various civil and military capacities, and consolidating their territorial position by a series of prudent alliances among the neighbouring gentry. The judge's son, John, married Joan of Cornwall, sprig of a bastard branch of the far-spreading Plantagenet tree and heiress to many rich manors around Lynn. Alice de Boys, wife of old William's grandson, John Howard the second, brought the manor of Fersfield into the family. Two generations later, another John Howard married another heiress, Margaret Plaiz of Toft, and through his second wife, Alice Tendring, acquired the Stoke Nayland estate in Suffolk and Tendring Hall, where his son Robert was born.

Robert Howard, a contemporary of that notable warrior King Henry V, commanded a fleet which 'kept the coasts of France about Calais' during the Agincourt campaign and was subsequently rewarded by a marriage more brilliant than any the family had yet been able to aspire to – his wife, Margaret, being the daughter of Thomas Mowbray, Duke of Norfolk, a lady in whose veins flowed the bluest blood in the kingdom, Plantagenet and Bigod, Warenne, FitzAlan and de Bohun. The only son of this momentous marriage, John Howard, the fifth of his name, was destined to live through troubled times, to play an important part in the affairs of the nation and to be the effective founder of his house.

At the outbreak of that bitter and complicated family feud known as the Wars of the Roses, John Howard followed the lead of his Yorkist Mowbray cousins and, when the Mowbrays died out in the male line, continued to support the Yorkist cause. But it was not until the coup of 1483, which brought Richard of Gloucester to the throne, that John Howard, 'a man of great knowledge and virtue as well in counsel as in battle', finally reaped the harvest of his loyalty to the White Rose when the new king created him Duke of Norfolk and conferred the courtesy title of Earl of Surrey on his son Thomas.

Enriched by the vast Mowbray estates and trusted as allies by Richard Crookback, the Howards, father and son had become great men, standing close to the centre of affairs. But in fifteenth-century England it was never wise to take your luck for granted. In less than two years the storm was ready to break over Richard III's head; and across the sea in Brittany Henry Tudor, last surviving representative of the House of Lancaster, was gathering his forces, waiting his opportunity to strike.

The 'unknown Welshman' came ashore at Milford Haven early in August 1485 and a few days later John Howard, Duke of Norfolk, wrote urgently to that other well-known East Anglian John Paston, letting him to understand 'that the king's enemies be a-land. Wherefore, I pray you that you meet with me at Bury . . . upon Tuesday night, and that ye bring with you such company of tall men as ye may goodly make at my cost and charge, beside that ye have promised the King. And I pray you ordain them jackets of my livery, and I shall content you at your meeting with me.'

When the armies met at Bosworth, the smell of treachery hung heavily over Richard's camp, and on the eve of the great battle the Duke of Norfolk found a placard fixed to his tent which bore the warning:

> Jack of Norfolk be not too bold,
> For Dickon thy master is bought and sold.

To his credit, though, Jack of Norfolk 'regarded more his oath, his honour and promise made to King Richard, and like a gentleman and a faithful subject to his prince, he absented not himself from his master.'

The first Howard Duke of Norfolk died fighting for the last Plantagenet king, but his son Thomas survived and spent the next three years as a prisoner in the Tower, while the family paid the penalty of having picked the losing side. Their rehabilitation began in January 1489, when Thomas was released from gaol and given a chance to prove his usefulness to the new dynasty by restoring order in the turbulent North Country. This he did with efficiency and moderation, demonstrating that his first loyalty was to the crown, no matter who happened to be wearing it, and he started to make slow but steady progress in royal favour.

Thomas Howard, Earl of Surrey, trained to soldiering from boyhood, was a man of limited intelligence, narrow and old-fashioned in outlook. But he was also a practical man of the world who knew which side his bread was buttered, and for the rest of his long life he served the House of Tudor as faithfully as his father had once served the House of York. His chief claim to fame is the crushing defeat he inflicted on the Scots at Flodden. In return, he was created Duke of Norfolk and Earl Marshal of England by letters patent dated 1 February 1514. (The title of Earl Marshal became hereditary in the Howard family with the sixth duke in 1672.) Thus after an interval of nearly thirty years, the Howards had redeemed at Flodden the status forfeited on the field of Bosworth.

Although the hostility between Thomas Wolsey and the aristocratic party (which was furiously jealous of the Cardinal's power and opposed to his foreign policy) temporarily barred the family's path to the highest places of political influence, the second duke's career of public service was by no means at an end. In 1515 he escorted the king's sister Mary on her wedding journey to France, in 1517 he and his son were called upon to deal with the Evil May Day riots in London, and in 1520 he acted as guardian of the realm during Henry VIII's absence at the Field of the Cloth of Gold. But Thomas Howard's last days were spent in retirement at Framlingham Castle, ancestral home of his Mowbray forebears, where he died, full of honours, in his eightieth year on 21 May 1524. The funeral of the victor of Flodden attracted a great host of mourners, who gathered from far and wide to pay their respects to a national hero and an honest man, of whom it was said that 'at his departing out of Framlingham Castle towards his burial, he could not be asked one groat for his debts, nor for restitution to any person'.

His eldest son, another Thomas, had no taste for the medieval discomforts of Framlingham and at once began to build himself a palatial new residence on the site of the old Mowbray hunting lodge at Kenninghall, some twenty miles south-west of Norwich.

Everything about Kenninghall, built in the shape of a letter H, was in the grand manner, with separate suites of apartments for the duke, the duchess, the children and for the duke's mistress Elizabeth Holland. Like all great households of the time, it was organised on generous lines with a staff of hundreds. Besides officials, such as the treasurer, the comptroller, the almoner and the master of the horse, there were chaplains, tutors, musicians, butlers, stewards, gentlemen ushers, grooms of the chamber, bedchamber women, nurses, cooks, clerks, pantlers, ewerers and hordes of lesser servants and servants' servants, down to the scullions and kitchen boys who worked naked in the fierce heat of the huge cooking fires. It was, in fact, a court in miniature over which the duke reigned – a petty king whose word, in his own territory, was law.

The family life at the centre of all this magnificence was not a happy one. The third Duke of Norfolk, gazing tight-lipped and cold-eyed out of Holbein's portrait, does not look an agreeable character, and nor was he. His wife, born Elizabeth Stafford daughter of the Duke of Buckingham, complained volubly about his 'shameful handling' of her, telling everyone who would listen that she had been born 'in an unhappy hour to be matched with so ungracious a husband', who flaunted 'that harlot Bess Holland' under her nose, kept her short of money, locked her up, took away her jewels and, another time, even 'set his women to bind me till blood came out at my fingers' ends, and they sat on my breast till I spat blood . . . and all for speaking against that drab Bess Holland, he put me out of doors'. Inevitably sides were taken on the domestic battlefield and deep and potentially dangerous rifts opened within the family circle.

The duke and duchess finally separated in 1533 – at a time when the fortunes of the house of Howard were becoming ever more closely intertwined with those of the house of Tudor. Norfolk's heir, Henry, the young Earl of Surrey, had been chosen as the friend and companion of the king's bastard son, Henry Fitzroy, Duke of Richmond, while his daughter Mary was to be Richmond's wife.

The Tudors and the Howards, though, were already connected by another marriage of immense historical significance, for in January 1532 the king had taken as his second wife Anne Boleyn, whose mother, Lady Elizabeth Howard, was Norfolk's sister. The duke had done his best to promote the match and by so doing had helped to destroy the detested Cardinal Wolsey, but Anne proved a serious disappointment to her Howard relations. She failed to give the king the legitimate son he so urgently needed and in the spring of 1536 she was arrested on charges of adultery, incest and high treason. The unfortunate queen received no help from her uncle Norfolk. On the contrary, it was he, in his capacity as Lord High Steward, who presided at her trial and, with no visible sign of emotion, pronounced the sentence of burning or beheading at the king's pleasure.

The third duke's recipe for survival in the bloodstained jungle of Tudor politics was a simple one – never at any time to oppose the king for any reason. He made no demur when Anne was executed, nor when her daughter, his great-niece Elizabeth, was declared illegitimate by Act of Parliament. Even though a devout Catholic himself, he apparently suffered no qualms of conscience over the king's break with Rome and showed no hesitation in accepting Henry Tudor as the Supreme Head of the Church in England. It was a philosophy perhaps best summed up by his famous warning to the less pliant Thomas More: 'By the mass, Master More, it is perilous striving with princes. And therefore I would wish you somewhat to incline to the King's pleasure. For by God's body, Master More, *Indignatio principis mors est* – the wrath of the King is death.'

Despite the setback caused by the Anne Boleyn episode and the annoyance of seeing another upstart – Thomas Cromwell – taking Wolsey's place as chief councillor, by the end of the 1530s the Duke of Norfolk was securely established as the acknowledged leader of the English nobility, Lord Treasurer and Earl Marshal, while the handsome, accomplished Earl of Surrey excelled among the younger generation. But it was another young, seemingly obscure member of the clan who brought the Howards briefly to a place of pre-eminence they were never to fill again.

Early in the year 1540 Katherine Howard – one of the numerous offspring of the duke's ne'er-do-well brother Edmund – made her début at court as a maid of honour to Henry VIII's fourth wife. Henry felt he had been shamefully deceived over poor plain Anne of Cleves and was labouring under an acute sense of grievance when his eye was first caught by the little Howard's plump, auburn-haired prettiness, her exuberant vitality and her winning ways. This was just the stroke of fortune which the family needed, and aunts and cousins descended in flocks to give Mistress Katherine sage advice on how to behave, 'in what sort to entertain the King and how often', while the Howards joined in chorus to commend their young kinswoman for her 'pure and honest condition'.

But having 'cast his fantasy' on this jewel of womanhood, who seemed to offer not only a 'very perfect love towards him' but also the desired fruit of marriage (Henry still had only one legitimate heir, three-year-old Prince Edward, to show for all his matrimonial exertions), His Highness needed no encouragement. The despised Anne of Cleves was divorced with more speed than ceremony and Mistress Katherine Howard elevated to the position once so disastrously occupied by her cousin Anne Boleyn.

The ageing Henry was openly besotted with his latest bride – his 'rose without a thorn'. 'The King is so amorous of her that he cannot treat her well enough,' commented the French ambassador, and while the honeymoon lasted the new queen was showered with expensive presents – dresses, furs, jewellery, valuable grants of land, manors and lordships pouring forth in an apparently inexhaustible stream – and life at court once more became a continual round of dancing and feasting. 'This King had no wife who made him spend so much money in dresses and jewels as did Katherine Howard, who every day had some fresh caprice,' recorded the gossipy author of the anonymous Spanish Chronicle. 'She was the handsomest of his wives and also the most giddy.'

Katherine was probably no more than eighteen or nineteen when she made her first public appearance as queen at Hampton Court in August 1540, so perhaps she was entitled to be a little giddy. Unfortunately, though, she seems never to have had the least conception of the fact that her marriage had thrust her into a world seething with violence and intrigue – the natural habitat of predators whose teeth and claws were very imperfectly camouflaged by the embroidered satin, the velvet and the jewels – a world where no quarter was asked or given, and which had just been the scene of a particularly ruthless coup. The circumstances surrounding the downfall of Thomas Cromwell remain more than a little obscure, but there is no doubt that the Duke of Norfolk, assisted by the king's timely infatuation for his niece, had been closely involved in the manoeuvres backstage, and he and his allies were now busy scrambling to power over the headless corpse of their former adversary.

Howard arrogance alone would have made the family unpopular but, as leaders of the reactionary right wing, they were feared and detested by the radical party, which favoured a far more sweeping programme of religious reform than anything the king had yet agreed to sanction. The progressives, who numbered many able and ambitious men among their ranks, watched morosely as the queen's relations dug themselves in around the throne, and meditated a counterattack. As it turned out, the flighty Katherine, symbol and source of Howard ascendancy, offered an easy target, for within a matter of months she was bestowing smiles and, so it was whispered, more than smiles on Master Thomas Culpepper, a gentleman of the Privy Chamber and another Howard connection.

By the summer of 1541 gossip was rife in the court and some people – people with special knowledge of the queen's reputation as a girl growing up in the household of her step-grandmother, old Duchess Agnes, widow of the Victor of Flodden – were beginning to wonder how best to put that knowledge to profitable use. Finally, John Lassells, a convinced member of the reformist faction, whose sister Mary could testify to the disgraceful goings-on which had been winked at by 'my old lady of Norfolk', laid certain information before the Privy Council. He told how one Henry Manox, a music master, had been familiar with the secret parts of Katherine's body when she was only thirteen, and how Francis Dereham, now one of the ushers of the queen's chamber, had been made welcome in her 'naked bed' and had known her carnally many times before her marriage to the King.

Gossip was one thing. Detailed accusations like these could not be suppressed and, although Henry's first reaction had been one of furious disbelief, the facts were presently found to be undeniable. There was no doubt at all that Katherine had been promiscuous before her marriage, nor that her behaviour since had been at best criminally foolish. Actual adultery was never proved conclusively but the presumption of guilt was very strong and in any case Thomas Culpepper confessed both desire and intention 'to do ill with the Queen', which was quite enough to condemn them both.

The king shed tears of maudlin self-pity over his young wife's betrayal, while the unhappy Katherine had fallen into such a 'fransy' of terror and remorse that Archbishop Cranmer, sent to bring her to a proper sense of her iniquity, was moved rather to pity and to fear for her reason. As for the rest of her family, the French ambassador remarked that 'the Duke of Norfolk may well be vexed, seeing that she is his brother's daughter and he was the author of this marriage'.

Norfolk, in fact, was terrified and wrote pathetically to the king from Kenninghall that the 'abominable deeds done by two of my nieces against your highness hath brought me into the greatest perplexity that ever poor wretch was in'. The duke feared lest His Majesty, 'having so often been thus falsely and traitorously handled', might now conceive a lasting displeasure against him and all his kin.

Things certainly looked bad for the Howards. Not only was Katherine under arrest but another of her uncles and his wife, the old Duchess of Norfolk and several lesser members of the clan were indicted for 'counselling the evil demeanour of the Queen to the slander of the King and his succession'.

In the end, though, the worst of the storm blew over. There was no mercy for Katherine, who was beheaded in the Tower on 13 February 1542 and went to join her cousin Anne under the stones of St Peter-ad-Vincula. But her relations were presently pardoned and released, and Norfolk himself survived with his influence only marginally diminished – later that year he was entrusted with the command of a full-scale raiding expedition over the Scottish border. When disaster did eventually overtake him, it was to be his son, rather than his erring nieces, who was cast in the role of nemesis.

The Earl of Surrey possessed none of his father's cunning, passive resilience. Hot-tempered, outspoken and stiff-necked – 'the most proud, foolish boy that is in England' – he was also a notable athlete, soldier, poet and hell-raiser who, though a married man in his mid-twenties, could still be caught playing such irresponsible pranks as breaking respectable citizens' windows and getting into fights in the brothels of Southwark. Such a handsome, high-spirited young lord naturally attracted notoriety and at Millicent Arundel's lodging-house in Laurence Lane, Cheapside, where Surrey and his cronies used to foregather, nothing was too good for him. For as well as being a peer of the realm, was he not a prince or next door to being a prince of the old royal house?

So at least they reasoned in Mistress Arundel's kitchen. But as Henry VIII began to fail, the question of who would rule England during his young son's minority was developing into a deadly power struggle between the 'new' men, headed by Edward Seymour, Earl of Hertford, and the Howards as leaders of the old nobility. Surrey's refusal to adopt a more conciliatory stance, his deliberate flaunting of his Plantagenet blood and provocative boast that his father, and by implication himself, would be 'meetest to rule the Prince' after King Henry's death, did nothing to advance the family cause, while his truculent contempt for upstarts like the Seymours had already made him some implacable personal enemies. By the autumn of 1546 they felt strong enough to strike, and in November the king was warned of the existence of a Howard conspiracy to seize control of the government.

As a result Norfolk and Surrey were both arrested and royal commissioners sent hurrying down to Kenninghall to take depositions from Norfolk's daughter, the widowed Duchess of Richmond, and from Bess Holland. Their evidence brought the dissensions long festering in the Howard family out into the open. The Duchess of Richmond, in particular, had scores to pay off, Surrey having been instrumental in preventing her projected remarriage to Thomas Seymour, and she told the commissioners that 'although constrained by nature to love her father and her brother, whom she noted to be a rash man, she would conceal nothing'. Nor did she. Her brother, she declared, hated all the Council and often reviled them. He had also urged her to try and entice the king into making her his mistress, so that she could bear 'as great a stroke about him' as Madame d'Estampes did about the French king.

While Mary Howard demonstrated her eagerness to betray her brother, Bess Holland, anxious to save her own skin, obligingly regaled the commissioners with various indiscreet remarks made by the duke about the plebeian origins of certain members of the Privy Council, and complaints that the king did not love him and was jealous of his power in his own country. None of this amounted to very much, and in the end the indictment against the Earl of Surrey resolved itself into a technical point of heraldry.

There had been controversy about Surrey's coat of arms for some time and Christopher Barker, a senior member of the College of Heralds, remembered an occasion nearly two years previously when the earl had shown him 'a scutcheon of the arms of Brotherton and St Edward' and said he would bear it. Barker claimed to have remonstrated that it was not in his pedigree and was 'not for his honour to do so', but Surrey had persisted, saying 'he would bear it and might lawfully do so'.

In fact, Henry Howard had every right to quarter the arms of his ancestors King Edward the Confessor and the Plantagenet Thomas of Brotherton, but it was a deliberate act of provocation to insist on exercising that right just then. At a time of acute political tension it could be taken as an open declaration of sinister intent and gave Surrey's accusers all the excuse they needed to charge him with traitorous abuse of the royal arms. He pleaded not guilty at his trial but had no illusions as to its inevitable outcome, exclaiming bitterly: 'I know the King wants to get rid of the noble blood around him and to employ none but low people, who would by their wills leave no noble man on life.'

The king was more probably motivated by doubts over Howard reliability in the matter of Royal Supremacy and the quarrel with Rome, and the Earl of Surrey was duly beheaded on Tower Hill in January 1547. A man of courage and 'excellent wit', a poet whose work is still included in anthologies of English verse, and a scholar who, with Thomas Wyatt, had been responsible for introducing the Shakespearean sonnet form into English literature, he typified the all-round brilliance of the Renaissance courtier – but he also typified the loser in the harsh world of sixteenth-century *Realpolitik*.

The Duke of Norfolk would undoubtedly have followed his son to the scaffold had not the old king died a matter of hours before the death sentence was due to be carried out. So the duke, that born survivor, lived on, a prisoner in the Tower, to see the Catholic Queen Mary Tudor come into her own, and died in his bed at Kenninghall in 1554 at the advanced age of eighty-one.

When Elizabeth Tudor succeeded her half-sister in 1558, Thomas Howard, fourth Duke of Norfolk, played a prominent part at her coronation in his capacity as Earl Marshal. The fourth duke, eldest son of the butchered Surrey, was still only twenty years old, but as England's premier nobleman and a close relative of the new queen, he looked a certain candidate for high office in the state. Yet, curiously enough, high office did not come his way. Although he became a well-liked and respected figure, the queen never admitted him to the innermost circle of her confidence. She bestowed honours on her cousin, as befitted his rank, but not power.

Norfolk had inherited all his father's obstinate pride of caste and, like his father, resented the rise of such 'new erected' men as the Secretary of State, William Cecil, and the queen's favourite, Robert Dudley, Earl of Leicester. The bad blood between Norfolk and Leicester was a matter of common gossip, and on one occasion in March 1565 they very nearly came to blows. They had been playing tennis at Hampton Court with Elizabeth looking on 'and my Lord Robert, being hot and sweating, took the Queen's napkin out of her hand and wiped his face.' Norfolk, outraged by the sight of this casual familiarity, had to be restrained from hitting his opponent over the head with his racquet. 'Whereat rose a great trouble, and the Queen offended sore with the Duke.'

As time went by, the duke grew increasingly dissatisfied. He felt himself slighted by the queen and thwarted ambition led to his disastrous involvement with that notorious *femme fatale*, Mary Queen of Scots. In the autumn of 1568 Norfolk's third wife Elizabeth, widow of Lord Dacre of Gilsland, had just died and a group of conservative peers, who shared his frustrations, suggested he might marry the Scottish queen, now a prisoner in England. This idea was first mooted as a possible means of restoring Mary to her throne by putting her under the control of a reliable English husband, but it was noticeable that no one, least of all the bridegroom elect, could quite bring themselves to mention it to Queen Elizabeth.

But it wasn't long before Queen Elizabeth got to hear about it and she wasted no time in confronting Norfolk. He emphatically disclaimed any desire to become King of Scotland. He preferred to sleep on a safe pillow, he said, and, in any case, counted himself as good a prince at home in his bowling alley at Norwich as the Queen of Scots, 'though she were in the midst of Scotland'. Besides, if he attempted to marry Mary, who pretended a title to the English crown, Elizabeth might justly accuse him of seeking that crown for himself.

This had already occurred quite forcibly to Elizabeth and when further talk of the marriage, linked with disquieting rumours of unrest in the North, persisted into the summer of 1569, she grew increasingly uneasy. When, at the end of the summer, the duke suddenly bolted to his East Anglian fastness, many people, including the queen, 'hung in suspense and fear lest he should break forth into rebellion'.

In fact, the shifty Norfolk, now deeply involved both with the Queen of Scots and the disloyal activities of his brother-in-law, the Earl of Westmorland, had lost his nerve. Instead of taking the field, he took, unheroically, to his bed with an ague. Elizabeth ordered him to return to London at once and by early October he found himself in the Tower, which was becoming almost a second home for the Howard family. There he remained, in his grandfather's old lodging, throughout the winter and the abortive Northern Rising, but by the following spring his friends at court were urging his release. In June 1570 he wrote to the queen, admitting his error in having listened to overtures on behalf of Mary Stewart and craving forgiveness from the bottom of his heart. 'I now bind myself upon the bond of my allegiance,' he wrote, ' . . . never to deal in that cause of marriage again, nor in any other cause belonging to the Queen of Scots.'

Two months later he was allowed to go and live under surveillance at his town house, but it seems that Thomas Howard had learned nothing from his recent experience. Fatally weak, fatally lacking in judgement, he allowed himself to become embroiled in further intrigues intended to secure the release of the Queen of Scots and the deposition of Elizabeth and these were to lead inexorably to his downfall.

By September 1571 details of the so-called Ridolfi Plot were coming to light and a search of Howard House revealed that the duke's solemn promise to have nothing more to do with the Queen of Scots was not worth the paper it had been written on. By the end of November the case against him was complete, and in January 1572 he was brought to trial in Westminster Hall, convicted and condemned.

The Duke himself maintained that he had been wrongfully

accused by traitors and foreigners and there is a school of thought which still maintains that he was framed. He had always been popular. 'Incredible it is how dearly the people loved him', remarked the contemporary historian William Camden. It was a popularity purchased, according to Camden, 'through his bounty and singular courtesy not unbeseeming a great prince'. But while 'some were terrified with the greatness of the danger which, while he lived, seemed to threaten by means of him and his faction', others 'were moved with pity towards him as a man of high nobility, goodness of nature, goodly personage and manly countenance, who might have been both a great strength and ornament to his country, had not the cunning practices of his malicious adversaries diverted him from his first course of life'. Norfolk may have been a reluctant conspirator. But he had allowed himself to be used by others for their treasonable purposes, forgetting that his exceptional rank and close relationship with the queen had given him a special position in the state and that he, of all people, should have held aloof from politics and self-seeking. In the last resort, it was his own greed and basic dishonesty which had trapped him.

Thomas Howard had always been a good family man and while waiting for death, he wrote a touching letter of farewell to his children, especially his eldest son Philip, then fifteen years old. 'Serve and fear God above all things. . . . Love and make much of your wife . . . show yourself natural and loving to your brothers and sisters and sisters-in-law. . . . When God shall send you to those years as it shall be fit for you to company with your wife, then I would wish you to withdraw yourself into some private dwelling of your own. . . . O Philip! Philip! then shall you enjoy that blessed life which your woeful father would fain ha' done and never could be so happy. Beware of high degrees. To a vainglorious proud stomach it seemeth at the first sweet. Look into all the chronicles and you shall find it brings only heaps of cares, toils in the state, and most commonly in the end utter overthrow.'

Yet again it looked like utter overthrow for the House of Howard, and with the execution of the fourth duke the family's hold on their East Anglian power base was permanently loosened. However, Philip's wife was his step-sister, the northern heiress, Anne Dacre, and he himself presently inherited the earldom of

Arundel through his mother, the fourth duke's first wife, who had been Lady Mary FitzAlan, together with Arundel Castle in Sussex. This later became the principal Howard residence, while Kenninghall and the great town house in Norwich fell into disuse and decay.

Philip's life was to turn into as sad a waste as his father's had been. The earlier Tudor Howards had conformed to the Protestant settlement (though they were often suspected of concealing Popish sympathies) but Philip, Earl of Arundel, openly professed the faith of his ancestors. In 1585 he was caught trying to leave the country and became the fifth generation of the family to enter the Tower of London as a state prisoner. He died there ten years later, at the age of thirty-eight, and in 1970 was canonised by the Catholic Church. The majority of his descendants who, in 1842, took the additional surname of Fitzalan, remained true to the Catholic faith and although the dukedom of Norfolk was revived in 1660 – Philip Howard's great-grandson becoming the fifth duke – their religion debarred the senior line from playing any significant part in the political life of succeeding centuries.

But the disgrace of the fourth duke did not prevent another member of his house from playing a noble part in the Elizabethan epic. Charles Howard of Effingham, grandson of the second duke's second marriage, was one of the queen's most trusted lieutenants and, as Lord High Admiral, commanded the fleet which defeated the Spanish Armada in 1588. When the battle at sea was over, an epidemic of typhus broke out in the English ships and Charles Howard, who took his responsibilities very seriously, was deeply distressed by the sailors' sufferings. 'It is a most pitiful sight', he wrote, 'to see here at Margate how the men, having no place to receive them, die in the streets. I am driven of force myself to come on land to see them bestowed in some lodging. The best I can get is barns and such outhouses, and the relief is small that I can provide for them. It would grieve any man's heart to see them that have served so valiantly to die so miserably.'

The Lord Admiral was with the Earl of Essex at the triumphant English raid on Cadiz in 1596 and on his return the queen created him Earl of Nottingham. Seven years later, when Elizabeth lay dying at Richmond, he was the only person with enough influence over her to persuade her to go to bed.

Like a sturdy plant constantly putting forth fresh shoots, the collateral branches of the Howard tree spread far and wide. Thomas Howard, second son of the fourth duke by his second wife, Margaret Audley, kept up the family's seafaring tradition. He it was who, according to Tennyson, exclaimed, 'Fore God I am no coward' when the English were surprised at Flores in the Azores by a superior Spanish force, but sensibly chose to make a dignified exit, leaving his second-in-command, Sir Richard Grenville, to win useless glory and lose a valuable ship in the epic fight of the *Revenge*.

Created Earl of Suffolk by James I, Lord Thomas inherited the Audley End estate in Essex on which he built a mansion covering five acres of ground and costing upwards of £80,000, a good proportion of which came from bribes and other illicit gains he extracted from his various offices of profit under the crown.

The brief Howard renaissance in the early years of the seventeenth century was largely due to the machinations of Henry, bachelor brother of the fourth duke, created Earl of Northampton in 1604, a sinister and twisted personality, whose peculiar and unappealing talents enabled him to flourish mightily in the snakepit of the Jacobean court. Nemesis, however, overtook the family once again when Suffolk's daughter, Frances, and her husband, the Earl of Somerset, were tried for the murder, by slow poison, of the unfortunate Sir Thomas Overbury. Three years later, in 1618, Suffolk himself was brought to trial in the Star Chamber and dismissed in disgrace, his rapacity and corruption having become too much even for Jacobean stomachs. He is said to have been making around five thousand pounds a year from various dishonest sources. But despite a mountain of debt and other vicissitudes the Suffolk line survived. The twentieth earl was killed in 1941 while attempting to defuse an unexploded bomb on the Erith Marshes and was awarded a posthumous George Cross for conspicuous gallantry.

Lord William Howard, third and youngest of the fourth Duke's sons, married Elizabeth, another of the Dacre heiresses, known as 'Bessie with the broad apron' in an allusion to her vast territorial possessions in the north of England. The couple lived in feudal state and wedded bliss at Naworth Castle in the wild Border country east of Carlisle, and William, who acted as Lord Warden of the Marches, figures as Belted Will in Walter Scott's *Lay of the Last Minstrel*.

From Belted Will descended the Howards of Corby Castle and the Earls of Carlisle. It was the third earl who, at the end of the seventeenth century, employed John Vanbrugh, dramatist and architect, to design a great house on the site of Henderskelfe Castle in Yorkshire. Today Castle Howard – stateliest of stately homes – stands as an enduring memorial to 'a very worthy old English peer', of whom his cousin the tenth Duke of Norfolk wrote approvingly: 'His noble works at Castle Howard are sufficient proof of his refined tastes, which works, he says on a monument erected there, were not only done, but *paid for* by himself. A proper lesson to those, whose thirst for improvement often makes them run beyond their incomes, and who show their taste at the expense of the ingenious and industrious people they employ.' The moral drawn by the tenth duke certainly underlines a remarkable achievement, considering that the earl had spent the enormous sum of £78,000 on his house before he died in 1738.

Unlike their Norfolk cousins, the Earls of Carlisle did not adhere so strictly to the Catholic religion and so were able to take an active part in public life. In 1663 the first earl was sent to Russia by Charles II to negotiate the restoration of privileges formerly enjoyed by English merchants at the port of Archangel. These concessions had been withdrawn by the Czar as a gesture of protest against the execution of Charles I and, according to John Evelyn's *Diary*, 'By means of the Czar's ministers the Earl was very ill received, and met with what he deemed affronts, and had no success as to his demands, so that at coming away he refused the presents sent him by the Czar. The Czar sent an ambassador to England to complain of Lord Carlisle's conduct, but his lordship vindicated himself so well that the King told the ambassador he saw no reason to condemn his conduct.'

His lordship was, in fact, entrusted with further diplomatic missions to Sweden and Denmark and later became Governor of Jamaica. He died in 1685 and was buried in York Minster.

His son and grandson both sat as Whig Members of Parliament, but Henry Howard, fourth Earl of Carlisle, lived abroad for most of his life and took little interest in politics. The fourth earl married into the Byron family and his son, Frederick, acted as guardian to his cousin, Lord Byron the poet.

Frederick succeeded to the earldom when he was only ten years old and was to have a long and distinguished public career. In 1778 he went as Chief Commissioner to North America to try unsuccessfully to reach a negotiated settlement of the War of Independence with the rebellious colonies. Two years later he was appointed Lord Lieutenant of Ireland, where his enlightened attitude and advanced views on the subject of Home Rule earned him considerable popularity among the native population.

Despite an expensive friendship with the profligate Charles James Fox, the fifth earl was an insatiable collector of pictures and other works of art and in 1804 he presented York Minster with a magnificent stained glass window which had originally belonged to the church of St Nicholas in Rouen. The ninth earl was also artistically inclined, a talented painter himself and a friend and patron of Burne-Jones and William Morris.

The Earls of Carlisle still live at Naworth Castle but in 1921, after the death of the ninth earl's widow, the family estates were divided and Castle Howard, once described by Horace Walpole as a 'sublime palace', passed to a younger son. The great house, which not long ago starred in the ITV production of *Brideshead Revisited*, is occupied today by George Howard, until recently Chairman of the Board of Governors of the BBC and now ennobled as Lord Howard of Henderskelfe.

While his relatives were enjoying their resurgence at the court of King James I and, incidentally, helping themselves to assets which properly belonged to the senior line of the family, the head of the house, Thomas Earl of Arundel, only son of the ill-fated Philip, faced the task of rebuilding his shattered fortunes. This he largely succeeded in doing by marrying the third daughter and eventual sole heiress of the immensely wealthy peer, Gilbert Talbot, seventh Earl of Shrewsbury. Aletheia Talbot's inheritance brought her husband huge estates in the North Midlands, rich in lead, iron and coal, and including the town of Sheffield, already becoming a significant industrial centre, as well as a fine house at Worksop.

A close friend of Henry Prince of Wales, until his untimely death, Arundel established himself as a prominent figure at court and in

1616, despite his heritage, he made a formal gesture of conformity to the established religion by receiving communion in the Anglican Chapel Royal. As a result, he was given a seat on the Privy Council and throughout the 1620s and '30s was regularly employed on diplomatic missions abroad. He also acquired an international reputation as a connoisseur and amassed one of the finest private art collections in Europe, which included drawings by Raphael, Leonardo and Holbein, woodcuts by Dürer, paintings by Rubens, classical sculptures and antique gems. He patronised contemporary artists such as Van Dyck, Daniel Mytens and Wenceslaus Hollar and is said to have been among the first to recognise the genius of Inigo Jones. The earl was also an enthusiastic and knowledgeable bibliophile and he numbered among his circle of acquaintances such renowned figures as Edward Alleyn, founder of Dulwich College, Dr William Harvey, who discovered the mechanism of blood circulation, and the antiquarian Sir Robert Cotton.

The earl's artistic extravagance did not extend to his personal appearance. Aloof and reserved by nature, he was a tall man, 'magestical and grave' with a stately presence such that, according to Garter King of Arms, it was a common saying of the Earl of Carlisle: 'Here comes the Earl of Arundel in his plain stuff and trunk hose and his beard in his teeth, that looks more like a nobleman than any of us.'

The outbreak of the Civil War put an end to the civilised pursuits of the Collector Earl. He left England for the last time in 1641 and died in Italy five years later. His eldest son, christened Henry Frederick in honour of the late Prince of Wales, married a daughter of the Duke of Lennox and fathered a numerous family, which was to turn out to be his most useful service to the Howard line. Brought up a Catholic, he, too, appears to have found it politic to conform to the established religion and fought for the King at Edgehill. But although he was later allowed to compound for his estates by the victorious Parliament, Arundel Castle had been reduced to ruins during the civil war and Henry Frederick was also faced with a mountain of debt inherited from his father. He wasted a good deal of time and energy in harassing his mother and trying unsuccessfully to contest his father's will (incurring a good deal of public censure in the process), but it was eventually left to his second son, another Henry, to put the family finances back on to a sound footing, the eldest son and heir to the title being incurably insane.

Henry Howard fortunately possessed both business acumen and a single-minded devotion to the family interests. He not merely succeeded in paying off his grandfather's debts, which amounted to some £200,000, but in August 1660 successfully petitioned the newly restored king to restore the dukedom of Norfolk. He also attempted, rather less successfully, to revive the Howards' connection with their county of origin. Kenninghall had long since fallen into disuse and disrepair, but Henry, created Lord Howard of Castle Rising in 1669, set about rebuilding the ducal palace in Norwich and entertained the king there in 1671. The house, though, was never finished, becoming an expensive white elephant, and another ambitious project for rebuilding Arundel House in the Strand had to be abandoned.

In 1677 Henry's mad brother Thomas died at last and the following January he took his seat in the House of Lords as sixth Duke of Norfolk, just over a hundred years since the fourth duke had been convicted of high treason in Westminster Hall. Henry had waited long and patiently for this moment, but the malign fate which seemed to dog the Howard family was to prevent him from enjoying his new dignity for long. In the years immediately following the Restoration the prospects of the English Catholics had looked brighter than at any time since the accession of Elizabeth. The king was sympathetic and would have been prepared to grant them a measure of toleration, but the tide of popular feeling was running against him. In the summer of 1678 the sensational disclosures of the 'Popish Plot' – a supposed Catholic conspiracy to kill Charles II, burn London and massacre Protestants – whipped up a storm of anti-Catholic hysteria and in November the duke, together with the other Catholic peers, was forced to withdraw from the Lords. He retreated to Flanders, having taken the precaution of putting his estates into the hands of a committee of Anglican trustees, but although he returned to England in 1682, when the frenzy of the great Popish panic had faded, he died two years later, a disillusioned and disappointed man.

The seventh Duke survived the further upheavals of the 1680s, conforming, at least outwardly, to the state religion, and contriving to officiate as Earl Marshal at the coronations of both the Catholic

James II and the Protestant William and Mary. His private life is chiefly memorable for a protracted and messy divorce from his wife, daughter of the Earl of Peterborough, on the grounds of her adultery with 'a Dutch gamester of mean extraction', though his own record as a husband was far from blameless. He died childless in 1701, to be succeeded by his nephew, Thomas Howard of Worksop, a zealous Catholic, a virtuous gentleman, a Tory and a Jacobite – not at first sight a very promising combination of qualities for the head of a great family in the unsettled political climate of the early eighteenth century. However, the eighth duke also managed to survive, although he has the distinction of being the last Duke of Norfolk to be imprisoned in the Tower, where he spent six months in 1722–3, suspected of having given financial assistance to the Pretender. He, too, died childless and his younger brother, Edward, became the ninth duke.

Another devout Catholic, a Tory and, in his earlier years, an active Jacobite, Duke Edward sensibly avoided any further involvement with the House of Stuart, which had proved so disastrous for the family in the past. Instead he was to render an unusual service to the House of Hanover or, at any rate, to Frederick Prince of Wales, son of George II and Queen Caroline. When, in 1737, the notorious quarrel between the prince and his parents was at its height and he and his wife were evicted from St James's Palace, the Norfolks offered the homeless royals the hospitality of Norfolk House in nearby St James's Square and there, the following May, the future King George III was born.

The Duke and Duchess had no children of their own, and so took an especially close interest in their nephews, Thomas and Edward, sons of Philip Howard of Buckenham. The steadily increasing revenues from the Sheffield estates enabled the duke and duchess to embark on an ambitious programme of rebuilding, enlargement and improvement of their various ducal properties, most notably at Worksop in Nottinghamshire, an Elizabethan 'prodigy' house built by the sixth Earl of Shrewsbury in the 1580s and brought into the Howard family by Aletheia Talbot. Worksop Manor had been adopted by the eighth duke as his principal country seat and the ninth duke and his energetic, masterful wife, Mary daughter of Edward Blount of Blagdon – rather unkindly described by Horace Walpole as 'my lord Duchess' – lavished taste, thought and tender loving care, as well as a great deal of money, on transforming the old mansion into a suitably magnificent show-case for future generations of Howard Dukes of Norfolk.

The new Worksop was finished in the summer of 1761 and the event celebrated by a grand housewarming party, but almost immediately the jealous fate which had in times past pursued the Norfolk Howards so relentlessly caught up with them once more. Fire broke out at Worksop and rapidly got out of control, destroying everything except the chapel and part of the east wing.

The duke and duchess, now both in their seventies, took this staggering loss philosophically and, undaunted, prepared to start again from the beginning. Then Thomas Howard, who was destined to inherit all this splendour, died in Paris while on the Grand Tour, leaving Edward, his younger half-brother and the Norfolks' favourite, to lay the foundation stone of the new building with the duke in March 1763. Work proceeded briskly under the close supervision of the duchess for another four years. Then Edward suddenly died of a fever and even the indomitable duchess finally lost heart and interest. Worksop, which would have been the greatest English country house after Blenheim, was left unfinished and was later sold off to the Duke of Newcastle.

The ninth duke lived on into his nineties, placidly attending to estate business and maintaining an informed interest in horticulture, history and architecture, but when he died in 1777 the main stem of the Howard tree had withered at last and the dukedom passed successively to the so-called Greystoke and Glossop lines – to descendants of younger sons of the philoprogenitive seventeenth-century Earl Henry Frederick. The eleventh duke, known as the Jockey, was the most colourful personality from this branch of the family. Nature, it appeared, had cast him in her 'coarsest mould', failing to endow him with any of the 'external insignia of high descent' such as grace or dignity, so that with his large, convivial, muscular person permanently crammed into a favourite shabby plum-coloured coat, he could, according to a disapproving contemporary, easily have been mistaken for a grazier or butcher.

The Jockey was notorious, among other things, for the awesome quantities of porter, claret and brandy which he put away in company with such equally hard-drinking cronies as Charles James

Fox and the Prince Regent, for his fondness for practical jokes and his aversion to even an external contact with water. It is said that his servants had to wait until he had passed out before they could heave him into the tub.

It was hardly to be expected that such a rumbustious individual would be content to stay in the political wilderness of Roman Catholicism and he apostatised in 1780, six years before succeeding to the dukedom. He also broke with recent family tradition by becoming an active member of the Whig party – a fact not entirely disconnected with his determination to score over the Tory Earls of Lonsdale, who were his neighbours at Greystoke. Despite his plebeian appearance, his robust sense of humour and his 'democratic' enthusiasms, the Jockey was very conscious and very proud of his high descent. He was also a shrewd businessman, a generous, kind-hearted friend and a bibliophile of some distinction – in short, an eccentric fortunate enough to have been born into an age and society where a wealthy duke could, within certain limits, do and say very much as he liked.

Although brought up at Greystoke Castle on the north-western fringes of the Lake District, brought into the family by Philip Howard's wife Anne Dacre, the eleventh duke's most notable achievement was his work in rebuilding Arundel Castle which was, of course, conveniently close to Brighton and the Prince Regent. Since passing into Howard hands in 1580, Arundel, ancestral home of the FitzAlans, had had an unfortunate history. 'Slighted' in the Civil War, it had been left in ruins for nearly a century, when the eighth duke, who used it as an occasional shooting lodge, did a little long overdue patching up of the old fabric. After the débâcle at Worksop, the tenth duke began to make plans, and the necessary financial arrangements, for the resurrection of Arundel as the principal family seat, but it was the Jockey who turned these plans into reality, expressing his peculiar 'feudal-radical' views by refurbishing the castle in romantic neo-medieval, eighteenth-century Gothic, complete with a Barons' Hall. This was finished in time for a grand neo-medieval jollification in June 1815, intended to celebrate the six hundredth anniversary of the signing of Magna Charta with, in the Duke's mind, its concomitant triumph of liberty over royal tyranny.

The occasion was also marked by a great gathering of the Howard clan. According to one account, the duke had originally wanted to invite all the traceable descendants of Jack of Norfolk who had fallen at Bosworth Field, but abandoned the idea when he discovered that this would mean entertaining about six thousand people! In the end, twenty-three representatives of the four main lines of the Howard tribe – Norfolk, Suffolk, Carlisle and Effingham – were present at a dinner of which the high point was the entry, to a fanfare of trumpets, of a whole roasted stag.

In 1829 the long-delayed passage of the Catholic Emancipation Act finally restored the English Catholic population's civil rights and enabled the twelfth duke, Bernard Howard of Glossop, cousin of the Jockey, to take his seat in the Lords – the first Catholic Duke of Norfolk to do so since 1678. But although the legal disabilities had been removed, popular prejudice remained and in 1851 a rather tactlessly worded papal bull, re-establishing the Roman hierarchy in England, resulted in a storm which, while not exactly comparable to the mass hysteria of the Popish Plot or the destructive rampage of the eighteenth-century Gordon Riots, was still capable of raising some influential Protestants' hackles.

In the row over Papal Aggression, the thirteenth Duke of Norfolk rather surprisingly supported Lord John Russell and the outraged Anglicans to the extent that, pious Catholic though he was, he resigned from his church in protest against what he saw as a piece of unwarrantable interference by the Holy Father. This reaction was no doubt due in part to a genuine fear that life would once more be made difficult for less privileged Catholics, but the duke also felt a strong aristocratic distaste for the so-called Oxford Movement for Catholic Revival and the missionary activities of enthusiasts like Cardinal Wiseman.

Over the centuries it had been the steadfast tenacity of a handful of noble and gentle families which, at the cost of much suffering, had kept the embers of the Old Faith alive in England. Native Catholicism had consequently evolved into something resembling an elite and exclusive social club surviving, by necessity, in virtual isolation from Rome, and the conservative and exclusive thirteenth duke would, in his heart of hearts, have preferred to keep it that way. But times were changing. The influx of Irish labourers into Liverpool and other parts of the new industrial north had to be catered for, converts were being made, Catholicism had come in from the cold and was ceasing to be a rather extra special distinction reserved for a few top people and their dependants.

The Howards, of course, remained the ranking English Catholic family as, despite a few unfortunate lapses, they had been ever since the days of Saint Philip Howard, Earl of Arundel, producing two cardinals as well as numerous priests and nuns – the devout Glossop line being particularly prolific in this respect. Most of the eighteenth-century and all the nineteenth-century Dukes of Norfolk used their influence to protect the interests of their co-religionists, the fourteenth and fifteenth dukes taking an especially conscientious view of their responsibilities as leaders of the English laity. Both played a prominent part in the continuing Catholic renaissance of their day, devoting themselves to good works and tirelessly building schools and churches – most notably a new Catholic cathedral at Arundel dedicated to St Philip Neri.

The fifteenth duke, Henry Fitzalan Howard, a close friend of Cardinal Newman, contributed heavily towards the cost of building the Brompton Oratory. He also undertook further major reconstruction work at Arundel, dismantling the Jockey's more embarrassing architectural whimsies (though his library remains) and seeking to create a dignified setting for England's premier dukes and hereditary Earl Marshals, so that the castle, which is now administered by a charitable trust under the chairmanship of the present Duke, has become a fitting shrine for the history of a noble house. It is also a matchless repository of family heirlooms, including the rosary which Mary Queen of Scots carried to her execution and a few surviving treasures from the fabulous collection amassed by Thomas Howard, the Collector Earl.

An undercurrent of personal tragedy persisted well into the nineteenth century. The twelfth duke's wife left him for another man and the saintly fourteenth duke died in his early forties of a painful and incurable disease. The fifteenth duke's first wife, Lady Flora Abney-Hastings, also died young, leaving him with a blind, epileptic and retarded son to whom he was pathetically devoted but who died at the age of twenty-three. Duke Henry, though, married again, his second marriage, to Gwendolen Baroness Herries, bringing him some years of late happiness and a family of three daughters and a son, Bernard Marmaduke, who succeeded his father in 1917.

As Earl Marshal and stage manager of the pageantry of numerous state occasions, the sixteenth duke was to become a familiar figure to television audiences all over the world – at the coronation of Queen Elizabeth II he officiated in the same capacity as the fourth duke at the coronation of Queen Elizabeth I almost exactly four centuries earlier.

Duke Bernard inherited a flourishing estate of nearly 50,000 acres and, although Norfolk House in London was given up in 1938, he continued to maintain the standards considered proper by his generation for the holder of a medieval dukedom, for the Lord Lieutenant of Sussex, a Knight of the Most Noble Order of the Garter and a Privy Councillor. His principal leisure interests were cricket and horse-racing: and again, as was only proper, he played a prominent part in both. He was President of the MCC and Senior Steward of the Jockey Club, winning the Ascot Gold Cup with Ragstone in 1974.

When he died in 1975, he left a family of four daughters and his cousin Miles, formerly a professional soldier, succeeded as seventeenth Duke of Norfolk, Earl of Arundel, Baron Beaumont, Baron Maltravers, Earl of Surrey, Baron FitzAlan, Clun and Oswaldestre, Earl of Norfolk, Baron Howard of Glossop, Hereditary Marshal and Chief Butler of England. The present Duke no longer uses Arundel as a family home, but he follows the family tradition of acting as watchdog over the interests of his fellow Catholics and was recently one of the prime movers in a successful campaign to preserve the right of free transport for Roman Catholic children to Catholic schools.

The Howard Dukes of Norfolk celebrated their quincentenary in 1983 and, no doubt, William Howard of King's Lynn, who set out to make a career for himself in the law some time in the mid-thirteenth century, would have been surprised and gratified had he known that he was founding a noble house and a family which would still be active in English public life seven hundred years later. But William Howard's achievement was by no means unique. Many another aristocratic English family can trace its origins to an ambitious, hard-working, hard-headed young man of yeoman stock, determined to win his way in the world with nothing but his own wits, his native stamina and resourcefulness to rely on.

The House of Cavendish

Cavendo tutus

Sir William Cavendish attributed to Sir John Bettes *The National Trust*

THE HOUSE OF CAVENDISH

Cavendo tutus

DERBYSHIRE is paradoxically Devonshire country, the home ground of a family whose surname comes from a village on the Essex/Suffolk border. It is more than likely that the Cavendishes can trace their ancestry as far back as the fourteenth century, to Stephen, draper and Lord Mayor of London in 1362, and to Sir John Cavendish of Cavendish Overhall, a Chief Justice of the King's Bench unfortunate enough to have been lynched by a Suffolk mob during the Peasants' Revolt of 1381. Their pedigree cannot, however, be conclusively proved further back than one William Cavendish, mercer of London, who died in 1433, and for all practical purposes the ducal house was founded by his great-grandson, another William, born about 1505.

This William almost certainly owed his start in life to his elder brother George, gentleman usher to Cardinal Wolsey and a valued and influential member of the great man's household. George Cavendish is known to have been on friendly terms with Wolsey's secretary, Master Thomas Cromwell, a busy man of affairs who could always find room on his staff for another promising young man, especially if it meant obliging a colleague at the same time. So, at least, it seems reasonable to assume, but if William Cavendish did indeed follow his brother into the Cardinal's far-reaching administrative empire he was wise, or lucky, in choosing to attach himself to the servant rather than the master. By 1530 Wolsey's career had come crashing down to end in lonely disgrace and George went home to Suffolk to devote his retirement to writing down his personal recollections of *The Life and Death of*

Cardinal Wolsey. George Cavendish was an old-fashioned romantic, quixotically loyal to the memory of his dead lord, to the old ways and the old religion. William, on the other hand, hard-headed thrusting and materialistic, preferred to look forward into a future where Henry VIII's quarrel with Rome was beginning to open up hitherto undreamt of opportunities for an enterprising young civil servant.

Certainly there could have been no better vantage point for an enterprising young civil servant eager to exploit these opportunities than the office of Thomas Cromwell, who had wasted no time in transferring himself from the cardinal's to the king's service and who, in the space of less than five years, had risen from relative obscurity to become the king's closest and most favoured councillor. Cromwell's astonishing success with the monarch was not only due to the dedicated efficiency with which he had helped to sort out Henry's matrimonial problems; he had also relieved his financial necessities by releasing the enormous wealth previously locked up in the iron-bound coffers of the Roman church.

It was on this work of nationalising church property that William Cavendish was principally employed during the revolutionary 1530s, and in April 1536 he was appointed one of ten auditors of the Court of Augmentations – a body set up to deal with the disposal of lands belonging to the larger monastic institutions. Energetic, unsentimental and endowed with the meticulously appraising eye of a natural-born property developer, William rode busily round the country taking the surrenders of abbots and priors, listing and selling off the moveable assets of each house, pensioning off the dispossessed religious and arranging the conveyancing of their estates to the Crown – all apparently without any inconvenient qualms of conscience.

Much of the land which thus changed hands was subsequently redistributed – some by outright gift but more often sold or leased on favourable terms – to the king's faithful servants, and who had shown himself a more faithful servant than William Cavendish? By 1535 he had already acquired the lordships and manors of Northaw, Cuffeley and Childwyke in Hertfordshire, formerly the property of the Abbey of St Albans, together with the advowson (the right of presentation to a vacant benefice) of the parish church at Northaw 'and all messuages, lands etc. in Meriden in the parish of Tewynge, Co. Herts'. Soon afterwards he received a grant of 'the house and site of the late Priory, Cell or Rectory of Cardigan S. Wales' which had once belonged to the monastery of Chertsey in Surrey, and in 1538 he was able to take a twenty-one year 'farm' or lease on the former abbey of Lilleshall in Shropshire. Appropriation on this scale was not, of course, to be compared with the kind of empire building currently being practised by those with real money to invest or valuable claims on the generosity of royalty, but it still represented a very satisfactory achievement on the part of a low-to-middle ranking government official and a promising basis for further expansion.

By 1540, when Thomas Cromwell's career also ended in disgrace and disaster, William Cavendish's reputation for zealous devotion to duty was too firmly established to be affected by his patron's misfortune. In the following year he was sent over to Ireland to conduct a survey of Crown property in the wake of the Dissolution. Here he quickly won a glowing testimonial from the Lord Deputy, Sir Anthony St Leger, who informed the king that 'Mr Cavendish took great pains' over his accounts and surveys, undaunted by shocking bad weather and 'such a man as little feareth the displeasure of any man in Your Highness' service'. Mr Cavendish was back in England in 1542 and no more is heard of him in his public capacity until the spring of 1546, when he was appointed Treasurer of the King's Chamber, knighted and sworn a member of the Privy Council.

The death of Henry VIII in January 1547 made no difference to his circumstances, but on 20 August that year the new knight and Privy Councillor took the step which was to ensure him his measure of immortality – his 'prudent and happy match' with the handsome, red-headed young widow Elizabeth Barley or Barlow, née Hardwick. The wedding took place quietly at Bradgate in Leicestershire, home of Henry Grey, Marquess of Dorset, and his wife Frances, a niece of the late king's, and far-reaching though its consequences were to be, there is no suggestion that it was anything other than a run-of-the-mill arranged marriage. William Cavendish was now in his early forties, a widower with three daughters who needed a wife. Elizabeth, or Bess as she was to become known to history, was about twenty, the orphan daughter of an impoverished country squire from Hardwick in Derbyshire. Widowed in her teens, with only a tiny jointure, she appears to have found herself a niche in the Dorset household while she looked out for another husband and, despite the difference in their ages, Sir William, a prosperous and respected royal official, would have been as good a match as she could hope to make.

In fact, the marriage turned into a mutually happy and profitable partnership. Bess's first child, a daughter christened Frances as a compliment to Frances Dorset who stood gossip or godmother, was born the following June and another daughter, Temperance, in 1549. Like so many babies of that time, Temperance failed to survive, but three sturdy sons – Henry, William and Charles – now began to arrive at punctual annual intervals. Then came Elizabeth, Mary and finally Lucrece, born in March 1557. Lucrece also died in infancy, but to have raised six children out of eight was an achievement of which any Tudor parent could be justly proud.

By the time her three younger daughters were born, Lady Cavendish was to be found spending less time at the family's London house in Newgate Street and rather more in her native Derbyshire. Within two years of their marrige she had embarked on a campaign to persuade her husband to dispose of all those properties wastefully scattered over the Home Counties, the north-west and Wales, and instead to concentrate his resources on the moors and dales of the Peak District where an opportunity had just presented itself to acquire the Chatsworth estate, lying no more than fifteen miles from Hardwick itself. Lady Cavendish carried her point – she usually did. As well as buying Chatsworth for six hundred pounds, Sir William bought and exchanged other land in the district and by 1553 the couple were ready to start building a fine new mansion on the site of the old Chatsworth manor house overlooking the River Derwent.

Bess Cavendish is always given the credit for the Tudor Chatsworth and no doubt hers was the moving creative spirit, but Sir William took a close interest in the progress of the work and in March 1555 addressed an appeal to his friend Sir John Thynne, who was also building down in the West Country.

> Sir, I understand that you have a cunning plasterer at Longleat, which hath in your hall and other places of your house made divers pendants and other pretty things. If your business

> be at an end, or will be by next summer after this, I would pray you that I might have him in Derbyshire, for my hall is yet unmade.

The Longleat plasterer never did get to Chatsworth, and Sir William's hall was not destined to be completed until more than ten years after his death, but large quantities of luxury furnishings – bedhangings, tapestries, plate and other household gear – were being ordered and despatched northwards. In their enthusiasm the Cavendishes were spending money they hadn't got, and in the summer of 1557 Nemesis finally caught up with the Treasurer of the Chamber, who found himself called upon to explain a staggering five thousand pound deficit in his accounts.

Although it is clear that Sir William had been systematically misappropriating government funds on a scale well beyond the generous limits tolerated by Tudor society, the motive behind the attack on him was almost certainly political. He and Bess had long been closely associated with the radical Protestant faction represented by powerful families such as the Greys and the Seymours. They were also known to be friendly with the Protestant heiress – Elizabeth Tudor had stood godmother to their eldest son. Ever since the accession of Queen Mary, William Cavendish's position had been growing increasingly precarious – a man whose fortunes were founded on the dissolution of the monasteries could hardly expect to be popular with a sovereign dedicated to the re-establishment of Catholicism – and now ruin stared him between the eyes. He made no attempt to deny the charge against him, simply throwing himself on the queen's mercy, but in describing himself as a 'poor sick man' he was not exaggerating, and Bess prepared to come to his side. She set out from Chatsworth on 20 August, her tenth wedding anniversary, ready to throw her strong, energetic personality into the task of nursing, supporting and generally breathing fresh life into her unfortunate spouse. All sorts of delicacies were tried to tempt the invalid's appetite, including necks of mutton, pigeons, oysters, whiting, capons and calf's-foot jelly. But it was no use and two months later Bess opened the pocket book in which Sir William had carefully recorded the details of their marriage, and the births and baptisms of their children, to make a sad, final entry of her own.

> Sir William Cavendish, knight, my most dear and well-beloved husband, departed this present life on Monday, being the 25th day of October, betwixt the hours of eight and nine of the same day at night, in the year of our Lord God, 1557. . . . On whose soul I most humbly beseech the Lord to have mercy and to rid me and his poor children out of our great misery.

Bess and William Cavendish had been ideally suited and she no doubt mourned him sincerely. His death also left her with practical problems. A widow with six young children and a crippling debt to the Exchequer would appear to have had little choice but to cut her losses, to sell up and pay off that shameful five thousand pounds and then hope to make at least a respectable marriage with what she could save from the wreckage. There is no evidence to suggest that Bess ever considered such a craven course of action. An ambitious and intelligent woman, she had learnt a great deal about finance, about the intricacies of buying and selling and the management of real estate from William Cavendish. She herself possessed an astute business brain and so far from cutting her losses was plainly determined to continue to build for the future. Time, in the winter of 1557, was on her side. The queen was a childless, ageing and ailing woman, the government ineffective, factious and bitterly unpopular. Bess had only to keep calm, exploit the law's delays, sit tight and wait. As it happened, she had to wait for no more than thirteen months.

The accession of Elizabeth Tudor came at just the right moment for the six young Cavendishes and their indomitable mother, who now reaped the reward of the friendship she and Sir William had shown Elizabeth at the time when she stood most in need of it. Bess came to court as a Lady of the Privy Chamber unashamedly husband-hunting, and once again she chose well. Sir William St Loe came from an old and wealthy West Country family. He, too, had been a loyal supporter of Elizabeth as princess and gave further evidence of his good taste by falling in love with the fascinating Lady Cavendish. Certainly he proved an unusually indulgent and generous husband. He showed no jealousy over Bess's renewed absorption in her building activities, now being paid for with his money. Indeed, he once began a letter to her as 'my honest sweet

Chatsworth'. At other times she was 'my own sweet Bess . . . more dearer to me than I am to myself'.

St Loe also helped Bess to sort out her tangled financial affairs, compounding her debt to the Crown for £1000 (provided by himself) and persuading the queen to forgive the balance. He was a model stepfather, arranging for Henry and William Cavendish to be admitted to Eton College, paying their fees and buying their school books. His devotion to Bess was absolute, and when he died in the winter of 1564–5 he left her in full possession of his considerable property, which included the lands of Glastonbury Abbey in Somerset to the considerable annoyance of his own relations.

The widowed Lady St Loe was now in her late thirties, self-confident, strong-willed and still physically attractive, with her slender upright figure, reddish hair and fine complexion. Thanks to St Loe's bequest and her own business acumen (she managed her estates with 'masculine understanding', keeping an unforgiving eye on every detail, every subordinate), she had become a wealthy woman and a matrimonial prize in her own right. There was always a brisk market in rich widows and Sir John Thynne, Lord Darcy and Lord Cobham were all mentioned as possible suitors. But Bess was in no hurry. She spent more than a year at court, looking round, and it was not until the late autumn of 1567 that she made her last and most brilliant marriage: to George Talbot, sixth Earl of Shrewsbury.

Like William Cavendish, Shrewsbury was a widower with children and like William St Loe he appears to have been besotted with his bride. He was also an immensely rich man himself with property scattered all over the north of England, no fewer than eight country mansions, and two London houses as well. It seemed as if everything Bess touched turned to gold and her enemies did not hesitate to accuse her of an insatiable lust for wealth and power. But the main drive of her ambition was always centred on the advancement of the family she and William Cavendish had founded, and in negotiating the Talbot marriage contract her overriding concern was to ensure that future generations of Cavendishes would profit from this important alliance. Before she finally accepted Shrewsbury's proposal, therefore, she stipulated that her eldest son Henry and her youngest daughter Mary Cavendish should also be married to the earl's daughter Grace and his second son Gilbert Talbot.

Bess's fourth marriage had brought her and her children into the highest social and political circles in the land, and early in 1568 the new countess found herself singled out for the doubtful honour of acting as 'hostess' to Mary Queen of Scots, now beginning her eighteen-year stretch as a state prisoner in England. Mary had driven her first guardian, Francis Knollys, nearly distracted with her tears and tantrums, but the first few months she spent in the Earl of Shrewsbury's custody passed comparatively peacefully. This was due in part to the friendship she struck up with Bess. They made a strange pair – the exquisitely feminine Mary Stuart, a queen from her cradle, already at twenty-seven a figure of romantic legend, and the shrewd, succesful yeoman's daughter, past forty now, who had doggedly fought and married her way up the social ladder. Yet they had a surprising amount in common. Both were skilled and enthusiastic needlewomen. Both had a discerning eye for beautiful surroundings and a developed taste in luxury. Both possessed devious and scheming brains. It is impossible to say exactly when the first inkling of a plan more daring and ambitious than anything she had yet attempted began to take shape in Bess's brain but it is tempting to believe it had its origin in the hours she spent sitting with the Scottish queen over their endless embroidery.

Mary's second husband, Henry Lord Darnley, spectacularly murdered at Kirk o'Field in February 1567, had been her first cousin as well as her husband. After the Queen of Scots and her son James, now crowned King of Scotland, Darnley's younger brother, Charles Stuart, could legitimately claim to be recognised as heir presumptive to the English throne. Mary was a prisoner, constantly complaining of how ill she felt. James was a mere baby in the hands of the Scottish nobility and his future must be considered uncertain at the very least. But Charles Stuart was in England, still in the care of his widowed mother, Margaret Countess of Lennox, niece of the late King Henry VIII. And the Countess of Shrewsbury had a daughter still in her early teens, still unmarried. . .

In the autumn of 1574 the Countess of Lennox left London on her way to visit her estates in Yorkshire, taking her son Charles with her, this was the opportunity the Countess of Shrewsbury had been waiting for. The Lennoxes were invited to break their journey at Rufford Abbey, not far from the Great North Road at Newark, and within a matter of days Elizabeth Cavendish and Charles Stuart had 'so tied themselves together upon their own liking as they cannot be parted'. Not that any attempt was made to part them. On the contrary, the young people were married as quickly and quietly as the bride's mother could contrive it. Only then did she blandly release the story of a whirlwind romance which had taken both families by surprise, leaving them with no choice but to sanction a hasty wedding ceremony.

Surprisingly enough, considering the queen's well-known sensitivity over anything even indirectly affecting the succession, Bess appears to have survived this remarkable act of dynastic piracy more or less unscathed. But it did her little good in the long-term. The much-prized royal son-in-law was a sickly youth who died less than two years later and Elizabeth Cavendish's only child, the ill-fated Arbella Stuart, grew up to cause her grandmother more heartache and expense than anything else. Indeed, as Bess herself grew older her personal relationships became less and less satisfactory, and the beginning of the 1580s was to see the irretrievable breakdown of her marriage to the Earl of Shrewsbury.

Shackled as he was by his responsibility for the Queen of Scots, the earl resented his wife's independence, her absorption in Chatsworth and her numerous Cavendish business interests with ever increasing bitterness. Worst of all was the horrid suspicion that Talbot revenues were being siphoned off into Cavendish coffers. Signs that 'there was no good agreement betwixt my Lord and my Lady' had been apparent within the family circle for some time before the couple finally separated in the spring of 1583, and matters came to a head the following summer when the earl attempted to seize Chatsworth by force. William Cavendish the second barred the doors and, halberd in hand, succcessfully defied his stepfather's raiding party, but by this time the quarrel had spilled over into the surrounding countryside. Tenants on the Chatsworth estate were harassed by Talbot bailiffs, property was damaged and feeling between the adherents of the rival families ran high.

Mary Queen of Scots was also embroiled in the great Shrewsbury Scandal. She and Bess were now at one another's throats (their friendship had not long survived the birth of Arbella Stuart) and scurrilous rumours that she was the earl's mistress were almost certainly spread by the Cavendishes. It was all very unseemly and by September 1584 Mary had been removed from Shrewsbury's custody, while Queen Elizabeth, who disapproved of marital disputes amongst her nobility, ordered the earl and countess to make up their differences. But the breach was now too wide for healing, even by royal command. 'As to my wife,' wrote Shrewsbury in 1585, 'she hath sought to impoverish me and enrich herself. She hath sought the ruin and decay of my house and posterity, to raise up her house and name into that honour.' These accusations of deliberate peculation, coming from a man who had been under too great a nervous strain for too long, should not be taken too seriously, but they are revealing of Bess's all-consuming obsession with family matters and an unendearing lack of sympathy for anyone else's problems.

Even the most dedicated dynasts are limited by the human material they have to work on, and neither Bess nor Shrewsbury had been especially fortunate in this respect. The earl's much loved eldest son, Francis, died in the plague epidemic of 1582 and his grandson, George, son of Gilbert Talbot and Mary Cavendish did not survive beyond his second year. Had he lived, the Shewsbury/Cavendish story might have ended differently. Bess had also been seriously disappointed in her eldest son, Henry. He and Grace Talbot had failed to have any children at all, though Henry fathered a whole tribe of bastards, earning the soubriquet of 'the common bull of Derbyshire' in the process. It wasn't until 1590 that William Cavendish and his wife Anne Keighley presented Bess with her first Cavendish grandchild – another William – and two years later Catherine Ogle, her youngest son's second wife, also gave birth to a boy.

Throughout the nineties, though, Bess was principally concerned with her grand-daughter Arbella, 'my jewel Arbelle' as she called her. Elizabeth Lennox died young, leaving Arbella to be brought up by Bess who spared no expense on her education, hoping the girl would make a brilliant marriage, even perhaps a royal marriage. If Queen Elizabeth were to take a fancy to her, there was no telling what her future might hold. But here again, over-optimism was destined for disappointment. Arbella, it is true, paid two visits to court in her teens, but on the second occasion she succeeded in offending the queen and was asked no more. Standing as close to the throne as she did, there would be no marriage for her, brilliant or otherwise. With Elizabeth now approaching the end of her reign, the government had no intention of giving Arbella Stuart any opportunity of interfering with a peaceful transition of power to the King of Scotland. So the unfortunate young woman was left to eat her heart out in Derbyshire until, growing desperate, she began a futile struggle to escape from home. This drew down official disapproval and led to a series of bitter rows between Arbella and her grandmother, culminating in an abortive 'rescue' bid by her uncle Henry Cavendish, Bess's 'bad son Henry', and some of his undesirable friends. By this time Arbella was on the brink of a nervous breakdown and even Bess had had enough, complaining pathetically that a few more weeks like those she had suffered of late would be the end of her.

The death of Queen Elizabeth in March 1603 brought release and a short-lived spell of favour for Arbella at her cousin James's court, while Bess, now in her mid-seventies, was left in peace to enjoy the last years of a long and crowded life. She spent them at Hardwick, the great house she had started to build within a month of the Earl of Shrewsbury's death in 1590, which had become the headquarters of her business and territorial empire. She cannot be said to have mellowed very much with age this formidable woman, part virago, part genius, part dreamer of dreams, whose career as a property developer, financier, farmer and merchant of lead, coal and timber had made her the richest and most influential woman in England next to the late queen. Litigation over property disputes with the Talbot family dragged on well into the new century and Bess never forgave her bad son Henry, who had been cut out of her will in 1603. But she was eventually reconciled with Gilbert Talbot and her daughter Mary who, with Charles Cavendish, visited her at Hardwick in December 1607 finding, according to Gilbert, 'a lady of great years, of great wealth and of great wit which yet still remains'. The old lady received them 'with all respect and affection' and kept them with her for a whole day 'without so much as one word of any former suits or unkindness, but only compliment, courtesy and kindness'.

Bess was now in her eighty-first year and to her relations must have begun to seem as much a permanent part of the landscape as the houses she had built, but even her amazing physique was failing at last. Gilbert Talbot noticed that her appetite had gone and that she was barely able to walk the length of the room with two people supporting her. On New Year's Day 1608 she was reported as looking 'pretty well' and she kept 'the blessing of sense and memory' to the end, which came quite peacefully at about five o'clock in the afternoon of 13 February. They buried her in All Saints Church, Derby, according to the minute instructions left in her will, under the splendid monument which she herself had commissioned and which had been ready and waiting to be erected for more than seven years. Bess had left nothing to chance in making her methodical preparations for eternity and felt reasonably confident that the Almighty would receive her into 'the most blessed company of his Elect'.

Although Chatsworth had been entailed on Henry Cavendish, it was on William, her second son, that Bess's mantle now fell. William had long been her trusted lieutenant – quiet, unassuming, apparently content to live in his mother's shadow while possessing her business acumen and his father's head for figures. He was a sound man, not one to take risks but knowing a good investment when he saw it; and in 1610 he seized the chance to buy back the Chatsworth estate from his insolvent brother. William had already been raised to the peerage as Baron Cavendish, an advance in social status which he owed to his niece Arbella, and in 1618 he laid out £10,000 or thereabouts to purchase the Earldom of Devonshire from an insolvent monarch. Why Devonshire, when the family owned no property and had no other interests in that part of the country, remains unexplained.

The first earl proved a first-rate managing director and caretaker of the Cavendish interests, but he was past fifty when Bess died and the future lay in the hands of Bess's grandson, William the third, who had begun to display ominous signs of favouring his scapegrace uncle Henry before he was out of his teens. Young William, at eighteen, had little relish for the sensible dynastic marriage being arranged for him. 'Poor Wylkyn', as his uncle Charles put it, 'desired and deserved a woman already grown.' Instead he found himself being hustled resentfully into matrimony with red-haired Christian Bruce, the twelve-year-old daughter of one of the king's Scottish cronies. Not that he ever allowed marriage to interfere with his pleasures to any noticeable extent, and he was soon off to Europe on the Grand Tour with his tutor-cum-companion, the philosopher Thomas Hobbes.

Like many another scion of a newly rich family, William the third was very much more interested in spending money than in making it, and he certainly showed an impressive talent for spending it, throwing himself wholeheartedly into the business of becoming a leader of fashion and of high society. This proved to be an exhausting as well as an expensive career and the second earl died in 1628 at the comparatively early age of thirty-eight – the result, so it was said, of 'excessive indulgence in good living' – leaving behind him a widow, three young children, 'a vast and increasing debt and upwards of thirty lawsuits'. Christian Cavendish was not a financial genius of the calibre of Bess of Hardwick, but fortunately for the survival of the Cavendish family she was a woman of charm, intelligence, strength of mind and great good sense who immediately set about the task of rescuing her son's inheritance. It was thanks to her strict economy and careful housekeeping that the estates were solvent again by the time William the fourth attained his majority.

Four years later the Cavendishes, in common with the rest of the English nobility, had to make up their minds whether to throw in their lot with king or Parliament. For the Earl of Devonshire and his younger brother Charles there was no decision to make and they were among the first to place themselves unreservedly at the disposal of the king. Nor was there any decision to be made by their cousin William – yet another William Cavendish – son of their great-uncle Charles, lord of Welbeck Abbey and Bolsover Castle, Baron Ogle, Viscount Mansfield and Earl of Newcastle, courtier and magnifico to his fingers' ends, whose devotion to the Crown was unquestioned and unquestioning.

In his late forties by the time the Civil War broke out, Newcastle was already one of King Charles's most trusted lieutenants and an old friend and servant of the royal Stuarts. During King James's reign he had more than once played host to royal hunting parties in Sherwood Forest, and in the summer of 1633 had entertained Charles at Welbeck 'in such a wonderful manner, and in such an excess of feasting, as had scarce ever before been known in England' until, that is, the summer of 1634, when he provided a still more stupendous and costly entertainment for both the king and queen at Bolsover, newly and palatially rebuilt. Their majesties were pleased to accept his hospitality, but it took another four years and much lobbying before the earl was finally rewarded by his appointment to the coveted office of Governor to the eight-year-old Prince of Wales.

In happier times this cultivated, polished, highly civilised man of the world, the most accomplished and knowledgeable equestrian of his day, would have been an ideal choice of guide and mentor to the heir to the throne. As it was, although their association lasted no more than three and a half years, the lively, affectionate child became devoted to the governor who taught him to ride and fence, and encouraged him to study 'things more than words, matter rather than language'. He also appears to have taken to heart the earl's rather cynical advice that one could never be too civil to the ladies.

In 1641 Parliament forced Newcastle's resignation from the prince's household and the following year the king appointed him to the key position of commander of the royal forces in the North. Considering that William Cavendish had no previous practical experience of war or generalship, he did rather better in his three-year contest with the Fairfaxes, Parliamentary father and son, than he is usually given credit for. Certainly he grudged no effort or personal expense in raising and equipping a volunteer army from the northern counties – in particular from the men of the Border lands of his mother's family, the Ogles. These were the famous Whitecoats, so-called because when no scarlet cloth could be found for their uniforms, they asked to be given white, promising to dye it in the enemy's blood.

The end of Newcastle's military career came with the Scots invasion of 1644 and the disastrous royalist defeat at Marston Moor in the summer of that year. Prince Rupert, German-born nephew of the king, a general in the royalist army and a tough professional soldier, was ready to rally his men and carry on the struggle, but the Marquess of Newcastle, as he now was, had had enough. Sickened by the slaughter of his valiant Whitecoats and moved to despair by the way in which he felt Rupert had squandered the army he had so painfully created and knew could not be replaced, he made up his mind to leave the country. No one ever questioned his physical courage, but his pride could not endure the thought of 'the laughter of the court' over his present discomfiture.

Newcastle's retreat to Holland, where he lived in exile in Rubens's house in Antwerp with his young second wife Margaret Lucas, and occupied his time producing a massive work on the art of *manège*, effectively marked the end of the whole Cavendish war effort. Charles, brother of the third Earl of Devonshire and the *beau ideal* of a young Cavalier officer – handsome, dashing and brave – had been tragically killed in a minor battle at the age of twenty-three, while Devonshire himself never saw any active service at all. He had slipped discreetly away to France when the fighting began, and in 1645 came discreetly home again to make his peace with the king's enemies and save his sequestered estates. This appears to have been at his mother's insistence, for although Countess Christian remained a convinced and active royalist to the end of her long life, there were some sacrifices she was not prepared to make, or allow the head of the family to make, for the royalist cause.

The Marquess of Newcastle returned to England after the Restoration and in due course was awarded a dukedom by his former pupil, but he played no further part in political life. He and his eccentric blue-stocking duchess, Mad Madge of Newcastle, passed their time chiefly at Welbeck writing bad plays and worse poetry, and at eighty the duke began to build himself a palace on the site of Nottingham Castle. The design was his own and would have looked more at home in northern Italy than the damply prosaic setting of the English Midlands.

The loyal duke's only surviving son, Henry Cavendish, presently succeeded to his father's numerous honours, but his line did not prosper. Of the second duke's four sons three died in infancy and the fourth (the same Lord Ogle who, to the distress of Dorothy Spencer, was matched with the little Percy heiress) died in his teens. The Newcastle title was later conferred on John Holles, Earl of Clare and husband of the duke's favourite daughter Margaret, but again there were no sons and the Newcastle/Cavendish property eventually passed by marriage to William Bentinck, second Duke of Portland.

But if the junior branch of the Cavendish tree was destined to wither away, the Devonshire family continued to flourish, despite the fact that the fourth earl, who succeeded in 1684, was an aggressive individual, forever getting into fights and brawls, a gambler and a notorious womaniser. In politics he emerged as a prominent member of the opposition Whig or 'Country' Party, though he did have enough sense not to become embroiled in the treasonable activities which culminated in the Rye House Plot and brought his unfortunate friend, Lord William Russell, to the scaffold. There was, however, no love lost between the fourth Earl of Devonshire and the last Stuart king, and the earl spent the greater part of James II's reign in Derbyshire, where he divided his time between corresponding with William of Orange and rebuilding Bess of Hardwick's Chatsworth.

The turreted Elizabethan house, now over a hundred years old, was certainly in urgent need of modernisation and repair. The earl's Clerk of the Works had already warned him that the fabric was 'decaying and weake' and in the autumn of 1686 he began on the reconstruction of the south front. This was all he had meant to do, but having started he became unexpectedly addicted to the building habit and for the next twenty years the transformation of Chatsworth into a mini-Versailles or, as the guidebooks were soon describing it, the Palace of the Peak, was to be the absorbing interest of his life and leisure.

His architect, at least for the south and east fronts, was William Talman, but it seems quite likely that the earl was his own architect for the second half of the great project, experimenting, building, getting a new idea halfway through and making his exasperated work force start all over again. The interior decorations – the painted ceilings, walls and frescoes – were entrusted to the Italian Verrio, the Frenchman Louis Laguerre, born at Versailles and a godson of the Sun King himself, and the English baroque painter Sir James Thornhill. The gardens were laid out after the formal French pattern. The famous cascade was constructed and a hill which was obstructing the view to the south was casually removed and replaced by the present Canal Pond. Daniel Defoe did not recognise the place: 'I was perfectly confounded at coming there a second time, and not knowing what had been done; for I had lost the hill, and found a new country in view, which Chatsworth itself had never seen before.'

Well before the transformation of Chatsworth and its surroundings was complete, in 1694, to be exact, the fourth earl had been created first Duke of Devonshire. This was the final instalment of his reward for the leading part he had played in the brilliantly successful and happily bloodless aristocratic *coup d'etat* known as the Glorious Revolution of 1688. The earl and his fellow conspirators had, of course, been acting to protect their own interests from the alarmingly absolutist tendencies of the post Civil War and Commonwealth monarchy, but they also expected – and received – the gratitude of the new style monarchs. Certainly the great-great-grandson of the first William Cavendish couldn't complain: Privy Councillor, Knight of the Most Noble Order of the Garter, Lord Lieutenant of Derbyshire, Lord Steward of the Royal Household and Lord High Steward of England on the occasion of the coronation of King William and Queen Mary, he had now unquestionably joined the first rank of the aristocracy.

Throughout the eighteenth century the Dukes of Devonshire and their eldest sons, the Marquesses of Hartington, were consistently active and influential on the political scene. The second duke, whose marriage to Rachel Russell, daughter of the dead patriot Lord William Russell, had cemented a useful alliance between two leading Whig families, had to consolidate and defend his position against Tory attack during the reign of Anne but thereafter, as a trusted ally of Robert Walpole and the new Hanoverian royal house, his prestige and influence in the corridors of power were unassailable. The second duke was also a discriminating art collector, especially of Old Master drawings, and the first of the family to buy pictures for their own sake rather than as suitably grand wall covering.

The Cavendishes had not so far made much of an impact on the intellectual front, though the earls of Devonshire had, to their credit, employed and sheltered the philosopher Thomas Hobbes, author of the *Leviathan*, and protected him in his old age from charges of atheism. The brother of the magnificent first Duke of Newcastle had been a gifted amateur mathematician and, at a time when it was fashionable to take an interest in scientific matters, the third earl and first duke of Devonshire were members of the Royal Society. But in the mid-eighteenth century the family unexpectedly produced a genius. Henry Cavendish, a grandson of the second duke, was known in his own times as a natural philosopher (today we should prefer the term physicist), who devoted his life to the study of anything and everything in the scientific field which happened to attract his interest – anything and everything from pure mathematics to meteorology, aeronautics to chemistry – and his researches into the composition of air and water broke entirely new ground, as did his work on the nature and properties of electricity.

His lifestyle and personal habits were unusual to the point of eccentricity. Avoiding all distractions such as the company of his fellow men and women (particularly women), he lived in hermit-like seclusion at his house in Clapham, emerging only to attend the dinners of the Royal Society (held at the Crown and Anchor Tavern and costing five shillings), or the *conversaziones* given by its president, Sir Joseph Banks. His contemporary, the Whig politician Henry Brougham, remembered the strange little man and

> the shrill cry he uttered as he shuffled quickly from room to room, seeming to be annoyed if looked at, but sometimes approaching to hear what was passing among others. His walk was quick and uneasy. He probably uttered fewer words in the course of his life than any man who ever lived to fourscore years, not at all excepting the monks of La Trappe.

Henry Cavendish did not, in fact, quite attain four score years, dying in February 1810 at the age of seventy-nine and leaving a fortune of around one million pounds. It was not that he had been exactly a miser, but, as with human relationships, money and its ordinary uses had simply never entered into his scheme of things. Anecdotes about his peculiarities are numerous: his only communication with his housekeeper was by means of notes left on the hall table; he always left a signed receipt when taking a book from his own library; and on one occasion he literally fled in terror from a Royal Society meeting when threatened with compliments from a visiting scientist. He was said 'never to express himself warmly on any question of religion or politics and indeed appeared to reject all human sympathy'.

Whether he was to be pitied or envied must depend on one's

point of view. Francis Bickley, whose history of the Cavendish family appeared in 1911, felt there was

> something pathetic about such an existence as Henry Cavendish's, so fruitful and yet so utterly barren. . . . He understood the structure of the universe. But the stars had no song for him, neither had earth any laughter.

On the other hand, John Pearson, the most recent family chronicler, takes the view that

> he was fortunate in being able to stay free from the cares and passions that enslave most lesser men . . . and was lucky to have lived in a period when a dedicated aristocratic amateur like him could make discoveries on such a scale and over such a range of subjects.

Obviously such a man – 'the man who weighed the world' by computing its mean density and yet apparently wanted so little to do with it that he chose deliberately to bury himself in solitude and insignificance – cannot be judged by any normal standard. Mr Pearson perceptively describes him as 'a Merlin figure' and he just has to be accepted as a sport of the generally prosaic Cavendish stock.

While the magus of Clapham was quietly engaged in pushing back the frontiers of knowledge, his relations were following the more characteristically Cavendish occupations of politics, gambling and marrying money. The third duke, who succeeded in 1729, a simple soul, 'plain in his manners, negligent in his dress', served for an uneventful stint at Dublin Castle as Viceroy of Ireland and married the daughter of a wealthy City merchant, who was as uncomplicated and homely as himself and bore him a numerous family. His eldest son, who succeeded in 1755, also married an heiress – one of the greatest heiresses going – the sixteen-year-old Lady Charlotte Boyle, daughter of the architect and connoisseur Earl of Burlington, who was to bring Burlington House in Piccadilly, a Palladian villa at Chiswick, romantic Lismore Castle in County Waterford and Bolton Abbey on the Yorkshire moors, together with the Burlington art collection, into the Cavendish family. As an added bonus, the heiress was pretty, sweet-natured and intelligent and the marriage turned out to be a very happy one, if short-lived, for sadly young Lady Hartington died of smallpox after less than seven years, leaving four young children and a disconsolate husband.

The fourth duke never remarried. When he succeeded his father in 1755 he was known as 'the Crown Prince of the Whigs' and held office as Prime Minister for an uncomfortable six-month period at the beginning of the Seven Years' War with France, with the elder William Pitt as his Secretary of State. Then, in 1762, he fell out with the new, brash young King George III, who was shockingly rude to him, and abandoned politics in disgust. Already in poor health, he died not long afterwards at the early age of forty-five – one of the last of the old-style Whig oligarchs.

Apart from his lacklustre political career, the fourth duke is remembered for effecting another transformation scene at Chatsworth. Having decided that the house should properly be made to face west over the Derwent valley, he demolished the old stables and other offices which had been obscuring the view. Since the village of Edensor now also obscured the view, he demolished that as well, with the splendid insouciance only possible for a rich eighteenth-century duke. Edensor was rebuilt round the corner discreetly out of sight, and the architect James Paine commissioned to design a new stable block. Paine also designed a handsome new bridge to span the river Derwent just below the reorientated house and, since the fashion in gardens was now for carefully contrived 'naturalness', the greatest practitioner of that particular art was called in to undertake the re-landscaping of the grounds. Capability Brown destroyed the first duke's formal terraces and parterres, creating instead the lushly wooded setting for the classical jewel which is Chatsworth as it appears today.

The fifth duke, William Cavendish the ninth in direct line from the founder of the family fortunes, was a somewhat lethargic youth of fifteen when his father died in 1810 and it is ironic that the Devonshires should have reached the zenith of their fame and glamour during the reign of this cold, dull, inhibited man. The reason, of course, lay in the personality not of the duke but the duchess. With an income of around £40,000 a year, four huge and profitable estates and a mansion for every day of the week, plus one or two to spare, the fifth duke was by far the most eligible bachelor in England, if not in Europe, and had only to speak twice to any young woman to start speculative gossip. While society waited eagerly to see where he would throw the handkerchief, the duke himself, who already had a perfectly satisfactory mistress, appeared in no hurry to embark on the tedious business of acquiring a wife. But at last, on Sunday 5 June 1774, he married Georgiana, elder daughter of the first Earl Spencer of Althorp, at Wimbledon parish church. He was in his mid-twenties, she was two days short of her seventeenth birthday: a tall, well-built girl with a fresh pink and white complexion, a luxuriant mane of reddish hair, bubbling high spirits and immense personal charm.

The teenage duchess made an immediate impact on the polite world which hastened to enthuse over 'the amenity and graces of her deportment . . . her irresistible manners, and the seduction of her society.' Horace Walpole pronounced her to be 'a lovely girl, natural and full of grace' and, after meeting her at a ball at Almacks in the year of her marriage, was in raptures over her 'flowing good nature, sense and lively modesty'. 'So handsome, so agreeable, so obliging in her manner' gushed the septuagenarian Mrs Delany, a doyenne of society, who was, nevertheless, a little anxious lest her young friend's 'superabundant spirits' would get her into scrapes; while Georgiana's mama, knowing her daughter to be 'giddy, idle and fond of dissipation', felt grave misgivings about the future.

Georgiana herself knew no such qualms and over the next couple of decades she was to turn Devonshire House in Piccadilly, headquarters of the influential Devonshire House set, into the headquarters of the beau-monde – especially of the *avant-garde* beau-monde. Here were to be found Charles Fox, Richard Sheridan, the young George Prince of Wales, Lady Melbourne, the duchess's sister Harriet Duncannon, later Countess of Bessborough, and, of course, her bosom friend Lady Elizabeth Foster.

Throughout the 1770s and '80s all the wit and brilliance, rank and beauty and fashion of that supremely civilised age found its way through the great wrought iron gates, across the courtyard and on into the elegant reception rooms, designed for the third duke by William Kent, to talk, dance, gamble, flirt and promenade under the blazing chandeliers – all drawn by the magnetic attraction of Georgiana's outgoing charm and the electric atmosphere generated by her 'superabundant spirits', her reckless enjoyment of life, her outrageous gaiety. The fifth Duchess of Devonshire is still probably best remembered for her taste in large feathered hats, immortalised by Gainsborough, and her enthusiastic canvassing for her friend Fox in the 1784 election, when she was accused of dispensing kisses to the butchers and draymen of Westminster in exchange for votes. Less well-known is the extraordinary story of her life behind the glittering public façade.

It had very soon become clear that the duke was immune to the charms of his seductive young bride, and after a few months' honeymoon at Chatsworth he had returned with relief to his usual London routine of drinking and gambling at Brooks's Club for most of the night, coming back to Devonshire House for breakfast and a good day's sleep. He was seemingly quite indifferent to Georgiana's social activities and, not surprisingly, she was soon in difficulties. In April 1775 she wrote to her mama:

> I begin to grow very uneasy about money for I don't think I can well tell the Duke. . . . If it was possible to borrow money just to get out of the scrape now, I think I could better tell him next year at anytime than at present.

This letter was the prototype of hundreds more written over the next thirty years ending in a note dictated on what became her deathbed, begging for the loan of a hundred pounds until Lady Day. Everyone in Georgiana's circle played high – even her strait-laced mama – but the duchess was not only a compulsive gambler, she was a compulsive loser too, and the rest of her life was to be punctuated by recurrent crises over gambling debts which she dared not disclose to the duke. She borrowed with increasing desperation from her family and friends, from the Prince of Wales, from the banker Thomas Coutts, from the former French finance minister, M. de Calonne, from servants and tradesmen, from anyone who could be cajoled into parting with a few hundred guineas. And all the time the debts, with their attendant festering muddle of dishonesty and shame, grew like some monstrous abcess.

The duke continued to be as impervious to his wife's financial problems as to everything else concerning her. Even the bestselling novel she published anonymously in 1779 which revealed so many intimate details of their private life – his adultery and neglect, her bitterness and total disillusion with the holy estate of matrimony – failed to provoke any reaction. The duke, it seemed, really did not care what the duchess did. All he asked was that she should perform her primary function of providing an heir to the family titles and estates: something she had so far conspicuously failed to do. The Devonshires' marriage appeared, in short, to be on the verge of collapse. Then, in the spring of 1782, Lady Elizabeth Foster came into their lives and nothing was ever the same again.

Daughter of Frederick Hervey, the eccentric Earl of Bristol, and separated from her unsatisfactory Irish MP husband, Elizabeth Foster seemed at first to be a legitimate object of compassion. But behind her wistfully feminine exterior there lurked a tough, calculating intelligence. Lady Elizabeth meant to get on in the world, using whatever means came most readily to hand. She had no scruples about trading on Duchess Georgiana's well-known weakness for a hard luck story, and within a matter of weeks she had succeeded in getting herself adopted into the Devonshire household.

The duchess was delighted with her new friend and protégée, and the torpid duke had been roused to quite unwonted enthusiasm by Lady Elizabeth's melting brown eyes, fragile prettiness and winning ways. Soon, after the Devonshire House custom, all three were on pet name terms: the dog-loving duke was Canis, Lady Elizabeth the Racoon, or Racky, and the duchess Mrs Rat. More significantly, by the end of that momentous year, the duchess was pregnant, and although the baby born in July 1783 was a girl, at least there was now a definite hope that boys might follow.

Some eighteen months later ducal hopes were rising again, but this time 'dearest Bess' was also in the family way and since it was essential to conceal the remarkable but undisputed fact that the duke was responsible for both pregnancies, Lady Elizabeth departed on a trip to Italy. There, in conditions of some discomfort but with a minimum of fuss, she gave birth to a daughter, to be known as Caroline St Jules, while at home in London the duchess produced another girl.

In the summer of 1786 the three friends were joyously reunited at Chatsworth and the following year Bess was once again carrying the duke's child – a boy this time, christened Augustus and given the surname Clifford – but it was not until May 1790 that Georgiana at last succeeded in presenting her husband with the longed-for legitimate male heir.

William Cavendish the tenth, Marquess of Hartington, always known in the family as 'Hart', was born near Paris at the *hôtel* belonging to the Marquis de Boulainvilliers at Passy. Yet despite the number of witnesses present and although Lady Elizabeth was pointedly displaying herself at the Opéra looking 'as thin as a Wrayle', slanderous rumours about the true maternity of the sixth Duke of Devonshire were to persist over many years. The unusual nature of his father's domestic arrangements, coupled with the fact that his birth had taken place abroad and in a country where a bloody revolution was in progress, not surprisingly aroused deep suspicion in some quarters. The ducal party seems, however, to have been little troubled by mob violence (which, admittedly, was still sporadic) and their prolonged stay on the Continent had a good deal to do with Elizabeth Foster's plans for integrating her own offspring into the Cavendish family circle.

In 1791 the duchess was pregnant again, the father being her lover, the promising young Whig politician Charles, later Earl Grey, who as Whig prime minister was to carry the Great Reform Bill of 1832. But what was sauce for the goose was emphatically not sauce for the eighteenth-century gander. There was never any question of Georgiana's bastard joining the 'orphan' Caroline St Jules, now cosily entrenched in the Devonshire House schoolroom presided over by that paragon of respectability Miss Selina Trimmer, and the duke, with a fine show of indignation, insisted on banishing his erring wife from his bed and board but unfortunately this also meant banishing Lady Elizabeth, who could scarcely remain unchaperoned by the duchess and who accompanied Georgiana into exile. The exile was in consequence comparatively brief and two years later Canis, Racky and Mrs Rat were together again, apparently as affectionate as ever.

The 'private history' of Devonshire House was naturally the subject of much prurient speculation and also led to painful stress and strain within the family. Apart from Harriet Bessborough, the Spencers detested 'Lady Liz' and as they grew up, Georgiana's own children made no secret of their dislike and scorn. But there was no shifting her now. 'Do you hear the voice of my heart crying out to you?' wrote Georgiana when her 'dearest Bess' was in Paris in 1802, and, to do her justice, dearest Bess remained loyal to her friend as Georgiana's looks and health began to fail. The unfortunate duchess was suffering from a lethal and agonising combination of acute eye trouble (she lost her left eye altogether after 'a dreadful operation which she bore with great courage'), gall stones and an abcess on the liver which finally killed her in March 1806.

To the disgust, but scarcely the surprise of his relations, the bereaved duke presently married Lady Elizabeth Foster, who for nearly a quarter of a century had studied to please him with more percipience, and certainly greater success, than his first duchess. She was still prepared to listen attentively to his anecdotes, to soothe him with her constant devotion and uncritical companionship, and never, never fell into 'high Hystericks' as Georgiana had been so distressingly prone to do. Lady Liz had waited long and patiently for her reward, and despite all her maddening little affectations and addiction to baby talk, it seems only fair that she should have had 'at last the name also'. She lived on until 1824, dying in Rome at the age of sixty-six, the longest survivor by fifteen years of that mysterious threesome which had once so shocked respectable society with its titillating exhibition of 'vice in its most attractive form'.

The fifth duke's natural habitat had been London and Brooks's Club. His son preferred Chatsworth. The sixth duke, who never married and played no part in politics, spent his life quite pleasurably doing nothing very much. He adored Chatsworth and lavished a great deal of money on it, as well as on collecting first folios, antique coins, neo-classical Italian statuary and any other elegant trifles which happened to catch his fancy. He is reputed to have been deaf – some say, almost totally – and yet this handicap does not appear to have prevented him from enjoying the performances of his private orchestra. It therefore seems at least possible that the ducal deafness was also a ducal alibi: a convenient pretext for avoiding the more disagreeable chores of public life.

The first Cavendish title-holder to fail in his duty of providing an heir, the Bachelor Duke was in many ways a survivor from an earlier, more relaxed age – a charming, extravagant, purely ornamental creature who, in the eyes of the censorious nineteenth century, sometimes appeared dangerously self-indulgent, irresponsible and frivolous. Although he himself would not have realised it, the Bachelor's most memorable achievement was his patronage of Joseph Paxton, gardener, engineer and pioneer, whose Great Conservatory – nearly half an acre of glass and iron built at Chatsworth in the 1830s to house the duke's collection of tropical trees and costing around £30,000 – was to supply Paxton with his inspiration for the construction of the Crystal Palace in Hyde Park for the Great Exhibition of 1851.

No one could accuse the seventh Duke of Devonshire of being irresponsible or frivolous. A middle-aged widower when he succeeded his cousin in 1858, the seventh duke was a deeply religious man, devoted to his four children, serious-minded, scholarly and possessing a well-developed Victorian social conscience. As the sixth duke is associated with Joseph Paxton, so the seventh is with Eastbourne. The Sussex estates had come into the family in the 1780s when the fifth duke's brother married the Compton heiress, but it was not until the 1850s, with the extension of the London/Brighton and South Coast Railway, that the possibility of expanding Eastbourne into a more refined alternative to Brighton began to open out.

Although the fifth duke had experimented with building some elegant crescents and assembly rooms at Buxton, the Cavendishes, unlike the Russells, had not so far attempted much in the way of urban property development. Now, under the benevolent autocracy of the seventh duke, Eastbourne began to blossom into an 'Empress of Watering Places' – a genteel family resort catering for the aspiring (and wealthy) upper middle class. The seventh duke also invested heavily in the industries of Barrow-in-Furness, close to his own favourite home of Holker Hall. But his most memorable achievement must be his endowment in 1870 of a new Laboratory of Experimental Physics at Cambridge University, to be known as the Cavendish Laboratory in honour of the long-dead genius of Clapham Common.

Like his immediate predecessor, the seventh duke took no interest in politics but his second son, Lord Frederick Cavendish, was to be murdered in Phoenix Park, Dublin on the very day he arrived to take up his appointment as Irish Secretary, and his eldest son and heir enjoyed (if that is the word for one who so carefully cultivated an air of bored world-weariness) a long and active political career.

Owing to his father's longevity, the eighth duke was known by his courtesy title, or by his nickname Harty-Tarty, until his late middle-age. First elected Liberal Member of Parliament for North Lancashire in May 1857, he sat for thirty-four years in the House of Commons. He held the offices of Postmaster General, Secretary for War, Chief Secretary for Ireland and Secretary for India in successive Liberal governments under Mr Gladstone, and in 1886 only narrowly missed becoming Prime Minister himself. Both as 'Harty-Tarty' and 'the Duke with the Whiskers', Spencer Compton Cavendish, eighth Duke of Devonshire, became an essential part of the late Victorian landscape – his casual, slumbrous, amateur approach concealing a sophisticated professionalism. His membership of the 'fast' Marlborough House set, his addiction to the turf, and his famous thirty-year-long liaison with a married woman, the Duchess of Manchester, did him no harm with his colleagues or, for that matter, with the public. The Duke was genuinely devoted to Louise Manchester, and their marriage, which eventually took place in 1892, was a very happy one, although the energetic and sociable German-born Louise (known, inevitably, as the Double Duchess) did force her lethargic spouse to dress up as the Holy Roman Emperor for a great fancy dress ball at Devonshire House to celebrate Queen Victoria's Diamond Jubilee. Both partners were approaching sixty by the time they reached the altar, but fortunately there was no need to worry about the succession since the duke's nephew and heir, Victor Cavendish, and his wife Lady Evelyn Fitzmaurice, soon began to produce a large family.

The ninth duke, first of the twentieth-century title-holders, inherited in 1908 and was fated to become the first Cavendish forced to preside over the breaking up of the family empire to appease that peculiarly twentieth-century bogeyman the tax collector. During the 1920s both Chiswick House and Devonshire House, opposite the Ritz Hotel, were sacrificed on the altar of economy. Nevertheless, the Cavendishes between the wars were still very comfortable and, in a relaxed and unassuming way, very, very grand. They still had Compton Place at Eastbourne, Bolton Abbey, Lismore Castle, Hardwick Hall and, of course, Chatsworth, which was still being run on lines which would have been perfectly recognisable to old Bess of Hardwick herself. Indoors, apart from the butler, the under-butler, the duke's valet, the duchess's maid, the housekeeper and the cook, there were still a platoon of liveried footmen, a groom of the chambers, a dozen housemaids, two or three kitchen maids, two or three scullery maids, laundry maids, stillroom maids and a dairy maid. There were 'odd men', scrubbing women, boilermen, sewing women, coalmen, firemen, porters, joiners, plumbers, carpenters and electricians. The house functioned as a self-contained, self-sufficient unit much as it had done in past ages, nor had the numbers to be catered for greatly diminished. Eighteenth-century dukes were accustomed to keep house for 180 persons at Chatsworth. At Christmas gatherings of the clan in the 1930s, there would be approximately 150 people to feed, from the dining-room to the servants' hall.

In 1925 the ninth duke was cruelly afflicted by a stroke accompanied by a personality change which turned a gentle, easy-going character into an unpredictable, intensely irritable, sometimes actually violent individual. Faced with this especially distressing personal calamity, Duchess Evie – 'Grannie Duchess' as she was known to her immediate descendants – strong-willed and indomitable, took over the running of the estate, kept up appearances, and kept an unforgiving eye on the accounts. When income tax went up to five shillings in the pound, Duchess Evie retaliated by stopping the payment of beer money, an age-old perquisite of the indoor staff. An implacable enemy of waste, woodworm, and dry rot, Grannie Duchess devoted many hours of her long widowhood, spent as châtelaine of Hardwick Hall, to repairing the priceless tapestries acquired in Bess's day. Her expertise and enthusiasm for this esoteric pastime was such that an admiring professional from the Royal School of Needlework was once moved to tell her that she was wasting her time as a duchess, thus pleasing the old lady immensely.

The ninth duke died in 1938 and his death marked the end of an era. Chatsworth was occupied by a girls' boarding school during the Second World War, while the tenth duke pursued his career as a member of the wartime coalition government and his two sons went into the Coldstream Guards. But William, or Billy, Hartington was killed in France in 1944, only four months after his wedding to Kathleen Kennedy, sister of the future President of the United States, who was herself to die tragically in a plane crash in 1948. The loss of his beloved elder son was a blow from which the tenth duke seems never quite to have recovered; nor had the malign fate which pursued the Cavendishes so relentlessly through the first half of the twentieth century yet finished with the family. The duke died quite suddenly at Compton Place of a massive coronary in 1950. He was only fifty-five and his death had taken place just three and a half months before the expiry of the five-year statutory period when the transfer of his assets to the Chatsworth Settlement would have protected the estate from the worst effects of death duties running at a crippling eighty per cent. This was the culminating disaster which left his surviving son, thirty-year-old Andrew, to pick up a bill from the Treasury for approaching five million pounds.

Although he had no nostalgic childhood memories of the place, the eleventh Duke of Devonshire was fiercely determined to keep Chatsworth in the family, but in order to save it much else had to be sacrificed. Some of the finest works of art in the Chatsworth collection, including a fifth-century Greek head of Apollo, the tenth-century manuscript Benedictional of St Aethelwold, the Memling Triptych, Rembrandt's 'Philosopher' and Rubens's 'Holy Family' disappeared into the tax man's insatiable maw. Compton Place became a girls' school and many thousands of acres of land in Scotland, Derbyshire and Sussex also vanished. Still it was not enough, and in 1954 the duke decided to offer Hardwick Hall, the great Elizabethan 'prodigy house', together with its contents and surrounding farmland to the nation. Today, Bess's masterpiece, miraculously preserved by time and chance very much as she left it, slumbers on in the charge of the National Trust, while Chatsworth, that other great showplace, is still a family home.

Chatsworth had been re-opened to the public at Easter 1949 (it has been open to visitors since its earliest days), but the tenth duke and duchess never considered going back to live there themselves. Nor, until the mid-1950s, did the eleventh duke and his wife Deborah (youngest of the fabled Mitford Girls). However, now that the house had been saved for the family, it was pointed out, reasonably enough, that the family might as well move back in. Not, of course, in anything like the pre-war style. Even if money had been no object, the unlimited supply of labour on which the pre-war life style had been supported no longer existed. But a nucleus of devoted, knowledgeable and professional staff had survived – had, indeed, done much to preserve the fabric of the building throughout the war years and after – and in 1958 work began on creating a set of modernised private apartments where the family could live the ducal life post-war style.

The sheer physical scale of Chatsworth is staggering: one hundred and seventy-five rooms, fifty-one of them very large, more than an acre of roof, seventeen staircases, nearly four hundred doors, more than two thousand electric light bulbs. In her book, *The House, A Portrait of Chatsworth*, the present duchess touches on some of 'the joys and problems of living in a huge house'.

> Everything is bigger than lifesize, the indoor distances, the faraway meals, the long passages and stairs for luggage all add to the complications of life. A bag put down in a rare bit of house can be lost for months. The master key can be forgotten in an attic door till panic sets in. It is a terrible place to house train a puppy. . . . On the good side children can roller-skate for miles without going out of doors; on a wet day you can walk for hours, be entertained and keep dry, gramophone, piano and loud singers can blast away in the drawing room without fear of waking angry sleepers. And there is always escape from people.

In the early sixties the Devonshires were briefly back in politics, when the duke held office as Minister of State for Commonwealth Relations in the government of Harold Macmillan, his uncle by marriage. More recently his ancestral Whiggism has reasserted itself, leading him into joining the SDP. Although they have a variety of other interests – for example, horse-racing and breeding, and gardening – the duke and duchess work seriously at the family business which is, essentially, Chatsworth, ironically more continuously occupied today than ever before in its history. Thanks to carefully worked out arrangements concluded in the early eighties, its financial future should now be secure and, significantly, the climate of public opinion is changing. In the 1950s there was little or no sympathy for a duke struggling to save his inheritance from the tax man. Now, as usual when it is almost too late, people are beginning to realise that houses like Chatsworth are not replaceable; that they and their contents, which have been assembled over so many centuries, are not, or need not be, dead things, time capsules of past glories; that they are still evolving and reflecting the personalities of their owners. The present duchess has turned the Orangery (which once contained trees from the Empress Josephine's collection at Malmaison) into a shop – a highly successful monument to her 'passion for commerce'. She has also taken over the Chatsworth home farm and set up a farm shop, as well as becoming internationally known as a breeder of Shetland ponies. The present duke has begun to add to the artistic treasures of his ancestors, to buy books and to commission work from living artists and sculptors.

So far as it is possible to be certain of anything in an increasingly uncertain world, the Cavendishes seem likely to stay with the house which William Cavendish and his wife Elizabeth first began to build for their growing family in the valley of the River Derwent just over four hundred years ago. 'Think of what the Cavendishes have done in days gone by,' said the Victorian Liberal statesman John Bright. 'Think of their services to the state.' By reviving and restoring Chatsworth, by keeping its contents together, above all by keeping it alive and 'in the family' for the pleasure of us all, the Cavendishes are still performing services to the state as uniquely valuable in their way as those of generations past.

The Russells of Woburn

Che sara sara

John 1st Earl of Bedford by Hans Holbein the Younger
reproduced by gracious permission of Her Majesty the Queen

THE RUSSELLS OF WOBURN

Che sara sara

'THE House of Russell derives its distinctive appellation from one of the fiefs which the first chieftain of that surname possessed, anterior to the conquest of England, in Lower Normandy in the ancient barony of Briquebec.' This, at least, was the conclusion reached by Josiah Wiffen, pursuing his enquiries into the origins of the House of Russell early in the nineteenth century. After many years of painstaking research and study of ancient charters, Wiffen felt fully justified in assuring his patron, the sixth Duke of Bedford, that he could trace his ancestry to the knightly Norman family of du Rozel, 'said by some authorities to have been known under that surname so early as the year 1012', and who, in their turn, could claim descent from a seventh-century Viking chieftain, Olaf the Sharp eyed, King of Rerik.

Modern scholarship, however, has provided the Dukes of Bedford with a less romantic, but more reliably documented pedigree. The first Russells, it seems, were merchants, shippers and distributors of the strong red wine of Gascony, established in a flourishing way of business at Weymouth in Dorset by the last decade of the fourteenth century. They were men of substance, prominent members of the trading and seafaring community and active in local politics.

Stephen Russell, otherwise known as Stephen Gascoyne, represented the borough of Weymouth in the Parliament of 1394, while his son Henry was three times returned to Westminster as burgess. Henry also held a variety of official appointments to do with the collection of taxes levied by the Exchequer on goods passing through the ports, and in 1440 received a royal commission giving him powers to conduct a special investigation into the evasion of customs duties – a popular pastime then as now.

Following the usual pattern of such successful entrepreneurs, the Weymouth Russells invested their money in land, married local heiresses and set themselves up as country gentlemen on estates at Berwick and Swyre, just inland from the strip of coast lying between Bridport and Portland Bill. And there they might very well have remained, had it not been for the great storm which swept across southern England in January 1506, when gales in the Channel forced the fleet which was carying Archduke Philip of Austria and his wife Joanna of Castile from Flanders to Spain to run for shelter in Weymouth Bay.

The unexpected arrival of a 'puissant navy' upon their coast caused considerable alarm among the people of the district and brought the nearest big landowner hurrying to the scene at the head of his tenantry. As soon as the situation was made clear to him, Sir Thomas Trenchard very properly took the drenched and seasick strangers under the shelter of his own roof and despatched messengers to inform the King of this 'accident'. He also turned for help to his neighbour and kinsman by marrige, young John Russell of Berwick, who had just returned from a spell of foreign travel which may or may not have been connected with the family's business interests, and who was known to speak fluent French and Spanish.

John Russell – he would then have been about nineteen or twenty – did so well as an interpreter that he presently accompanied the royal visitors to Windsor, where King Henry VII was so taken by the promising newcomer, that he offered him a place at court. This, at any rate, is the traditional story and there is nothing inherently implausible about it, for it was on the ability to seize and profit by just such a chance opportunity, that many sixteenth-century careers were founded. Certainly John Russell was ensconced as a junior member of the royal household before 1509, and he certainly appears to have been endowed with qualities worthy of royal notice, being by all accounts an exceptionally attractive and talented youth, well-educated, noticeably good-looking and possessing the sort of endearing personal charm which 'exacted a liking, if not a love from all that beheld him'.

When Henry VIII succeeded to the throne as an exuberant and

energetic seventeen-year-old, Russell retained his post of Gentleman Usher and no doubt played a creditable part in the jousting and dancing, pageants and 'disguisings' which occupied so much time at the new, gay young court; but it was the king's determination to pick a quarrel with France which marked the beginning of his rise in the royal service. Early in 1513 he was sent over to join the garrison at Calais, and later that year transferred to Tournai, captured by the English in the summer campaign. Here he was able to prove his usefulness as a courier and intelligencer, riding about on the king's business, delivering letters and other messages best not committed to paper, gathering and passing on information, gaining valuable experience and making valuable contacts.

John Russell was present at the Field of the Cloth of Gold in 1520, and two years later was a member of an expeditionary force which seized and destroyed the town of Morlaix on the Breton coast. He lost an eye in this action and was knighted for gallantry by the Earl of Surrey. His real work, though, lay in the subtle, unprincipled world of international diplomacy and he was being increasingly employed as a special envoy or special agent, travelling round the courts of war-torn Europe on a variety of confidential missions.

It was an adventurous life and at times an actively dangerous one – Sir John was more than once obliged to leave town in his socks – but it was also one for which his linguistic skills, his tact, discretion and shrewd business brain fitted him admirably. In 1527 he was in Rome, entrusted with handing over 200,000 gold ducats, which, it was hoped, would buy papal support for Cardinal Wolsey's foreign and domestic policy. His Holiness, Russell reported enthusiastically, esteemed himself 'as greatly bound to the King's highness as ever Pope was to any prince', and everyone was exclaiming that the King of England was proving a true Defender of the Faith. 'I think verily', he concluded, 'the King never spent money that shall sound more to his fame and honour than this' – a comment, which, as things turned out, might qualify as the misstatement of the century. But John Russell could hardly have been expected to foresee the remarkable events of the next decade.

Now in his early forties, the pattern of his career was changing.

In 1526 he had married the widowed Lady Jerningham, daughter and heiress of Sir Guy Sapcote, who brought him the manors of Thornhaugh in Northampton and Chenies in Buckinghamshire. The Russells did not go back to Dorset and Chenies, pleasantly and conveniently situated in the Chess valley, became their home. Sir John needed a base close to London, for in the year of his marriage he had been promoted to become one of the six Gentlemen of the Privy Chamber and was thus brought into close daily contact with the king throughout Henry's long drawn out battle for his divorce from Catherine of Aragon, the fall of Wolsey, the rise of Thomas Cromwell and the final breach with Rome. It was a period of intense social and political upheaval, a world in which a public man's first error of judgement was frequently his last. But John Russell survived unscathed, still inching his way upwards, never putting a foot wrong, never making an unnecessary enemy, hard-working, single-minded, unswervingly loyal, the model of a dedicated professional diplomat, courtier and civil servant.

For all that, he had to wait until he was fifty, late middle age by the standards of the time, before reaping any really substantial reward for his years of devoted service. But when they came, rewards came thick and fast. In 1537 he was appointed Comptroller of the Household and two years later raised to the peerage as Baron Russell of Chenies and created a Knight of the Garter.

The end of the 1530s found John Russell back in the West Country, sent as the king's lieutenant to quell rumblings of religious and economic discontent. To enhance his standing in the area and enable him to support the dignity of his position, he now received valuable grants of land belonging to the former abbeys of Tavistock and Dunkerswell, also Torre Abbey in South Devon and a house in Exeter, which he renamed Russell House and made his headquarters in the West. These new properties, added to the manors he already owned in the Midlands and Home Counties, had the effect of doubling his income, but equally important was the royal trust and favour they so comfortingly represented. Lord Russell had become one of the king's closest confidants, and it was to him that Henry poured out his angry disappointment after his first sight of Anne of Cleves.

The disastrous Cleves marriage was followed by the fall of

Thomas Cromwell, but although Russell tried to intercede for his old friend, Cromwell's disgrace and execution and the consequent temporary rise of the reactionary Howard faction, in no way affected his own position. In 1542 he became Lord Privy Seal and two years later, a man of nearly sixty, was once more in France with the army besieging Boulogne. When Henry VIII died in 1547, he appointed his faithful servant to be a member of the council which was to rule during his son's minority and bequeathed him further lands, including the abbey and manors of Woburn in Bedfordshire.

John Russell, Father Russell as he was known at court, was now a rich, respected and venerable figure, still leading an active public life. Remarkably active in fact, for the first service he rendered the new government was to suppress a serious rebellion in the West Country, protesting, amongst other things, against the new Book of Common Prayer, and which culminated in a fierce encounter at the village of Sampford Courtenay. Here, as he reported to his fellow councillors, he found the rebels, led by one Humphrey Arundel, strongly encamped and offering strong resistance. When Lord Russell arrived on the scene, he ordered and himself took part in a three-pronged assault, 'upon the sight whereof the rebels' stomachs so fell from them, as without any blow they fled'. 'All this night we sat on horseback', wrote the old gentleman energetically, 'and in the morning we had word that Arundel was fled to Launceston. . . . I have sent incontinently to keep the town in a stay, and this morning I haste thither with the rest.'

His reward was another step in rank. In January 1550 he was created first Earl of Bedford and shortly afterwards yet more property was added to his already formidable list of assets – Thorney Abbey in the fen country and the site of the former convent, or Covent Garden in London, once part of the estates of the Abbey of Westminster. Still he was not ready to retire. The spring of 1554 saw him travelling to Spain, to Santiago de Compostella to escort Prince Philip – grandson of that Austrian Archduke whose enforced sojourn in the West Country was perhaps responsible for his present eminence – over to England, and the new earl performed his last service to the Crown at Winchester Cathedral on 25 July, when he was one of a group of five senior peers who gave Queen Mary Tudor in marriage to the Prince of Spain. He died the following March at his house in the Strand after a career as a courtier, soldier, diplomat and administrator, which had spanned four reigns and almost half a century, and was 'carried to his burying place in the country, called Chenies' with all the solemnity of banners of arms, black-hooded mourners and black-draped horses due to a great man.

The first Earl of Bedford had apparently never found any difficulty in adjusting to the fluctuations in the religious climate of his day, but his son Francis, a sober, rather homely young man, succeeding to the title in his twenty-seventh year, was of a more uncompromising turn of mind. The second earl held inconveniently advanced Protestant views and after his father's death found it prudent to travel abroad during most of the remainder of the Catholic Mary's reign.

The accession of Elizabeth fortunately put an end to any problems of conscience. The new queen made the Earl of Bedford a member of her Privy Council and, with William Cecil and the Marquis of Northampton, he was brought in to help with the revision of the prayer book and the drawing up of a new liturgy which would satisfy the queen's conservative leanings as well as the more radical aspirations of the younger clergy.

Francis Russell had inherited his father's gift for languages, which made him useful as a diplomat, and in 1561 he was sent over to France on a formal visit of condolence to the newly widowed Mary Queen of Scots. As governor of the frontier town of Berwick he became something of an expert on Scottish affairs and acted as Queen Elizabeth's representative at the baptism of Mary's son James, although, true to his principles, he refused to attend the popish christening ceremony itself.

Bedford was always a popular and influential figure on the Elizabethan political scene and one of the queen's trusted aides, but he was a man of wider interests than his father, a noted patron of letters in fact. The first earl had, after all, had to strive to build up his career and fortune. His son could afford to take life a little more easily and spend more time with his family. The Russells were now securely established among the English nobility. The second earl's eldest daughter, Anne, married Ambrose Dudley, Earl of Warwick, and became one of the queen's closest friends. Another daughter married George Clifford, Earl of Cumberland, and became the mother of Anne Clifford, later Countess of Dorset. In 1600 his granddaughter, another Anne Russell, married Lord Henry Herbert and the queen, then quite an old lady, danced at her wedding.

The second earl was also able to devote more attention to the management of his estates. A considerate and conscientious employer, he once wrote rebuking his steward, Edmund Yard, for negligence in paying the household bills. 'A thing whereof you are not ignorant how careful I have been that poor artificers should ever be paid at the week's end or fortnight's at the most. And myself having so often moved you that the same order might be kept, cannot but marvel to see poor men driven to such sums, as not so much as the Rushes discharged.'

The earl spent some of his time at Russell House in Exeter. He improved the buildings at Tavistock and, possibly for sentimental reasons, acquired the manor of Kingston Russell in Dorset from the Crown. When in London, he lived at Russell House in the Strand and owned another house by the river at Chiswick. But his principal home was still Chenies. It was not quite on the scale of some of the great Elizabethan mansions, perhaps; yet, judging from the inventory drawn up in 1586, Chenies, with its tables of walnut tree, its joined cupboards, chairs and stools upholstered in tawny velvet, its carved and gilded bedsteads with their coverlets of crimson damask or green and white silk, its silver jugs and basins and oak wainscotting, was obviously a comfortable, well furnished family house.

Francis, second Earl of Bedford, died in July 1585 and was buried at Chenies beside his father. He had never held any of the great offices of state, apparently by his own wish, and wisely declined the honour of acting as the Queen of Scots's custodian after her flight into England. Always a prominent member of the ultra-Protestant faction on the Council, he made no effort to shine among the peacocks of the court and left a reputation among his contemporaries as 'a true lover of Religion and Vertue'. A little too consciously self-righteous perhaps, and a bit of a prig, but, wrote the eighteenth-century commentator Edmund Lodge, 'he loved his country entirely and devoted himself to it on the only just principles of public service – loyalty to his prince, reverence to religion and submission to the laws. . . . The vast wealth which he inherited in his youth from his father seduced him neither into indolence, debauchery nor pride. His charity was as pure as his patriotism, and as free from vanity as that from ambition.'

The second earl was succeeded by his grandson who was confined to his estates after his involvement in the Essex rebellion, and took little or no part in public life, spending most of his time at Moor Park in Hertfordshire cultivating his garden, although his wife Lucy Harrington, a talented and literary lady, the friend of Ben Jonson and John Donne, expensively ornamented Jacobean society.

The first members of the family to make their home at Woburn were Francis, Lord Russell of Thornhaugh, cousin and heir of the childless third earl, his wife Katherine and their ten young children. The Francis Russells did not go to Bedfordshire from choice, but had fled there in some haste and disarray in August 1625 as refugees from the plague currently raging in London. Neither the first or second earls had taken much interest in Woburn, though the second earl did once entertain Queen Elizabeth there. The third earl would have sold it, had he not been prevented from doing so by his heirs, and the house, already in a bad state of repair, had been left standing empty and neglected.

The Russells did not stay long on that first occasion: as soon as it was safe to do so, they returned to their home in Chiswick. But Francis had evidently seen the possibilities of Woburn, for when he succeeded to the title in 1627, he announced that he intended to make it his principal residence and at once set about the task of restoration. The old decaying abbey buildings were demolished and soon a grand new mansion began to rise on the site.

As well as putting Woburn on its feet, the fourth Earl of Bedford turned his attention to another previously neglected family property, Thorney Abbey in the 'marishy' country east of Peterborough, and by the early 1630s he had embarked on an ambitious drainage programme. 'The earl saw before him the brightest prospects,' wrote a nineteenth-century historian of the area. 'Hope dawned over a dreary waste; in the ardour of his imagination a new world arose to crown his efforts, and enable him to deserve from posterity a monument of its unceasing gratitude and admiration.'

At the time, however, the prospects were often very far from bright. Although the earl was chiefly concerned with draining the southern half of the Great Fen, known today as the Bedford Level, it was still, given the limited technical resources available, an enormous undertaking and was to prove enormously expensive. Thirteen other 'adventurers' or speculators took shares in the project, but it was a long time before either the Russell family or their co-adventurers saw any return on their investment.

Apart from a chronic shortage of capital and the obvious practical difficulties encountered by the Dutch engineer in charge, Cornelius Vermuyden, progress was constantly impeded by fierce local opposition. The fenmen, who lived by summer grazing, fishing and fowling, going about their daily business on stilts, saw their livelihoods threatened by this alien interference. According to the Elizabethan historian William Camden, they were anyway people of 'brutish, uncivilised temper' and they reacted by seizing every opportunity to sabotage the construction of the new drainage channels.

The earl, however, refused to be discouraged and, in spite of every obstacle, Cornelius Vermuyden and his work force, many of them Walloons from Picardy and northern Flanders, laboured grimly on. The work continued into the second half of the century and well beyond the lifetime of the fourth earl, but eventually both the Old and New Bedford Rivers were complete, together with the cut known as Vermuyden's Drain, and as a result some 600,000 acres of reclaimed land were gradually brought into cultivation, so that the prosperity of the fen country today may fairly be said to stand as a monument to the courage and vision of Francis, fourth Earl of Bedford.

Around this time the Russells were also beginning to develop their London property. The original Russell House in the Strand by Temple Bar had been abandoned for the larger and grander Bedford House just across the way, and the fourth earl commissioned Inigo Jones to design a church, dedicated to St Paul, and a handsome piazza in the Italian style on his Covent Garden estate.

The fourth earl's numerous family was now growing up and in 1634 his eldest son returned from the Continent after making the obligatory Grand Tour, a 'handsome and genteel' young man and a most eligible *parti*. William Russell, however, paid no attention to any of the hopeful young ladies being brought to his notice. His mind was already made up and he presently informed his parents that he meant to marry Lady Anne Carr or no one. This was unfortunate, for Anne Carr, though herself a delightful girl, was the daughter of the notorious Countess of Somerset, née Frances Howard, who with her husband had been tried and convicted for the murder of Sir Thomas Overbury. The Bedfords were, not unnaturally, strongly opposed to the connection. The earl refused his consent and went on refusing. Lord William was equally stubborn, the young people remained 'all in a flame with love' and eventually, with many misgivings, his father relented. The marriage took place in July 1637 and proved a triumphant success, Lady William soon winning the affection even of her formidable father-in-law and presenting him with two grandsons in a satisfactorily short space of time.

But although the earl could take comfort from knowing that his family was happily settled and a new generation beginning to grow up, the last years of his life were deeply troubled by the approaching confrontation between king and Parliament. While in favour of constitutional reform, his personal inclinations were for compromise and moderation – he had, after all, too much to lose to want to see matters pushed to extremes. The other moderates had great hopes of him as 'the greatest person of interest in all the popular party, being of the best estate and best understanding of the whole number', and he was prominent in various eleventh-hour attempts to divert the opposing factions from their collision course. For a time the king seemed disposed to listen to his advice, offering to negotiate through him and to make him Lord Treasurer. Had he lived, he might have exercised a restraining influence, 'as he had in truth more authority with the violent of his party than any body else', but instead he succumbed to a fatal attack of smallpox in the hysterical weeks preceeding the Earl of Strafford's execution, and in May 1641 he was borne in state from Bedford House to be laid to rest among his ancestors at Chenies, which remained the family burial place.

The untimely death of the 'Great Earl' of Bedford came just a year before the outbreak of the Civil War, and perhaps he was well out of it. Lord Clarendon certainly thought so. 'He was a wise man,' he wrote in his *History of the Great Rebellion*, 'and would have proposed moderate courses; but he was not incapable, for want of resolution, of being carried into violent ones, if his advice were not submitted to. Therefore, many who knew him well, thought his death not unseasonable, as well to his fame as his fortune.'

William Russell, who now succeeded as fifth earl, played an active, if somewhat erratic part in the fighting. In 1642 he took up an appointment as a general in the Parliamentary army commanded by the Earl of Essex, and was rather embarrassed to find himself called upon to lay siege to Sherborne Castle, home of his sister Anne and her Royalist husband George Digby. In 1643, having failed in an attempt to arrange a peaceful settlement of the war, he changed sides and joined the king at Oxford, but the coldness and suspicion with which he was received soon drove him back into the Essex camp. After this he sensibly abandoned fighting and politics and retired to devote himself to the continuation of his father's work in the fens.

The fifth earl spent the period of the interregnum living quietly at Woburn. The Russells had managed to avoid the financial disaster which struck so many great landed families as a result of the war, but they were still obliged to be cautious for a while as a result of the considerable debts incurred in raising capital both for the fen drainage schemes and speculative building in London. It was, however, only a temporary difficulty. By the mid-1640s the Covent Garden development began to show a steady profit as the Piazza became a fashionable place to live, and by the mid 'fifties the rent-roll from the property amounted to rather more than £1500 a year. The area was already popular with vendors of fruit and vegetables and in 1671 the earl applied for a royal licence to hold a regular market 'within the Piazza at Covent Garden'.

In the late 1660s the earl's second son, another William, began to pay his addresses to Rachel, Lady Vaughan. 'I hope you will excuse me if, having no other means to do it, I trouble you with a little scribbling, to let you know how much I am your servant,' he wrote in 1668. William's courtship was not exactly headlong, but 'I assure you that it has not been for want of inclination to render you my respects, that I have deferred thus long the giving you most humble thanks for your manifold kindnesses and testimonies of affection,' he told the widowed Lady Vaughan, 'but only out of fear not to be able to do it as it ought to be'.

William and Rachel were married the following May and, as well as being an ideally happy marriage, it was to prove a momentous one for London and the Russells, for Rachel, daughter and coheiress of Thomas Wriothesley, fourth and last Earl of Southampton, brought the manors of Bloomsbury and St Giles into her new family.

The couple moved into Southampton House on the Bloomsbury estate and Rachel bore her 'dear lord' two daughters and a son, christened Wriothesley for his grandfather. She wrote to William during one of their rare separations, 'Your boy will please you. You will I think find him improved, though I tell you so beforehand. They fancy he wanted you; for, as soon as I alighted he followed, calling Papa. But I suppose 'tis the word he has most command of, so was not disobliged by the little fellow. The girls were in remembrance of your birthday and we drank your health after a red-deer pie. Would fain be telling my heart more things – anything to be in a kind of talk with him, but I believe the messenger stays for my despatch. 'Tis written in bed, thy pillow at my back, where thy dear head shall lie, I hope, tomorrow night and many more.'

Just two years after that letter was written, William Russell was arrested and charged with complicity in the so-called Rye House Plot – a conspiracy to assassinate King Charles II and his unpopular Catholic brother James, Duke of York, on their way back to London from the Newmarket races. King Charles's government had a long score to settle with William Russell, a vocal and active member of the newly christened Whig opposition party, led by Lord Shaftesbury, which was doing its utmost to wrest political power from the throne and setting the country in an uproar by a crude appeal to sectarian prejudice under its 'No Popery' banner.

William himself, sincerely religious, a little too confident of his own righteousness and at best dangerously naïve, may not have realised that murder was in the air, but he had undoubtedly been dabbling in treason against a king who, he was convinced, would end by leading England into Catholicism and slavery. He was a close friend of the Duke of Monmouth, Charles II's bastard son, who later attempted to raise a Protestant insurrection against James II, and Southampton House had been used as a regular meeting place for the Council of Six, the inner caucus of the opposition, which had for some months been discussing detailed plans for a general insurrection.

Rachel, needless to say, flung herself wholeheartedly into the preparations for her beloved husband's defence. 'Your friends believing I can do you some service at your trial,' she wrote to him in prison, 'I am extreme willing to try. My resolution will hold out. Pray let yours.' And at the trial at the Old Bailey on Friday, 13 July 1683 she sat below him in the court, a touchingly gallant figure, earnestly making notes to help his memory.

William pleaded not guilty to the charges against him, indignantly denying that he had ever been a party to a murder plot. He had 'ever looked upon the assassination of any private person as an abominable, barbarous and inhuman thing, tending to the destruction of all society – how much more would be the assassination of the prince!' As for making or raising rebellion, that was something so abominable and wicked that it had never entered his thoughts. 'I have always been for preserving the government upon the due basis and ancient foundation,' he declared, 'and for having things redressed in a legal, parliamentary way . . . and so I shall be, I am sure, to my dying day, be it sooner or later'.

It was to be sooner, for William Russell was convicted and condemned to death. His family made frantic efforts to save him. The Earl of Bedford is said to have offered £100,000 for a pardon, telling the king that he would think himself, his wife and children happier to be left with but bread and water than lose a dear son for so foul a crime as treason. 'May God incline Your Majesty's heart to the prayers of an afflicted old father and not bring grey hairs with sorrow to my grave.'

Although petitions for clemency poured in and there was some talk of allowing William to go into exile with the Duke of Monmouth – he himself offered to live in any part of the world which might be appointed and never meddle again in the affairs of England – no reprieve was forthcoming. The second Charles Stuart was not normally a vengeful man, but he had suffered a good deal at the hands of William Russell and his friends and he perhaps remembered what many people seem to have forgotten – that three years earlier the stainless Whig patriot had led a particularly vindictive hue and cry against William Howard, Viscount Stafford, a personally dislikable but politically inoffensive Catholic peer, falsely accused of treason by Titus Oates and subsequently executed.

On 20 July William and Rachel said their goodbyes in Newgate Prison, and when she had gone he told Bishop Burnet, 'now the bitterness of death is past'. His execution was a gentlemanly affair. He was driven in his own coach from Newgate to Lincoln's Inn Fields and there beheaded before a large and sympathetic crowd. The corpse, the head having been carefully reattached with a black ribbon band, was later buried in the family vault at Chenies, and for Rachel a long lifetime of mourning had begun. 'My heart . . . cannot be comforted,' she wrote, 'because I have not the dear companion and sharer of all my joys and sorrows. I want him to talk with, to walk with, to eat and sleep with. All these things are irksome to me now; the day unwelcome and the night so too; all company and meals I would avoid, if it might be. When I see my children before me I remember the pleasure he took in them and this makes my heart shrink.'

The old Earl of Bedford also withdrew to the seclusion of Woburn, but five years later he was ready to welcome Dutch William and his wife Mary to the English throne. The Glorious Revolution of 1688, which ousted James II, brought fresh honours to the Russell family which, in the person of Admiral Russell, the earl's nephew and later Earl of Orford, had done a good deal to ensure its success. The new sovereigns quickly reversed the attainder on William Russell, now a national hero, and in 1694 the fifth earl became the first Duke of Bedford, the preamble to the patent of creation explicitly stating that, 'It is not the least that he was father to the Lord Russell, the ornament of his age. . . . Therefore, to solace his excellent father for so great a loss, to celebrate the memory of so noble a man, and to excite his worthy grandson, heir to such mighty hopes, to follow the example of his illustrious father, we entail this high dignity upon the Earl and his posterity.'

The worthy grandson and heir of the new duke was Wriothesley, son of William and Rachel, who now received the courtesy title of Marquess of Tavistock. Rachel had done well by her dear lord's children. The girls married into the families of Cavendish and Manners, both later becoming duchesses, and Wriothesley's wife, although a commoner, was a great heiress. From her father, the prosperous City draper, Elizabeth Howland inherited the manors of Streatham, Tooting Bec and Rotherhithe, while her maternal grandfather was the East India Company tycoon, Josiah Child. The marriage took place at Streatham in 1695 when Wriothesley was fourteen and his bride a year younger, and was solemnised by Bishop Burnet, who had supported William Russell at his execution.

After the ceremony the boy and girl returned to their respective schoolrooms, but during the next five years a close friendship and profitable business partnership grew up between the Russells and the Howlands. Mrs Howland came frequently to stay at Woburn (always paying meticulously for her own and her servants' board), and she and the Duke of Bedford between them planned and financed the building of a wet and dry dock at Rotherhithe. The duke, though now over eighty, also began to interest himself in the lucrative East India trade, taking shares in the company and building two ships of his own in the new Rotherhithe dock, so that when Wriothesley succeeded in September 1700, he was reputed to be the richest peer in England.

But the second duke, 'heir to such mighty hopes', made little impact on the commercial or political scene being, unusually for a Russell, of more artistic and musical tastes. Nor, it must be said, could his son, another Wriothesley, who succeeded in 1711, be considered an ornament to any age. A compulsive gambler, he fell disastrously into the hands of cardsharpers, and Lady John Russell told her grandmother, the Duchess of Marlborough, 'I fancy you will scarcely give credit to it, but it is most certain that he has lost £30,000 at Newmarket at one sitting'.

It was as well for the Russell fortunes that Wriothesley the Second did not long survive such excesses, dying on a therapeutic sea voyage to Lisbon in 1732, when he was still only twenty-four. His younger brother John, sometimes known as 'the merry little Duke', was a far more typical Russell, sturdy, shrewd, strong-minded and well qualified to fill the position of head of a family in the front rank of the Whig aristocracy.

Duke John's first wife, the gentle, consumptive Lady Diana Spencer, died only three years after his succession and in 1737 he married Gertrude Leveson-Gower and brought her home to Bedford House in Bloomsbury Square. The old Bedford House in the Strand had been given up after the first duke's death. The site was becoming unacceptably noisy and, with the development of the Covent Garden estate, too cramped for satisfactory rebuilding, so Southampton House was rechristened and Bloomsbury became the Russells' London headquarters.

The fourth duke led an active public life, holding a string of political appointments – First Lord of the Admiralty, Lord Lieutenant of Ireland and ambassador to France – though he was frequently out of sympathy with the government of the day. A shrewd businessman, he maintained the family connection with the East India trade, as well as investing in the whaling ventures of the Greenland Company. He also found time to enlarge and improve the Woburn estate and early in the 1750s embarked on a major programme of rebuilding and renovation of the Abbey itself, now in a serious state of decay.

His architect was Henry Flitcroft, master carpenter to the board of works, and although the duke insisted on keeping the old north front and the two corner pavilions on the west front unaltered, Flitcroft remodelled the south and east wings and rebuilt the centre of the west front along Palladian lines, as well as designing two new stable blocks. Horace Walpole considered the result to be 'plain like a College', but there was nothing plain about the interior of the new Woburn, where decorators and upholsterers vied with one another to create an atmosphere of opulent luxury using the finest raw materials: the bales of silk, the rolls of Chinese wallpaper, the carpets, porcelain and inlaid furniture which came back to Rotherhithe in the tall ships of the East India Company. A new system of plumbing was also installed, including a water closet for the duke's exclusive use.

The duke spent a good deal of his time commuting between Woburn and Bloomsbury, and the surviving account books give a fascinating picture of life in a grand eighteenth-century town household. In 1753 there were forty servants on the payroll at Bedford House, their wages amounting to nearly six hundred and fifty pounds a year. Changing social habits are reflected in the sums spent on tea, coffee and chocolate and, of course, all the paraphernalia of silver teapots, kettles, spirit lamps and coffeepots which had to be acquired as well. A man in the duke's position was expected to do a good deal of entertaining, and a ball at Bedford House involved Mr Butcher, the agent-in-chief, and his second-in-command, the house steward, in mighty feats of organisation. Extra glasses had to be hired – a guinea for twenty-one dozen on one occasion – while plate was borrowed from friends and neighbours, but the sedan chairmen who carried it to and fro had to be paid and the under-butler at the lending household suitably recompensed for his trouble. Extra footmen, too, were borrowed and received a guinea for an evening's work. Clothes are another recurring item in the accounts. In 1757 six guineas was paid out for a blue hoop petticoat for the duke's daughter, Lady Caroline Russell,and in 1761 the duke himself was obliged to spend nearly thirty pounds on new robes and thirteen pounds two shillings on a coronet for the coronation of King George III.

The fourth duke enjoyed a particularly happy and united home life, and in June 1764 he welcomed a charming daughter-in-law when his much loved only son and heir, by his second wife Gertrude Leveson-Gower, married Lady Elizabeth Keppel. The young couple went to live at Houghton on the Ampthill estate near Woburn. Two sons were born and another baby was on the way when the twenty-eight-year-old Lord Tavistock was thrown from his horse, fractured his skull and died within a fortnight. Barely a year later his heartbroken widow had followed him to the grave, leaving her three little boys to the care of their grandparents. The duke never recovered from the grief and shock of this double bereavement and his last years were further shadowed by his own blindness and infirmity. He died in 1771, to be succeeded by his eldest grandson, Francis, then a child of six.

Following in the liberal Whig tradition of his forebears, the fifth duke grew up to be a close friend of the Prince Regent, and a staunch supporter of Charles James Fox, vigorously denouncing the war with revolutionary France and forming one of a group of five peers who signed a protest against the emergency wartime suspension of habeas corpus in 1794.

Following also in the Russell tradition of devotion to Woburn, he employed the fashionable architect Henry Holland to make further alterations and improvements to the house. A terrace was added to the south front and the chilly north-facing rooms, used by the family since the days of the Great Earl of Bedford, were at last abandoned in favour of new accommodation on the sunny side. Holland also designed a Chinese Dairy, and an indoor riding school and a tennis court were added to the amenities of the abbey.

True to his advanced social principles, Duke Francis allowed the public free access to his park and when one of his acquaintances commented on the loss of privacy this entailed, replied that he considered himself as a steward with the duty of doing the best he could with the money placed in his hands for the benefit of others. 'If I were to shut up this place,' he said, 'many people who enjoy it as much as I do would be shut out of much innocent enjoyment and healthy amusement. . . . If I were to close my gates, from a selfishness of feeling, I, who have a thousand gratifications in my power, should deprive these poor people perhaps of their only one or greatest.'

By the end of the first quarter of the nineteenth century, development of the Bloomsbury estate was virtually complete. It had started back in the 1660s, when Rachel Russell's father, the Earl of Southampton, had built himself a 'little town' in the neighbourhood of Holborn and St Giles. Great Russell Street, linking the new Southampton, later Bloomsbury Square, and its houses with Tottenham Court Lane soon followed, as did further building in Southampton Row and its vicinity, but the area north of Bedford House and Montagu House, which presently became the first British Museum, remained open grazing land until the middle of the 1750s. Then London's first bypass, now the Marylebone and Euston Roads, was constructed and – literally – paved the way for the second stage of the Bloomsbury development.

Planned by the fourth duke, this continued during the minority of his grandson when the Bedford estates were administered by trustees, closely supervised by the strong-minded Dowager Duchess Gertrude (known as the 'Old Begum' by Horace Walpole and his friends). Work on Bedford Square began in 1774, and the long street running parallel with Tottenham Court Road was named Gower Street in honour of the dowager's brother. In 1800 Duke Francis demolished Bedford House to make room for further building in Bloomsbury Square. Russell Square followed in 1805, and Tavistock, Gordon and Woburn Squares had all been laid out by the end of the 1820s. Times have changed and Bloomsbury with them, but enough of those handsome Georgian streets and squares still survive to serve as yet another monument to the enterprise, business acumen and enlightened self-interest of the Russell family.

The London properties naturally formed the most profitable part of the Russell estates, but despite their numerous urban and political preoccupations, the Dukes of Bedford remained countrymen and farmers at heart. In his short lifetime the second duke gained the reputation of being 'a great husbandman' and the fourth duke took the lead in promoting new methods of farming, adopting the four-year rotation system of corn, clover, turnips and fallow at Woburn and using his private resources to initiate valuable programmes of agricultural research. His grandson, the fifth duke, followed in his footsteps, becoming a member of the Board of Agriculture in 1794. He established a three-hundred-acre model experimental farm at Woburn and also instituted annual sheep-shearings and ploughing matches – the forerunners of today's county agricultural shows – which attracted farmers and landowners from all over the country and even from abroad.

The other estates were not neglected – in 1820 Thorney alone was yielding a net income of about £12,000 a year, but Woburn was always the centre of Russell family life, and the sixth duke John Russell, who succeeded his childless brother in 1802, was very much a family man, having three children by his first wife and ten by his second, Lady Georgiana Gordon. He dispensed princely hospitality at the Abbey, which in his day was considered one of the greatest of the English country houses, and Frances Lady Shelley has left a vivid account of an energetic evening spent there in 1812, when after dinner the duchess led a raiding party of girls and young men who pelted the whist players with cushions. 'They defended themselves by throwing cards and candles at her head; but the Duchess succeeded in throwing over the card table, and a regular battle ensued, with cushions, oranges and apples.' The horseplay was finally brought to an end when Lady Jane Montagu was hit in the eye by an apple and nearly blinded.

On a rather more decorous occasion, in the summer of 1841, the young Queen Victoria became the second queen regnant to be entertained at Woburn. 'We are eleven of us Dukes or Duchesses,' wrote Sarah Lyttelton, née Spencer, to her daughter Caroline, 'and most dukefully dull indeed we are. The Queen must carry away with her a strange idea of what society and conversation mean. The material is all very fine. That is, the place is handsome, the house most comfortable and huge, and the dinner also, after a great and unconcealable effort, contrives to be *almost* as sumptuous as our daily fare at Windsor.' Things did improve, though. A musical entertainment helped to pass the time, as did a tour of the house and park. 'The former was interesting,' reported Lady Lyttelton; 'ought to have been more so, but the Queen seems always afraid (like a girl just out of school) of asking questions about pictures and portraits, for fear of being thought ignorant, so the part of the business she liked best was peeping into everybody's own rooms, which are, indeed, the most comfortable and best arranged imaginable, and worth admiring.' Before the visit ended, on 29 July, the High Sheriff of Bedfordshire, 'a burly squire', read the county address to the queen with some difficulty, the wearing of spectacles before royalty being forbidden by etiquette. Her answer was a relief. 'She read it most enchantingly, her pretty emphasis and half smile to the Duke, as she uttered "the noble and patriotic house of Russell" made his eyes glisten, and the good natured Duchess had to hide a tear or two behind a geranium.'

The family's political traditions were now being carried on by Lord John Russell, a younger brother of the seventh duke. Lord John, created first Earl Russell in 1861, was an ardent champion of Parliamentary reform and in 1822 declared that 'the liberties of Englishmen, being founded upon the general consent of all, must remain on that basis, or must altogether cease . . . . We cannot confine liberty in this country to one class of men.' Although he was to enjoy a long and distinguished political career as Home Secretary, Colonial Secretary, Foreign Secretary and Prime Minister, his greatest achievement was undoubtedly the vital part he played in helping to steer the Great Reform Bill through Parliament. His grandson, Bertrand Russell, was another crusader – for progressive education and nuclear disarmament, among other causes – though is probably best known as one of the leading mathematicians and philosophers of his day, and made, in the course of a long lifetime, his own very individual Russell mark on the history of his times.

Throughout the nineteenth century, the Woburn estate continued to lead the way in agricultural methods and research. An experimental farm, set up in 1875 at the expense of the ninth duke, did immensely valuable pioneer work on soil enrichment and fertilisers generally. A fruit farm, established on the same principles twenty years later, was the first of its kind in the country. Despite the slump in British farming and the falling rent-rolls of the seventies and eighties, the Russells maintained their reputation as enlightened landlords. During the tenure of the ninth duke a total of nearly £20,000 pounds was spent on school buildings on the Bedfordshire, Buckinghamshire and Thorney estates, although the passage of the 1870 Education Act had at last made it the responsibility of the state to provide primary education for all.

Herbrand Russell, who succeeded as eleventh duke in 1893, was destined to be the last of the traditional Dukes of Bedford. An exceedingly shy and withdrawn personality, characteristics which were to become more pronounced as he grew older, he applied himself conscientiously, if joylessly, to the business of being a duke and earned a reputation for eccentricity by his stubborn insistence on keeping up all the old ducal state at Woburn until his death early in the Second World War. Duke Herbrand was, perhaps surprisingly, an earnest advocate of land reform, actively encouraging, and helping, his tenant farmers to buy their freeholds. In 1910 he also electrified his fellow peers by speaking against the hereditary principle in the House of Lords. This, however, appears to have been his only venture into politics and, apart from those functions which he deemed to be part of his duty, he shunned all public and social life. Indeed his only interest outside the management of his estates was in stocking the park at Woburn with rare animals and birds, building up herds of threatened species such as Père David's deer and Prejevalski wild horse.

The duke's interest in animals was one of the few hobbies he shared with his wife. He had met and married Mary Tribe, a clergyman's daughter, while serving with the army in India as a young man, but as the years passed husband and wife led increasingly separate lives. The duchess's restless spirit found no fulfilment in the stultifying routine in which the duke took refuge and she sought an outlet for her energies in an astonishing variety of pursuits, which ranged from painting and needlework to ornithology, ice-skating and hospital nursing. She became a crack shot, was the first woman to wear a ride-astride habit, was a pioneering motorist – driving herself without a chauffeur in attendance and doing her own running repairs – and made a number of adventurous bird-watching trips to the far north. But the greatest and most enduring concern of her life was undoubtedly the cottage hospital, which she first opened at Woburn in 1898, and where for more than thirty years, under the name of Sister Mary, she worked devotedly in all departments – from scrubbing floors to acting as surgical nurse and radiographer. During the First World War the riding school and tennis court at the abbey were converted into a military hospital with eighty beds, the duchess working up to sixteen hours a day as administrator and organiser. After the war she reorganised the cottage hospital to take only surgical cases, enticing some of the most eminent surgeons of the day to come and give their services.

In the mid-1920s, when she was already over sixty, the duchess took to the air, finding that the change in atmospheric pressure brought relief from the tinnitus which accompanied her increasing deafness. To begin with she was a passenger only, but this passive role did not satisfy her for long. In 1928 she began to take flying lessons and the following year completed a record breaking flight to India and back in eight days with her instructor Captain Barnard. In 1930 they achieved another notable trip to Cape Town and back in seventeen days, which included two forced landings, and the intrepid co-pilot earned the inevitable nickname, the Flying Duchess. By 1933 she had become a qualified pilot in her own right and in March 1937 took off from Woburn in her De Havilland Gypsy Moth on a short routine journey intended to complete her two hundred hours of solo flying. She never returned and the few pieces of wreckage which were later washed up on the Suffolk coast left no clue as to what had happened, except to show that the duchess, whether deliberately or not, must have turned her little plane out to sea. Her deafness was by this time almost total, her beloved hospital was faced with closure, and she may simply have chosen to seek oblivion in her own way.

Despite their curiously semi-detached relationship, there had been a strong bond of mutual respect and dependence between husband and wife, and the duke, now in his eightieth year, was shattered by the duchess's death. His impenetrable reserve prevented him from taking any comfort from the rest of his family and, in any case, his only son, Hastings, had long since proved an acute disappointment.

A lonely, unhappy child, Hastings Russell had grown up

increasingly alienated from the society and the age into which he had been born. Blindingly sincere and possessing much of the visionary idealism of his cousin Bertrand, he yet had no vestige of the personal magnetism necessary to make an impact on his generation, or any impression on what he called the 'Appalling Stupidity of the Ordinary Person'. Nevertheless, with true Russell determination – or pigheadedness – he struggled on, dedicating his life to charitable work and the promotion of the various causes in which he believed. These included monetary reform, international brotherhood and, of course, pacificism.

It was his pacificism which had led to the break with his father at the beginning of the 1914–18 war, a period which Hastings spent contentedly washing up at a YMCA canteen at Portsmouth. The rupture was so complete, that the present Duke of Bedford tells in his autobiography how he himself was sixteen years old before he discovered, through a chance conversation with a chatty parlourmaid, that he was Duke Herbrand's grandson and eventual heir to the title. As a result, young John Russell – or Ian, as he was known in the family – made a few brief formal visits to Woburn, but never succeeded in establishing anything approaching ordinary human contact with his grandparents.

The old duke died in 1940. His wealth and his obstinacy had enabled him to hold the twentieth century at bay, but he was well aware that he was as much of a threatened species as the Père David's deer roaming his park. The hungry predators of war and social change were already prowling at the gates of Woburn, and his death brought them heavy-footed into the house itself.

The twelfth duke never lived in the abbey, which was occupied by an ultra-secret government department throughout the Second World War. He did what he could to manage the estate, although he knew next to nothing about it, and was further hampered by battles with the War Agriculture Committee, which strongly disapproved of precious, strictly rationed fodder being wasted on the bison, wapiti and other inedible denizens of the park. However, Russell stubbornness prevailed, and enough breeding stock was preserved to ensure the long-term survival of these irreplaceable herds. Less admirable was the new duke's refusal to part with the iron railings in his Bloomsbury squares to help the war effort – a futile gesture of defiance which resulted in reprisals by angry

Londoners. His persistent dissemination of anti-war propaganda also gave rise to suspicions that his enthusiasm for the brotherhood of man extended to the country's enemies so that he attracted much adverse press publicity, as well as the unfriendly notice of the Home Secretary.

With the return of peace, Duke Hastings planned to restore his ancestral home which was once more in a very bad state of repair. The whole of the east wing was riddled with dry rot and had to be demolished, together with the riding school and tennis court. Work proceeded slowly, complicated by further acrimonious disputes with officialdom over building licences, and was still unfinished in October 1953 when the duke died as the result of a shooting accident on the Devonshire estate.

His elder son, rejected as unfit for military service, had meanwhile been supporting himself as a rent collector for a firm of estate agents, a journalist on the *Sunday Express* and director of an Indian based export-import agency. In 1947, after a harrowing tragedy in his private life and finding himself permanently estranged from his father, he decided to try and make a new life outside England, and with his second wife, Lydia Lyle *née* Yarde-Buller, left for South Africa, where he embarked on a career as a fruit farmer in Cape Province. This happy and relatively carefree existence came to an end in the spring of 1954, when John Russell brought his family home and started to face up to the realities of being thirteenth Duke of Bedford.

The prospect was not encouraging. The break-up of the Russell estates had begun when the eleventh duke disposed of Covent Garden, Thorney and the Bedford Level. Now Chenies had to be sold to help meet a bill for death duties amounting to around four and a half million pounds, and it seemed more than doubtful whether Woburn itself could be saved.

The duke's first visit there shortly after his father's death had been, in his own words, 'a shattering experience'. 'The abbey,' he wrote, 'looked as if a bomb had fallen on it. . . . There were piles of stones and building materials lying in a haphazard fashion all over the place, and the courtyard in the centre of the house was full of Nissen huts. . . . The interior was freezing cold and desolate. It looked as if it belonged to a series of bankrupt auction rooms. . . . There were beautiful Louis XV chairs with kitchen-table legs straight through the seat; the walls and cornices were peeling and everything was covered in dust and filthy. The whole house reeked of damp. It looked as if no general maintenance work had been done at all . . . and after one quick tour I despaired of ever breathing life into the place again.'

But he did not despair for long. Despite the fact that he had no happy childhood memories of Woburn, or indeed any happy memories of it at all, the thirteenth duke made up his mind that the abbey must at all costs be kept in the family and strenuously resisted proposals that it should be handed over to the National Trust. It was his belief that, 'if a place like Woburn means anything in terms of history and tradition, then it is only because of the personal identification with it of the family that has built it up'.

It was obvious, though, that if the house were to be kept, it would have to be made to pay for itself. The complexities of successive family trusts had given the duke's trustees complete power of veto over every item of capital expenditure and they now had to be persuaded, rather against their better judgement, to sanction the initial outlay necessary to turn the abbey into a public showplace. The duke and his wife, helped by a handful of devoted estate workers and personal staff, themselves undertook the enormous task of cleaning up, clearing and sorting out the chaos indoors.

'Any friends who were unwise enough to come and see how we were getting on', the duke remembered, 'were immediately shanghaied as working parties or made to help with the washing-up of the vast collection of filth-encrusted china and glass that kept being turned up in nooks and crannies, not only in the house but in outlying buildings as well.' A treasure which turned up in one of Flitcroft's stable blocks was the Sèvres dinner service, presented to the fourth duke and duchess at the time of their embassy to Paris. Unwilling to give the responsibility to anyone else, the thirteenth duke and duchess nervously washed and dried all eight-hundred-odd priceless pieces themselves.

Woburn Abbey opened its door in April 1955 and the venture was an immediate, runaway success. In that first year 181,000 visitors passed through the gates and the abbey has remained in the top league of the stately homes business ever since. It is, of course, a most beautiful house and contains a glorious collection of art treasures amassed by the Russell family over the centuries, but it undoubtedly owes its immense and lasting popularity with the general public to the duke's determination to 'give the people what they want'. Quite undeterred by accusations of commercialism, he set out to do just that and people who are uninterested in pictures, even by the greatest artists, who are unmoved by Chinese porcelain of the K'anghsi period, eighteenth-century French furniture or family history can still be assured of a warm welcome and a good day out at Woburn.

From the very beginning there was a 'fun for all the family' atmosphere, with a children's playground and zoo, boating on the lake and a good cup of tea. Soon other attractions and amenities were added, including a funfair, drives round the park in a coach and four, licensed restaurants, an antiques centre, galleries for arts and crafts and an exhibition centre. The abbey also became a favourite venue for special events of all kinds – scooter, traction engine and caravan rallies, jazz festivals, Elizabethan banquets, beauty contests and fashion shows. Many other stately home owners now offer their visitors additional attractions – the lions at Longleat and the motor museum at Beaulieu, for example – and safari parks and pop festivals have become almost commonplace. But Woburn blazed the trail, and in the 1950s the thirteenth Duke of Bedford's unashamedly 'popular' approach was something quite revolutionary.

For almost twenty years the duke threw himself heart and soul into the business of 'selling Woburn to the world'. He made television appearances, gave lectures and went on promotional trips abroad, seeking publicity wherever it was to be found without regard for his ducal dignity. As he said himself, 'if you take your dignity to a pawnbroker he won't give you much for it'. In his campaign to preserve his inheritance by sharing it with as many people as possible, he wooed coach and tour operators, shook hands and chatted tirelessly with the payers of half-crowns, and was constantly on the lookout for new and imaginative ideas which would keep the customers coming back for more. It is an astonishing story of enterprise, dedication and sheer, gruelling hard work. As a result, although nearly all the once vast Russell estates have now been dispersed, Woburn Abbey with its three thousand acres of parkland has been saved for the enjoyment of the nation and the family, for whom it is still a home.

In the mid 1970s John Duke of Bedford retired to live in the South of France with his third wife, the former film producer Nicole Milinaire, handing over the running of the family business to his eldest son, Robin. This move was something of a shock to the present Marquess of Tavistock who had always expected that the running of Woburn would leapfrog to *his* eldest son – the age difference between himself and his father being only twenty-three years – and he had meanwhile embarked on a career in the City, becoming a partner in one of the largest firms of stockbrokers, the chairman of an investment trust and a director of Trafalgar House. Since moving to Woburn he has added two championship golf courses and built his wife, the former Henrietta Tiarks, a stud in the park, thus re-establishing the Bedford racing silks on the British turf. (The seventh duke, in fact, won the Derby three times, and on one occasion with an unnamed horse.)

Fifteen generations and nearly five hundred years have passed since the first John Russell, great-grandson of a Weymouth wine-shipper, left the Dorset countryside to make his career and his fortune in the king's service. During that time the family he founded has thrown up its quota of eccentrics and misfits – as well as the odd genius – among the sober politicians, diplomats and agriculturists. It has made an important and valuable contribution to the life of the community and still has a special place in the rich variety of the English social scene. The family flair for publicity keeps it regularly in the public eye and the colour supplements – Lord Tavistock's latest project is the organising of an exhibition of goats and 'goatabilia' (a goat figures on the ducal crest) and he is also breeding a herd of miniature Cameroon goats to add to the attractions of the Park at Woburn. One way and another, England would be a sadder and poorer place without the Russells of Woburn.

The Spencers of Althorp

Dieu defend le droit

John 5th Earl Spencer by Sir Francis Carruthers Gould *National Portrait Gallery*

The Spencers of Althorp

Dieu defend le droit

ON 20 July 1639 there was a wedding at Penshurst Place in Kent. The bride was Lady Dorothy Sidney and the groom Henry, third Baron Spencer of Wormleighton in the county of Warwick.

They were an exceptionally attractive and promising pair. Lady Dorothy, eldest daughter of Robert Sidney Earl of Leicester, came of a line of courtiers, soldiers, diplomats and administrators who had served their country nobly throughout the Elizabethan Age and was a very lovely girl – the Sacharissa so eloquently adored by the poet Edmund Waller. Dorothy Sidney also possessed great charm, intelligence and sweetness of nature, being admired by her contemporaries for her 'wit and discretion' as well as her good looks and long remembered by those who knew her as the ideal type of great lady.

Much anxious thought had naturally been devoted to the marriage of this paragon of maidenly modesty, beauty and grace, and several suitors had been considered by the family, among them Lord William Russell, the Earl of Bedford's heir, the young Earl of Devonshire and Lord Lovelace. But William Russell had already set his heart on Lady Anne Carr, the Devonshires were curiously lukewarm and Lord Lovelace, whose claims were strongly pressed by Lady Leicester's brother the Earl of Northumberland, was rejected by Dorothy and her mother on the grounds of his addiction to bad company, drunkenness and debauchery. Nothing but the best was good enough for Doll and Lady Leicester wrote to her husband, 'My dear Hart, let not these cross accidents trouble you, for we do not know what God has provided for her.'

As it turned out, God provided Henry Spencer, who appeared to combine all the qualities of character, rank and fortune demanded by the fastidious Lady Dorothy and her careful parents.

The Spencers claimed to be able to trace their pedigree from Robert Despencer, cupbearer to the Conqueror, but in the mid-seventeenth century they were still a comparatively 'new' family, owing their position to the shrewd business sense of John, son of William Spencer of Rodbourne in Warwickshire, who, some hundred and fifty years earlier, had taken note of the rising price of wool and the profits to be made from converting arable land to pasture and sheep-rearing. In 1506 John Spencer bought the manor of Wormleighton and two years later he acquired the neighbouring estate of Althorp in Northamptonshire. His grandson, another John, further increased the family fortunes by marrying Katherine Kytson, eldest daughter of a prosperous City merchant who was related to the Washingtons of Sulgrave. It was this John Spencer who enlarged and modernised the medieval moated manor house at Althorp. He married his daughters into the aristocracy and was several times Sheriff and Knight of the Shire for Northampton.

By the beginning of the new century, Robert, fifth in line of succession from the first John Spencer, owned enormous flocks and broad acres and was reputed to be one of the richest men in England. In July 1603 he was raised to the peerage as Baron Spencer of Wormleighton, being just the type of wealthy county magnate the Crown most needed to attach to its interest, and later made his presence felt in the House of Lords by quarrelling with the Earl of Arundel. Robert's son William married Penelope Wriothesley, daughter of that Earl of Southampton who had once been William Shakespeare's patron, and their son, named Henry for his maternal grandfather, succeeded as third Baron Spencer in December 1636.

As well as being an exceedingly rich young man, Henry Spencer had inherited the good looks and cultivated tastes of his mother's family. He was studious, thoughtful and serious minded beyond his years, showed no signs of addiction to debauchery and altogether seemed 'a most happy match' for the exquisite Sacharissa.

Dorothy was twenty-three, Henry just nineteen at the time of their marriage, and the bride's old admirer Edmund Waller took up his pen to write in jocular vein to her younger sister Lucy:

> May my Lady Dorothy (if we may yet call her so) suffer as much and have the like passion for this young Lord whom she has preferred to the rest of mankind, as others have had for her! . . . May she, that always affected silence and retiredness, have the house filled with the noise and number of her children; and hereafter, of her grandchildren! And then may she arrive at the great curse, so much declined by fair ladies – old age! . . . And when she shall appear to be mortal, may her Lord not mourn for her, but go hand in hand with her to that place where we are told there is neither marrying nor giving in marriage; that being there divorced, we may all have an equal interest in her again!

Waller's last wish for Sacharissa and her Lord was to be cruelly mocked by fate, but in the 'common joy at Penshurst' in the high summer of 1639 the future looked bright with hope.

After the wedding Lord Leicester returned to his post as ambassador in Paris and was joined in the autumn by his wife, his two next daughters and 'my new son-in-law and his wife'.The young Spencers remained in France for two years and there, in the summer of 1640, Dorothy gave birth to her first child, a girl also christened Dorothy. A son, Robert, followed a year later. Her third child, another girl, was born in 1642, but by this time the family had returned to England where the confrontation between king and Parliament was fast approaching the point of no return.

Henry Spencer was no courtier and his political sympathies were inclined to be radical, but he was soon alienated by the violence of the Parliamentary party, declaring that no power on earth would ever induce him to draw his sword against the king. During his brief career in the House of Lords he joined the group of loyal peers, led by Lord Falkland, who were still vainly trying to heal the breach and, when the moment of decision arrived in the summer of 1642, young Lord Spencer was among the thirty-two peers who rode to join the king at York.

He plainly hated the whole business, dreading the consequences of a royalist victory almost as much as those of a Parliamentary one but, as he wrote to Dorothy from Shrewsbury in September, 'unless a man were reduced to fight on the Parliament side, than which, for my part, I had rather be hanged, it will be said without doubt that a man is afraid to fight. If there could be an expedient found, to save the punctilio of honour, I would not continue here an hour. The discontent that I, and many other honest men, receive daily is beyond expression.'

A month later Spencer was present on the field at Edgehill, having entertained Prince Rupert at Wormleighton on the eve of the battle. In the lull in the fighting which followed he was able to get leave of absence to see his family at Penshurst, where his second daughter, Penelope, had just been born, but by the spring of 1643 he was back with the king at Oxford and in June was created Earl of Sunderland in consideration, so it is believed, of a large loan to the royal exchequer.

The new earl was now hoping to be able to send for Dorothy and the children to join him, but before this could be arranged the army was off to lay siege to Gloucester. He wrote on 25 August.

> My dearest Hart,
>
> Just as I was coming out of the trenches on Wednesday, I received your letter of the 20th of this instant, which gave me so much satisfaction that it put all the inconveniences of this siege out of my thoughts. At that instant, if I had followed my own inclinations, I had returned an answer to yours; writing to you, and hearing from you, being the most pleasant entertainment that I am capable of in any place.

He was quartered, he told her, in one of the many little private cottages scattered about the country, and its solitariness made a welcome change from the noise of the trenches, the 'tin-tamarre of guns and drums', and the distressing sights and sounds of dead and wounded men. It also made him often reflect 'how infinitely more happy I should esteem myself quietly to enjoy your company at Althorp, than to be troubled with the noises and engaged in the actions of the Court, which I shall ever endeavour to avoid. . . .' One more letter survives, written from Oxford on 16 September, in which he sends his blessing to 'Popet', his three-year-old daughter, tells Dorothy he has such a bad cold that he does nothing but sneeze, and signs himself 'most passionately and perfectly yours'.

Four days later he was killed at the first Battle of Newbury. 'A lord of great fortune, tender years – being not above three-and-twenty years of age – and an early judgement; who, having no command in the army, attended upon the King's person under the obligation of honour; and putting himself that day in the King's troop as a volunteer, was taken away by a cannon bullet.'

They brought the news to Dorothy, waiting at Penshurst for the birth of her fourth child. She and her mother clung together in the first agony of bereavement, and her father wrote to his 'deare Doll':

> I know you lived happily and so as no one but yourself could measure the contentment of it. . . . That now is past, and I will not flatter you so much as to say I think you can ever be so happy in this life again; but this comfort you owe me, that I may see you bear this change and your misfortune patiently. . . . [For her dead husband's sake she must take care of those he had loved so tenderly – herself and the children] They all have need of you, and one especially, whose life as yet doth absolutely depend on yours.

The baby, another son, was born safely some three weeks later, but in March 1649 Dorothy had to face another grief when, as Lord Leicester recorded in his journal: 'The sweet little boy, Harry Spencer, my grandchilde, five years old from October last, died at Leicester House.'

The widowed countess remained with her parents until after the end of the Civil War and in the autumn of 1650 went to live at Althorp, where her portrait by Vandyck still hangs, to devote herself to bringing up her two daughters and Robert, who had succeeded to the earldom when he was barely two years old.

The second Earl of Sunderland grew into a handsome, brilliant, wayward young man. In 1663, the year after he came of age, he was about to be married to Lady Anne Digby but at the last moment when, as Samuel Pepys heard, 'the wedding clothes were made, and portion and everything agreed upon and ready', my lord suddenly changed his mind. He went away, 'nobody yet knows whither', sending a message to his fiancée breaking off the engagement and telling his friends he had had enough of it. They could say what they liked about him 'so that they do not demand the reason of his leaving her, being resolved never to have her'.

Dorothy was left with the embarrassing task of picking up the pieces, while her son disported himself in Spain and Italy with his uncle Henry Sidney, only a year older than himself, and other congenial spirits. Nevertheless he presently began to regret his impetuous jilting of Lady Anne and to petition for forgiveness. 'All I can allege of him', wrote his mother loyally, 'is that often rebels have turned to be good subjects, and libertines the best Christians, and that I believe he will be as true a convert in his kind as any of them. . . .' The Digbys allowed themselves to be placated. The marriage eventually took place in 1665 and turned out happily and well, despite the strains it was put to throughout the earl's chequered political career.

The earl now embarked on an ambitious rebuilding programme at Althorp. Already a seasoned European traveller, he was determined to transform the old Elizabethan house into a little Italianate palace, and at the end of the 1660s the Grand Duke of Tuscany described it as the best planned and best arranged country seat for its size that he had seen in England. Inside, a magnificent staircase of polished walnut ascended to the piano nobile – 'this staircase dividing itself into two equal branches leads to the grand saloon, from which is the passage into the chambers, all of them regularly disposed after the Italian manner'.

The diarist John Evelyn, who came on a visit of inspection in 1675, was also pleased to approve. The setting was delightful, 'a pretty open bottom, very finely watered and flanked with stately woods and groves'. The house itself, in the form of a half 'H' and built in the modern style of red brick dressed with the local Weldon stone, was 'nobly furnished' within, the original long gallery having been repanelled and used to house the earl's growing collection of pictures. Outside, the moat had been drained and turfed, and Evelyn particularly admired 'the several ample gardens, furnished with the choicest fruit and exquisitely kept'.

All this splendour, though, had to be paid for. Thanks to the influence of Dorothy Sidney's Parliamentarian brothers, Philip and Algernon, the Spencer estates had escaped a heavy delinquency fine after the Civil War, but they had suffered from the general disorganisation and high taxation of the war years, while the Tudor manor house at Wormleighton had been destroyed in the fighting. And the second earl was a man of expensive tastes, a compulsive gambler and spendthrift with no idea of management, as he himself confessed. He was soon in serious financial trouble and, as a result, began to consider a career in the royal service.

In 1671 Sunderland went as an envoy extraordinary to Madrid and subsequently to Paris, but these diplomatic adventures did nothing to improve his financial position. On the contrary, his debts and constant demands for supplies became an embarrassment to the government and he returned home under something of a cloud. He spent most of the next five years hanging on at court, hoping to be given another job, sponging on his friends and making himself agreeable to anyone whose patronage might be useful.

His chance came at last in the emergency caused by the Popish Plot. Sunderland had a number of potentially valuable connections with the opposition or Country Party – the Earl of Shaftesbury was his uncle by marriage, Lord Halifax was his brother-in-law and his wife's mother had been a Russell. He would, therefore, be qualified to act as a mediator with Shaftesbury's dreaded Green Ribbon Club if all else failed. He was still a relatively insignificant figure who had not yet offended anyone (an omission he more than made up for later on) and in February 1679, the much harassed Charles II confirmed his appointment as a secretary of state.

Having achieved office, he clung to it with the tenacity of one who could not afford the luxury of a conscience. In order to keep his influence with the Catholic James II, he began to flirt with Catholicism himself, and the Princess Anne, who loathed both the Sunderlands – she was the greatest jade, he 'the subtillest workinest villain that is on the face of the earth' – told her sister, the Princess of Orange, that, 'to complete all his virtues,' the earl was working with all his might to bring in popery. 'He is perpetually with the Priests, and stirs up the King to do things faster than I believe he would of himself.'

But it was not until James's queen unexpectedly gave birth to a son, so unexpectedly that it gave rise to the legend of a baby smuggled in in a warming pan, that Sunderland publicly announced his conversion to Rome. It did him no good. Distrusted by the Catholics and reviled by the Protestants, he was dismissed from his post in October 1688 and in December – the month after William of Orange landed at Torbay – he fled precipitately to

Holland, where he proceeded to publish a long-winded justification of his inglorious part in the Glorious Revolution.

'My greatest misfortune', he declared, 'has been to be thought the promoter of things I opposed and detested . . . and I was often foolishly willing to hear what my master would have done, though I used all possible endeavours against it.' He now had leisure to reflect on the cause of his present afflictions – the loose, negligent, unthinking life he had hitherto led, 'having been perpetually hurried away from all good thoughts by pleasure, idleness, the vanities of the Court, or by business'.

In his Dutch exile Sunderland became an ostentatious member of the congregation at the Protestant church and in March 1689 he wrote to the new King William III, saying that if he had followed his own sense rather than the advice of his friends, he would never have left England, but nothing made him regret his absence so much 'as that I could not give my vote for placing Your Majesty on the throne, as I would have done with as much joy and zeal as any man alive'.

The whole letter reeks of the anxiety of one who fears he has left it too late to declare for the winning side, and the earl's antics during this period of his life not surprisingly earned him a lasting reputation for double-dealing, time-serving and hypocrisy, if not actual treachery. More likely, though, he had just panicked. Seventeenth-century politicians needed strong nerves, cool heads and iron digestions, and Sunderland, naturally volatile and highly strung, with 'too much heat both of imagination and passion' as one contemporary put it, appears to have cracked under an intolerable strain.

In 1690 he was allowed to return home with his long-suffering wife, who had stood by him through banishment and disgrace. They went back to Althorp, but in spite of everything the earl had not yet finished with the vanities of the court or its business, for three years later he was called out of retirement to serve as King William's political manager.

In 1698 he was preoccupied with family matters. Of his five children, two daughters were now dead, as was his elder son Robert, after a life apparently entirely devoted to gambling, duelling and drink. There remained Charles, born in 1674, 'a youth of extraordinary hopes', and his parents were now trying to negotiate a marriage for him with Anne Churchill, the Earl of Marlborough's younger and favourite daughter.

The Churchills had reservations about the match. The Spencer finances were still precarious, while Charles himself held some dangerously extreme opinions. He had become a violent, doctrinaire Whig and, according to Jonathan Swift, 'would often, among his familiar friends, refuse the title of lord, swear he would never be called otherwise than Charles Spencer, and hoped to see the day when there should not be a peer in England'.

His mother, rather as the first Lady Sunderland had once had to do, tried to reassure his prospective in-laws. 'He is very good natured and strictly honest,' she wrote to Lady Marlborough, 'and the heats that he shows – though I don't pretend to excuse them – I am certain proceed from an honest heart that has had the misfortune to fall into the acquaintance of a party that are of a crucifying temper.'

But although the countess might have felt certain that Charles's faults were due to no more than youthful impetuosity, soon cured by a little experience, the Marlboroughs were not easily convinced and the matter hung fire for some time. However, the marriage was eventually arranged and took place during the first week of the new century. It was to have momentous consequences for the Spencer family, but the second Earl of Sunderland did not live to see them. He had remained an influential, if consistently unpopular figure on the political scene, famed for his arrogance, his cynicism, his bitter tongue and his 'Court tune', an affected nasal drawl possibly cultivated to camouflage a speech impediment: 'Whaat maatters who saarves his Majesty, so lang as his Majesty is saarved?' He retired from public life for the last time in 1702 and died that September, safe in the bosom of the Church of England. His wife, always a devout Anglican, was able to tell her old friend John Evelyn that during near a month's sharp pains and tedious sickness he never showed the least impatience and called for prayers twice a day 'to which he did attend with a very great devotion'. The great apostate was laid to rest in the parish church at Great Brington where, all those years ago, his father's heart had been carried from the battlefield at Newbury.

Charles Spencer succeeded to the earldom, apparently untroubled by any scruples about titles, although he remained a fanatical and outspoken Whig and played a prominent part in government until his death at the age of forty-eight. In 1720, in an attempt to liquidate part of the national debt, he was responsible for granting special concessions to the South Sea Company – an enterprise having a monopoly of trade in the Pacific. As a result, the value of its hundred-pound shares shot up to a thousand pounds, triggering off a wild orgy of speculation. By August the South Sea Bubble had burst. Thousands of small investors were ruined in the stock market crash which followed and Sunderland was forced to resign his office as First Lord of the Treasury, although he had made no personal financial profit out of his scheme. A connoisseur like his father, he amassed a famous library said to be the finest in Europe, and also inherited his father's extravagance, love of gambling and irritable temper. His wife, by all accounts a girl of great charm and intelligence, supported him in his politics, but failed to restrain his gaming and overspending. She died, sadly, in her early thirties of what was described as 'a pleuritic fever', leaving a young family to be brought up by her mother, the famous and formidable Sarah, now Duchess of Marlborough.

Of all her grandchildren, it was Anne's youngest daughter Diana who held the first place in Sarah's heart. The duchess doted on 'dearest Di', but her dislike of George II and Queen Caroline and her unconcealed loathing of the prime minister, Sir Robert Walpole, were to cause her to involve Lady Diana in a remarkable piece of plotting with the unappetising Frederick, Prince of Wales, who was already on the worst of terms with his parents.

According to Horace Walpole, writing some fifty years later

> Money he soon wanted and old Sarah, Duchess of Marlborough, ever proud and ever malignant, was persuaded to offer her favourite granddaughter, Lady Diana Spencer, to the Prince of Wales with a fortune of a hundred thousand pounds. He accepted the proposal and the day was fixed for their being secretly married at the Duchess's Lodge in the Great Park at Windsor. Sir Robert Walpole got intelligence of the project, prevented it, and the secret was buried in silence.

A piece of gossip perhaps, but a fascinating footnote to history. No one knows what Lady Diana herself thought of the scheme, but it was lucky for her that nothing came of it. Instead, in 1731 she married John Russell, younger brother of the third Duke of Bedford, with a dowry of £30,000 provided by her grandmother. Sarah took a close interest in the young couple's affairs and, after paying a visit of inspection to their newly decorated town house in Grosvenor Street, warned Diana, who was now pregnant: 'If you come into a room that is but just washed, you will get a cold which will be very troublesome to you at this time. I don't doubt but that you'll take care not to lie upon a new feather bed and to have all the quilts well aired.'

Lady John Russell, who became Duchess of Bedford shortly after receiving this piece of grandmotherly advice, seems to have been an exceptionally sweet-natured girl – a least she was the only member of the family who managed never to quarrel with Sarah – and the cantankerous old lady began to call her Cordelia, 'which I think is the name of King Lear's good child, and therefore a proper title for you, who have been always good to me'.

Some years earlier, Sarah had acquired a property in Wimbledon, where she built a house intended for Diana. In 1735, after all the rows with architects and workmen which always attended the Duchess's projects, she was happily occupied putting the finishing touches to her creation and wrote to her granddaughter on 24 June: 'I have now full employment in furnishing Wimbledon, and it is a great pleasure and amusement to be dressing up and making a place pretty that I designed for my dear Cordelia. The furniture I think extremely handsome and will be almost all new.'

Diana's first baby had died at birth, but that summer she believed she was pregnant again and once more her grandmother was ready with advice. 'I hope you will continue to drink but very little wine; for I have reason to think that is a right method from several accounts I have heard of women that miscarried till they tried that way of drinking a great deal of water and sometimes milk.'

It was soon obvious that all was not well, and Sarah wrote again anxiously at the end of July: 'I am extremely uneasy at the account my dear Cordelia gives of her being so sick – you call it a perpetual sickness at your stomach – because that is something that I never heard of before. It is mighty common to have people sick in a morning, vomit sometimes, and till they are half gone with child have no inclination to eat anything. But to have a perpetual sickness in the stomach is what I have never heard of and therefore hope you will give me a better account in your next.'

Sarah wanted her dearest Di to get as much fresh air as possible and arranged to send her the tent which the great Duke of Marlborough had used on his campaigns. But neither her grandfather's famous tent nor her grandmother's tender solicitude could help Diana. She died that September of a 'galloping consumption' at the age of twenty-five and Sarah, typically enough, sought relief from her distress by picking a series of furious quarrels with the widowed Duke of Bedford.

Two years earlier there had been a considerable change in the fortunes of the Spencer family. With the death of John Duke of Marlborough in 1722 the Churchill family had died out in the male line and the duke's eldest daughter, Henrietta, became duchess in her own right. When she died in 1733, her son having predeceased her, the dukedom, together with Blenheim and the Marlborough estates, passed to Anne Churchill's eldest surviving son – Charles Spencer, Earl of Sunderland. It was not until 1817 that his grandson, the fifth duke, revived the old Churchill name by royal licence.

Duchess Sarah disapproved of Charles Spencer, whom she considered weak, vain and extravagant, but his younger brother John, an engaging scamp, was another of her favourites – she had told Diana that she thought he had 'good nature, sense, frankness in his temper (which I love) and, in short, a great many desirable things about him'. As Charles was to succeed as Duke of Marlborough, it had been settled in the family that Althorp and the Spencer estates should fall to John and he also became the principal legatee in Sarah's will. This was a honeyfall for the Spencers, as Sarah was an extremely rich old lady and John, or Jack Spencer as he was usually known, inherited her estate at St Albans, a great deal more landed property, cash, pictures and plate, together with many of her personal possessions which are still at Althorp. Jack Spencer was every bit as extravagant as his brother, but he did not live long enough to run through his grandmother's money. Indeed he only survived her by two years, dying at the age of thirty-eight because, according to Horace Walpole, 'he would not be abridged of these invaluable blessings of an English subject – Brandy, Small Beer and Tobacco'.

His son, another John, who was only twelve when his father

died, was considered a very delicate child, but he survived to become the first Earl Spencer, owing his peerage to the recommendation of the elder William Pitt. He appears to have inherited quite a few of the family characteristics, as his grandson the third Earl Spencer, was later to recall in a fragment of autobiography:

> My mother . . . told me that my grandfather's manners, when he wished to please, were so fascinating that it was scarcely possible to resist his influence; at the same time, she mentioned many instances which proved that he had no command of temper whatever. From what is indeed notorious, he must have been a man who never put any restraint upon himself. He succeeded to an enormous property in money, as well as land, before he was of age; and he died at forty-nine years old, very much in debt. He spent extravagantly large sums in contested elections . . . and he played very deep.

The unconventional marriage of Earl – then still plain Mister – Spencer to Georgiana, daughter of Stephen Poyntz, took place at Althorp on 27 December 1755, the day he came of age. He informed her father that he was determined to make her his wife as soon as he was master of himself and was as good as his word, carrying out his plan so secretively that, although there were fifty guests in the house at the time, no one knew what was happening. 'On the 27th December, after tea, the parties necessary for the wedding stole by degrees from the company, into Lady Cowper's dressing-room, where the ceremony was performed,' wrote Miss Granville, afterwards Mrs Delany, to her sister Ann, 'and they returned different ways to the company again, and joined dancing with them. After supper, everybody retired as usual to their different apartments. Miss Poyntz and her sister lay, from their first going to Althorp, in the best apartments, and Miss Louisa resigned her place on this occasion.'

The marriage was a happy one and produced three children – all destined to make their mark on the history of their times – Georgiana, later the famous and fascinating Duchess of Devonshire, whose total inability to understand the value of money was to cause her so much unhappiness; Harriet, her intelligent and devoted sister, who married the Earl of Bessborough, and a son, named George John. Earl Spencer had built himself a town house in St James's Place, and he and his wife were indefatigable travellers, following the second Lord Sunderland's example by bringing pictures and statuary back from Italy, but their only son was born in September 1758 at the house in Wimbledon which old Sarah Churchill had once so enjoyed making pretty for her dear Cordelia.

George John, who received the courtesy title of Viscount Althorp on his father's elevation, was educated at Harrow and Trinity College Cambridge, and made the obligatory European Grand Tour before taking his seat in the Commons as member for Northampton, which he occupied until he succeeded to the earldom in 1783. Although brought up in the family Whig tradition and closely connected with the so-called Devonshire House Set, the second Earl Spencer crossed over into the Tory camp on the outbreak of the war with republican France and became one of Mr Pitt's most valued supporters.

The earl was appointed First Lord of the Admiralty at a time when the safety of the nation depended entirely on the strength of the navy, and in the spring of 1797 he found himself faced with the makings of an appalling crisis on the ships of the Channel Fleet. On 17 April he informed George III 'of intelligence received in the course of yesterday and this morning from Portsmouth of representations from the companies of your Majesty's ships at Spithead on the very delicate subject of an increase of pay, which appears to have been brought forward and enforced in an unpleasant manner'. Lord Spencer therefore thought it his duty himself to go down at once 'in order to take such measures as may appear the most advisable for putting a stop to, and if necessary, for redressing the grievance complained of without suffering the disaffection which seems to have arisen to proceed any further'.

The naval mutinies at Spithead and the Nore rocked the country to its foundations. Many people were convinced that they heralded bloody revolution and the establishment of a 'system of terror' on the French pattern. Even so, no reasonable person could deny that the sailors did have a genuine grievance and Spencer told Lord St Vincent that their wages were 'undoubtedly too low in proportion to the times'. An ordinary seaman was paid nineteen shillings a month and that was frequently months in arrears. The First Lord was also surprised that 'the purser's deduction [the purser's customary perquisite of an eighth of all rations] and the system of short weights and measures depending on it, should have been so long tolerated'. But while he could sympathise with seamen forced to leave their families to starve on a pittance while they served their country in conditions often of incredible hardship, Lord Spencer still clung to the comforting conviction that 'this business has certainly originated from the admission of some mischievous plotting persons into the fleet'. He remained convinced that the troublemakers were in a small minority and that the rest followed, 'many of them most unwillingly'.

However, apart from immediate pay rises wrung from a badly frightened government, the mutinies did also lead to serious efforts to improve the lot of the common sailor and credit is due to Earl Spencer for his part in introducing a number of long overdue reforms in naval discipline and conditions of service. The earl was a humane man and is said to have been so distressed when obliged to pass sentence of death on Richard Parker, leader of the mutineers at the Nore, that he personally allowed Mrs Parker a pension for the rest of her life 'by way of compensation and some alleviation of her grief'.

During his six years at the Admiralty the battles of St Vincent, Camperdown and the Nile were fought and won, and it was Earl Spencer who wrote to Admiral Jervis in March 1798: 'I am very happy to send you Sir Horatio Nelson again, not only because I believe I cannot send you a more zealous, active and approved officer, but because I have reason to believe that his being under your command will be agreeable to your wishes.' A month later Spencer recommended Nelson for independent command in the Mediterranean, and in October Lady Spencer was writing to the victor of the Nile: 'Joy, joy, joy to you, brave, gallant immortal Nelson! May the great God whose cause you so valiantly support, protect and bless you to the end of your brilliant career.'

A warm friendship developed between the First Lord and the admiral and they kept up a steady, semi-official correspondence over the next two years. But in May 1800 the earl was anxious to try and detach England's hero from the unfortunate friendship with Lady Hamilton he had formed at the court of the King of Sicily.

> It is by no means my wish or intention to call you away from service but having observed that you have been under the necessity of quitting your station off Malta on account of the state of your health, it appeared to me much more advisable for you to come home at once, than be obliged to remain inactive at Palermo, however pleasing the respect and gratitude shown to you there may be. . . . I trust you will take in good part what I have taken the liberty to write to you as a friend, and believe me when I assure you that you have none who is more sincerely and faithfully so than
>
> Spencer

In 1801 Mr Pitt went out of office and Earl Spencer went with him. He found plenty to occupy him in private life, being a man of scholarly tastes, civilised and cultivated. 'He had lived', said his contemporary Lord Brougham, 'with the very best society all his life, foreign as well as English. He was full of anecdote accordingly and his mode of relating was excellent, being both succinct and accurate, and so were all his political recollections, of which he had the richest store of almost any man I have known.'

The earl took an informed interest in the new, improved methods of agriculture now being practised by men like his friends the great Coke of Norfolk at Holkham Hall and Francis, fifth Duke of Bedford at Woburn, and he was encouraged to turn his attention to Althorp. There had been very few changes since the days of the second Earl of Sunderland and in 1786 the fabric was found to be in an advanced state of decay. The fashionable architect Henry Holland was summoned to the rescue but money, as usual, was a problem and Earl Spencer told his mother in December, 'in my present circumstances I must be content with making the apartment we live in weatherproof, which it really hardly is at present, and saving the house from tumbling down. . .'

Mr Holland, however, succeeded in persuading his client to agree to an extensive rebuilding programme which completed the transformation of ancient moated manor house into Georgian mansion. The moat itself was finally filled in, the windows enlarged and the exterior faced with white brick tiles. Inside, the rooms were remodelled to accord with prevailing notions of taste and comfort. The Carolean panelling in the Long Gallery disappeared under paint and wallpaper, which Lady Spencer considered a great improvement, and Lord Spencer was given new accommodation for his precious books. In another letter to his mother, dated April 1789, he wrote:

> I was over at Althorp yesterday and went into the library there where I was much pleased at finding some books, the value of which I was unacquainted with before my late researches into the bibliographical science. Three or four of the most valuable I have had packed in a small case and shall bring up to town with me in order to collate them with other copies and to preserve them from any damage they might be exposed to in the general rummage that will happen when the Library is transferred from one room to the other.

And a few months later:

> Althorp goes on charmingly – the Library is beginning to be fitted up with bookcases and promises to be as comfortable and good looking a room as we could wish it. . . .

Earl Spencer's researches into 'the bibliographical science' were to win him an international reputation as a scholar and bibliophile, and over the years his matchless collection of rare and beautiful books spread until it came to take over nearly all the ground-floor rooms at Althorp.

The Spencers were a good-looking family. The second earl was described by Fanny Burney as 'very handsome' and his portrait by Reynolds at Althorp bears her out. They had also been generally fortunate in their choice of wives and again the second earl was no exception. Soon after coming of age he had married Lavinia Bingham, daughter of Lord Lucan, a woman of beauty and spirit much admired by her contemporaries, although her fiery temper and strongly expressed opinions could make her formidable. She seems to have been the sort of woman who gets on better with men than with other women – there was never much love lost between her and her sisters-in-law, and her children stood very much in awe of her – but she and her husband were a devoted couple and he was desolate when she died in 1831.

They had eight children, two of whom died in infancy. Of the survivors, two sons had distinguished careers in the navy and another went into the church, although he later caused consternation in the family by becoming a Roman Catholic and a Passionist monk.

Lord Spencer's eldest son and heir, John Charles, was born at Spencer House in 1782. Viscount Althorp received the usual education of his time and class, being sent away to school at Harrow when he was eight years old:

> 'Dear papa',
> 'You cannot think how many eggs my two grubs have laid, and I am very glad I did not bring the rest, as I should not have known what to do with them. There are four boys now below me, and one is having a struggle with me, for he is to be flogged if he does not keep up with me, and I shall not get my lessons ill to save him. How many brace of partridges did you kill, when you was out a shooting? I am, dear Papa, your dutiful son,
>
> Althorp.

Lord Althorp did not grow up to share his father's rarefied intellectual interests, although he was not stupid. When his mother said to him 'Jack, we expect you to take honours' as he was about to go up for his second term at Cambridge, he was much taken aback, but nobly sold his hunters and applied himelf earnestly to his studies. The brief lull in the Napoleonic Wars during the Peace of Amiens in 1802 enabled him to make a truncated version of the traditional Grand Tour, but even a sight of the art treasures of Rome and Florence failed to awaken any spark of the family connoisseurship.

In the general election of 1806 he was returned to the Commons as member for Northamptonshire, a seat he held for nearly thirty years, but he showed few signs of enthusiasm for a political career either. Like so many of his contemporaries in Regency England, young Lord Althorp was sporting mad. His idea of bliss was a good day out with the Pytchley and he never missed an opportunity of attending a prize fight. Many years later one of his friends remembered him waxing eloquent on the subject of the 'noble science', apparently the only time he was heard to speak with enthusiasm about anything.

> He described the fight between Gully and the Chicken. How he rode down to Brickhill, – how he was loitering about the inn door, when a barouche-and-four drove up with Lord Byron and a party, and Jackson the trainer, – how they all dined together, and how pleasant it had been. Then the fight the next day: the men stripping, the intense excitement, the sparring; then the first round, the attitude of the men – it was really worthy of Homer.

Unlike his father and grandfather, Lord Althorp seemed in no hurry to get married. A big, robust, rather diffident young man, who had already earned the nickname of 'honest Jack Althorp', he was happier in the undemanding company of dogs and horses than in society drawing-rooms. But the matter was taken out of his hands when Miss Esther Acklom, the heiress of Wiseton Hall in Nottinghamshire, fell in love with honest Jack and 'contrived to let him know it' – they were married in April 1814 and were ideally happy together. Lord Althorp used to say that his wife was the only woman he had never felt shy with, and she was obviously exactly right for him. Rather stout and 'without pretensions to regular beauty', she still possessed a great attraction, being intelligent, cheerful, perceptive and altogether 'not a common or every day character'.

The newly-weds made their country home at Wiseton Hall, although it cost £10,000 to make it habitable, and lived there in contented rural retreat, Lady Althorp laying out a new flower garden, while her husband took the home farm under his management. They read together, went out driving together and, in the words of Lord Althorp's biographer, 'a more attached and united couple perhaps never existed'. But their idyll was to be tragically brief. After several miscarriages, poor Esther died in June 1818 giving birth to a stillborn son and leaving Jack inconsolable. He shut himself up at Wiseton and told his sister Sarah, now Lady Lyttelton, that nothing but Christian faith and religious feelings could make him endure to live. That September he wrote pathetically to his old tutor, 'I am really not able to describe the present state of my feelings . . . . If I was confident that I should be able to persevere – so as to go to Heaven and again be with Esther – I should feel happier; but I have no confidence in myself if my time of trial here is to be a long one. You see by what I am saying that I really do not know how to answer you as to whether my mind is really recovering its tone or not.'

In some ways it never did fully recover. Lord Althorp remained unswervingly faithful to the memory of his Esther and from the day of her death always wore black, then considered suitable only for clergymen and 'persons in mourning'. He continued to avoid any kind of social life and spent some part of every year at Wiseton, where Esther's rooms were kept exactly as she had left them. Gradually, though, he began to take up the threads of his political career again – more from a sense of duty than from inclination. As leader of the Whigs in the House of Commons, he worked closely with Lord John Russell in helping Lord Grey to steer the Great Reform Bill through Parliament, and held the office of Chancellor of the Exchequer under both Grey and Melbourne.

Viscount Althorp was always disarmingly unassuming and quite without illusions about his own abilities. Certainly he possessed no intellectual brilliance and was a hesitant speaker, but his transparent honesty, his good sense and unfailing good humour won him many admirers. In the words of one of them: 'There is something . . . quite delightful in his calm, clumsy, courageous, immutable probity and well-meaning, and it seems to have a charm with everybody.'

When the second Earl Spencer died in 1834, his son at once retired gratefully both from the Commons and from affairs of state. 'You must be aware,' he had previously written to Lord Brougham, 'that my being in office is nothing more or less than misery to me. I am perfectly sure that no man ever disliked it to such a degree as I do; and, indeed, the first thing that usually comes into my head when I wake is how I am to get out of it.'

The new earl had never concealed his general boredom with the expensive, high society life-style taken for granted by his parents and the discovery, after his father's death, that the estates were heavily mortgaged, gave him all the excuse he needed to embark on a programme of stringent economy. The property at Wimbledon was sold, Spencer House shut up, and at Althorp the park and gardens were let, the household staff reduced to a minimum and only a few rooms kept open for the family's occasional use. But at Wiseton, the undistinguished house that was now his home, the third Earl Spencer spared no expense on the upkeep of the cattle-breeding establishment which usually ran at a loss of £3000 a year.

As he grew older, farming, especially stockbreeding, became the great interest of his life. Jack, according to his mother, was famously well 'and up to his ears in shorthorned cattle, monsters of sheep and wallowing hogs. . . .' Jack indeed took the greatest pride in the Wiseton herd of shorthorns and, as president of the Smithfield Club, would work happily all day in his shirtsleeves, helping to get the beasts into their stalls ready for a show. He was a co-founder and first President of the Royal Agricultural Society, contributing papers on the comparative nutritional merits of mangelwurzels and Swedish turnips, and other subjects connected with the niceties of raising pedigree cattle. It was also said on good authority that few people could compete with his lordship in his knowledge of sheep.

He had given up hunting after his wife's death, but the old chase books at Althorp record in loving detail those golden days when 'we found a fox in Hothorp Hills, and went away at the bottom over Marston field, up the hill, through Marston Wood, pointed to Nethercoat's Gorse, but turned a little to the left and checked, and were brought to hunting, went on, left Clipstone on the left and hunted up to him in Tallyho, took a turn there, left Haselbeech on the left, and went away again at the best pace over a corner of Naseby Field. . . .' Names which poignantly recall other days and old battles, and that long dead Henry Spencer, the brave but reluctant Cavalier.

The third Earl Spencer continued to resist all attempts to persuade him to return to public life, rejecting Lord Melbourne's offers of the Lord-Lieutenancy of Ireland and governorship of Canada. But in an important and widely reported speech at a local function in 1843, he threw the weight of his reputation as an honest man and practical agriculturist on the scales in favour of a repeal of the Corn Laws, stating his conviction that it would not materially lower the price of corn and that a policy of protectionism must in the end be self-defeating.

Two years later, in October 1845 Lord Spencer died, and was buried wearing a locket containing Esther's hair. He had been taken suddenly ill during the Doncaster Races and carried home to Wiseton, where he 'prepared himself in the calmest manner for death', dispassionately discussing arrangements with his heir – his brother Frederick, or Fritz – and saying to those around him, 'Don't feel for me, I am perfectly happy; and the happiness I have enjoyed in this life makes me think that it will be granted to me in the next.' Apparently he had for some time been living on a near starvation diet in order to ward off the gout, of which he was morbidly afraid. 'He used to weigh his breakfast, and then, having eaten the very small portion he allowed himself, rush half-famished from the room to escape further temptation'. His biographer considered that 'nothing but his great power of self-denial could have enabled him to persevere in a mode of life so trying', and obviously believed such eccentric conduct to be gravely injurious to health.

'My dearest brother died as he had lived,' wrote Sarah Lyttelton, 'in earnest piety and simplicity. . . . He remained entirely placid, and death came like a gentle sleep upon him, like that of a child.' Sarah Spencer, who had married William Henry, third Lord Lyttelton in 1813, was the model of a devoted wife and mother. 'Sal is up to her ears in alphabets, copybooks and gamuts [scales]', Lavinia, Lady Spencer had observed, just a shade scornfully, in 1823. 'Her babies are really uncommon fine ones . . . and they will be admirably brought up, for she thinks and does nothing else.'

Widowed in 1837, Sarah became a Lady of the Bedchamber to the youthful Queen Victoria, thus marking the beginning of the Spencers' close domestic friendship with the royal family. Lady Lyttelton, a shrewd and humorous observer, was a voluminous correspondent and her letters paint a finely detailed picture of life at the young queen's court. One of the lady-in-waiting's duties was to accompany Her Majesty to the play: 'if her Majesty would wear less than *four* different wraps (all to be taken care of and put on), and go there without a bouquet, *and* a bag, *and* an opera-glass, there would be no difficulty at all'.

A few months later, on the occasion of the prorogation of Parliament, the new Lady of the Bedchamber found her responsibilities unexpectedly important and arduous. 'After the Duchess of Sutherland had changed her Majesty's robe, with the help of the dressers, *I* had, in the presence of the whole Court, and surrounded by all the great officers of State, to unpin and remove from her Majesty's head her diamond diadem, and taking the great Crown of England (weighing 12 pounds) from some grandee (whom I did not see very distinctly) to place it and *pin it on* with two diamond pins through the velvet and her hair at the back of her head!' This alarming operation was successfully performed but when it had to be done in reverse, the queen was in a hurry and poor Lady Lyttelton, fumbling with nervousness, *could* not get the last pin into place and came perilously close to sticking it into the royal head, getting a 'comical arch look of entreaty' from Her Majesty. These little 'boggles' over shawling and pinning became something of a standing joke: 'Oh dear! Didn't I wrap up her Majesty at bedtime last night in my shawl, and wrap up myself in her Majesty's shawl. . . ! This morning brought the treason to light.'

Early in 1842 Sarah Lyttelton was asked to take over as governess of the royal nursery, a post she was to hold for nine years. The children called her by the pet name of 'Laddle' and flourished under her kind, commonsensical rule. 'I own I am against punishments; they wear out so soon, and one is never *sure* they are fully understood by the child as belonging to the naughtiness.'

In the summer of 1846 Frederick, fourth Earl Spencer, was appointed Lord Chamberlain to the royal household and his sister had the satisfaction of being able to pass on some complimentary remarks by Prince Albert's Private Secretary to the rest of the family. 'Mr Anson told me a night or two ago that he (Fritz) was most incomparable in his place . . . and had already done lasting good. I fully believe it; he took his place in the light of the command of a ship, and set to work in earnest with old habits of discipline and order.'

Sarah, Lady Lyttelton lived on into serene old age, being spared 'to see the children of her children's children'. She also saw her brother's son, Frederick 'a very nice civil gentlemanlike boy', succeed as fifth Earl Spencer in December 1857 and marry the exquisitely pretty Charlotte Seymour, who became known as Spencer's 'Faery Queen'.

Having progressed through all the usual channels – Harrow,

Trinity College, Cambridge and the family seat in the House of Commons – the fifth earl accepted the Lord-Lieutenancy of Ireland in Mr Gladstone's first administration, formed at the end of 1868. In the spring of 1882 he was sent to occupy the hot seat at Dublin Castle for the second time, with Lord Frederick Cavendish as his chief secretary. Both men were sworn in on the morning of 6 May and that same afternoon Lord Frederick was murdered by the so-called Irish 'Invincibles' as he walked back through Phoenix Park to Viceregal Lodge. Ironically enough, Earl Spencer's appointment had been intended as a conciliatory gesture to the nationalist leaders in Ireland as he had made himself well-liked during his previous period of office, but the outrage in Phoenix Park forced his hand so that for the next few years he was chiefly concerned with the suppression of terrorism. However, when Gladstone came out in favour of the principle of Home Rule, Spencer supported him actively during his six years in the wilderness and in the Grand Old Man's fourth and last government he held his grandfather's old office of First Lord of the Admiralty.

Bred in the sporting and farming, as well as the political traditions of his family and his caste, the fifth Earl Spencer was three times Master of the Pytchley, a member of the Royal Agricultural Society and its president in 1898. But, like most of the great landed proprietors – the Spencer estates amounted to some 26,000 acres – he felt the effects of the agricultural depression of the seventies and eighties and in 1892 opened negotiations for the sale of his grandfather's magnificent library. The prospective purchaser, the widow of a leading Manchester cotton manufacturer, intent on creating a worthy monument to her husband's memory, was a hard bargainer and the Spencer Collection, with all its fifteenth-and sixteenth-century treasures, its fifty-seven Caxtons, its Gutenberg Bible, two Mainz Psalters and hundreds of Aldines, was eventually sold for a mere £210,000. Today the collection forms the nucleus of the John Rylands Library in Manchester and, according to one of its custodians, is still the subject of most of the enquiries which come from abroad.

After Gladstone's final retirement from politics, Earl Spencer's name was several times canvassed as a possible future Liberal prime minister, but although his integrity was unquestioned, he was an awkward and hesitant speaker and in all probability would not have been able to cope with the premiership. In any case his health was beginning to fail. The death of his wife in 1903 caused him great grief and two years later he suffered a mild stroke which effectively brought his public life to an end. He died in 1910 at the age of seventy-five and, as there had been no children of the marriage which his aunt Sarah had once described as '*lucky* – that is, blessed . . . as far as his wife goes', the earldom passed to his half-brother, Charles Robert.

The fifth earl was the last of the political Spencers but his nephew, who succeeded in 1922, revived another even older family tradition of interest in and patronage of the arts; by now it was sadly no longer a question of amassing any great new collections, but of battling to preserve and conserve the treasures at Althorp. Indeed, finding how expensive it was to get needlework-covered chairs repaired, the seventh earl learnt the art of working *gros point* himself, and many of the chairs to be seen at Althorp today bear witness to his initiative and his skill with his needle.

Few members of the family have known so much or cared so deeply about its artistic heritage. The seventh earl devoted a great deal of his life to the care, arrangement and display of that heritage, especially the pictures – no other English country house possesses so many fine Reynolds – and it was during his tenure that Althorp was first opened to the public. He also turned his attention to the calendaring of the family papers, making the Althorp muniment room into one of the best arranged record offices in private hands. The seventh Earl Spencer may have played no part in national politics and held no post at court, but he took his full share in the less glamorous business of running local affairs – holding the record as longest-serving member of the Northamptonshire County Council. His artistic tastes were reflected in his membership of the Standing Committee on Museums and Galleries and he was also a Trustee of the Wallace Collection.

His eldest son, the present Earl Spencer, eighth of his line, succeeded in 1975. A former captain in the Royal Scots Greys he had been, as Viscount Althorp, equerry to King George VI and to Queen Elizabeth II for the first two years of her reign. Lord and Lady Althorp were, in fact, long-standing members of that exclusive inner circle of familiars which surrounds the royal family. They lived in a house on the Sandringham estate where their four children were brought up. It was there that Lady Diana Frances, youngest of the three Althorp daughters, first met the Prince of Wales; although, when their engagement was announced in February 1981 Lady Di, as she was dubbed by the popular press, was 'roughing it' in Kensington where she shared a flat with two other girls, working as a kindergarten teacher.

Her parents' marriage had broken up in 1969 and seven years later Earl Spencer married Raine, daughter of the romantic novelist Barbara Cartland, and who, as Lady Dartmouth, had once attracted some notoriety by her pungent comments on the state of the teacups at Heathrow Airport. She channelled her considerable energies into the task of improving Althorp's standing as a stately home, and in December 1981 was guest of honour at a function organised by the English Tourist Board to launch a scheme intended to persuade businessmen to make more use of the country's historic houses as venues for seminars, conferences and product launches. Lady Spencer has certainly made full use of Althorp's resources with her house parties for wealthy American tourists, her musical evenings and candle-lit dinners at thirty pounds a head and other fund raising events. In fact, she has been accused of deliberately seeking to exploit public interest in the family's connection with royalty.

During the early eighties Althorp underwent an extensive programme of restoration and redecoration which, according to the Earl, cost about £750,000 and in order to help finance the running of the house and its five-hundred-acre estate, a number of treasures from the Spencer collection had to be sold during 1982. Two late seventeenth-century gold wine coolers were bought by the British Museum, a seventeenth-century suite of black and gold lacquered table, mirror and candle-stands went to the Victoria and Albert, while a number of pictures, including a Reynolds portrait of Angelica Kauffman and several Van Dycks, found their way to the salerooms of various London dealers, causing some concern among the heritage lobby.

The Spencers of Althorp rose to peerage and prominence not by any special deed of valour, not by the spoils of the Reformation or a fortune made in trade, but on the broad woolly back of the Warwickshire sheep, said to be 'most large for bone, flesh and wool about Wormleighton'. As individuals, of course, they have varied widely – from Robert, the brilliant but unstable second Earl of Sunderland, to lucky Jack Spencer, the younger son who inherited Althorp, of whom it was said that he never soiled his hands with silver coins but used only gold ones; from the first Earl Spencer, in whose time Althorp became 'almost a gambling house', to his son the urbane and erudite bibliophile. But together they represent continuity. A strong, unbroken chain links the eighth Earl Spencer with his Tudor ancestors, those hardheaded sheep farmers, enclosing their land, multiplying their flocks and increasing their own and their country's wealth. The same continuity, the same strong chain of blood and bone links that earlier Diana Spencer, Sarah Churchill's beloved Cordelia, dying so young at Russell House more than two centuries ago, with the present Princess of Wales. Families like the Spencers, with their roots buried deep in the soil of the great Midland plain, are a part of England – tough, resilient and durable as the land that bred them.

BIBLIOGRAPHY

THE PERCY OUT OF NORTHUMBERLAND

Brenan, Gerald, *History of the House of Percy*, 2 vols, 1902
Burne DSO, Lt. Col. A. H., *More Battlefields of Britain*, 1952
Concise Dictionary of National Biography, to 1900, 1982
Davison, William, *Descriptive and Historical View of Alnwick*, facsimile edition, 1973
The Diaries of a Duchess, ed. James Greig, 1926
The Earl of Northumberland's Household Book, ed. Thomas Percy, 1827
de Fonblanque, Edward, *Annals of the House of Percy*, 2 vols, 1887
Froissart, Jean, *Chronicles*, ed. W. P. Ker, trans. Lord Berner, 1901
Letters of Hugh, Earl Percy, from Boston and New York, ed. C. K. Bolton, 1902
Memorials of the Rebellion of 1569, ed. Cuthbert Sharpe, 1841
Merrick, M. M., *Thomas Percy, Seventh Earl*, 1949
Percy, Thomas, Bishop of Dromore, *Reliques of Ancient English Poetry*, 1864
Round, J. H., *Studies in Peerage and Family History*, 1901

THE SACKVILLES OF KNOLE

Bridgman, John, *An Historical and Topographical Sketch of Knole in Kent*, 1821
The Diary of Lady Anne Clifford, ed. V. Sackville-West, 1923
Glendinning, Victoria, *Vita*, 1983
Holmes, Martin, *Proud Northern Lady, Lady Anne Clifford, 1590–1676*, 1975
Phillips, C. J., *History of the Sackville Family*, 2 vols, 1929
The Poems of Charles Sackville, 6th Earl of Dorset, ed. Brice Harris, 1979
Sackville-West, V., *Knole and the Sackvilles*, 1922
Pepita, 1937
Scott-James, Anne, *Sissinghurst*, 1974
Stevens, Michael, *V. Sackville-West*, 1973
Swart, J., *Thomas Sackville, A Study in 16th Century Poetry*, from *Groningen Studies in English*, 1949
Valentine, Alan, *Lord George Germain*, 1962

THE STANLEYS OF KNOWSLEY

Apsden, T., *Historical Sketches of the House of Stanley*, 1877
Churchill, Randolph S., *Lord Derby, King of Lancashire: Official Life of Edward, 17th Earl of Derby, 1865–1948*, 1959
Cox, Millard, *Derby: The Life and Times of the 12th Earl of Derby* 1974
Creevey, ed. John Gore, 1948
Jones, Wilbur Devereux, *Lord Derby and Victorian Conservatism*, 1956

Lutyens, Lady Emily, *A Blessed Girl*, 1953
Pollard, W., *The Stanleys of Knowsley*, 1868
Rowsell, Mary C., *Life of Charlotte de la Tremoille, Countess of Derby*, 1905
Saintsbury, George, *The Earl of Derby*, 1892
The Stanley Papers I, Chetham Society, XXIX, 1853
II, Chetham Society, XXXI, 1853
III i, Chetham Society, LXVI, 1867
III ii, Chetham Society, LXVII, 1867
Strickland, A., *Lives of the Tudor Princesses*, 1868
de Witt, Mme Guizot, *Lady of Lathom, Charlotte Countess of Derby*, 1869

THE NOBLE HOUSE OF HOWARD

Brenan, G. and Statham, E. P., *The House of Howard*, 2 vols, 1907
Chapman, Hester, *Two Tudor Portraits*, 1960
Edwardes, F., *The Marvellous Chance*, 1968
Howard, Charles, 10th Duke of Norfolk, *Anecdotes of the Howard Family*, 1769
Howard, Henry, *Memorials of the Howard Family*, 1834
MacElwee, William, *The Murder of Sir Thomas Overbury*, 1952
Robinson, John Martin, *The Dukes of Norfolk: A Quincentennial History*, 1983
Smith, Lacey Baldwin, *Tudor Tragedy*, 1961
Williams, Neville, *Thomas Howard, Fourth Duke of Norfolk*, 1964

THE HOUSE OF CAVENDISH

Bickley, Francis, *The Cavendish Family*, 1911
Brodhurst, Rev. R., 'Sir William Cavendish', from *Journal of the Derbyshire Archaeological Society*, vol XXIX, 1907
Calder-Marshall, Arthur, *The Two Duchesses*, 1978
Collins, A., *Historical Collections of the Noble Families of Cavendish*, 1752
Devonshire, Duchess of, *The House: A Portrait of Chatsworth*, 1982
Durant, David, *Bess of Hardwick*, 1977
Foster, Vere, *The Two Duchesses*, 1898
Georgiana, *Extracts from the Correspondence of Georgiana, Duchess of Devonshire*, ed. Earl of Bessborough, 1955
Leach, Henry, *The Duke of Devonshire: A Personal and Political Biography*, 1904
Masters, Brian, *Georgiana, Duchess of Devonshire*, 1981
Newcastle, Margaret Duchess of, *The Life of William Cavendish, Duke of Newcastle*, ed. C. H. Firth, 1886
Pearson, John, *Stags and Serpents: The Story of the House of Cavendish and the Dukes of Devonshire*, 1983
Round, J. H., 'The Origin of the Cavendishes', from *Family Origins and Other Studies*, 1930
Stuart, D. M., *Dearest Bess*, 1955
Thompson, Francis, *Chatsworth, A Short History*, 1951
Trease, Geoffrey, *Portrait of a Cavalier, William Cavendish, 1st Duke of Newcastle*, 1979

THE RUSSELLS OF WOBURN

Bedford, John Duke of, *The Flying Duchess*, 1968
A Silver-Plated Spoon, 1959
Blakiston, Georgiana, *Woburn and the Russells*, 1980
Burnet, Gilbert, *A History of His Own Times*, 1838
Diary of Frances Lady Shelley, ed. Richard Edgcumbe, 1912
Letters of Rachel, Lady Russell, ed. Lord John Russell, 1853
Lloyd, David, *State Worthies*, 2 vols, 1766
Memoirs of Sir Philip Francis, ed. J. Parkes and H. Merivale, 2 vols, 1867
Nicole Nobody, the Autobiography of the Duchess of Bedford, 1974
Prest, John, *Lord John Russell*, 1972
Thomson, Gladys Scott, *Family Background*, 1949
Life in a Noble Household, 1937
The Russells in Bloomsbury, 1940
Two Centuries of Family History, 1930
Trent, Christopher, *The Russells*, 1966
Wiffen, J. H., *Historical Memoirs of the House of Russell*, 2 vols, 1833

THE SPENCERS OF ALTHORP

Cartwright, Julia, *Sacharissa: Some Account of Dorothy Sidney, Countess of Sunderland, her Family and Friends*, 1893
Correspondence of Sarah Spencer, Lady Lyttleton, ed. Mrs H. Wyndham, 1912
Kenyon, J. P., *Robert Spencer, Earl of Sunderland, 1641–1702*, 1958
Marchant, Denis le, *Memoir of John Charles, Viscount Althorp*, 1876
Round, J. H., *Studies in Peerage and Family History*, 1901
Rowse, A. L., *The Early Churchills*, 1956
The Later Churchills, 1958
Sidney, Henry, *Diary of the Times of Charles II, including his Correspondence with the Countess of Sutherland*, ed. R. W. Blencoe, 2 vols, 1843
Spencer, Seventh Earl, 'Althorp', from *Country Life*, 11, 18 and 25 June 1921
The Spencer Papers, Navy Records Society, 1913–14, 1924
Thomson, G. Scott, *The Russells in Bloomsbury, 1669–1771*, 1940
Letters of a Grandmother, 1732–1735 – Being the Correspondence of Sarah Duchess of Marlborough with her Granddaughter Diana Duchess of Bedford, 1943

INDEX